THE LIFE EVERY
MAN DREAMS OF

Berner was very cautious when he outlined his demands to the Druggish. He knew all the fables, the fairy tales—rub the magic lantern or get three wishes and what happens? Disaster! Start out rich and powerful and end up behind the 8-ball.

Well, it wasn't going to happen to him. Not after a lifetime of failure.

He covered every angle, every possible loophole, when he asked for the strength of a superman.

His wordage was precise, exact, when he requested superhuman intellectual powers.

And when he came to sex, he made them understand *exactly* what he wanted—endowments unmatched in all of human history; powers that put Casanova to shame!

Only then was he satisfied—only then did he place himself in the hands of the alien creatures.

His life, once they reassembled him, would be a dream of power and pleasure.

And for a while it was—until Fate once again stepped in to play its ancient role. Then the fable of Edward Berner rushed toward its inevitable conclusion.

THE REASSEMBLED MAN

by Herbert D. Kastle

WILDSIDE PRESS

for
Barbara
and
John Stanley

"O, it is excellent
To have a giant's strength; but it is tyrannous
To use it like a giant."

MEASURE FOR MEASURE
Shakespeare

chapter 1

BEFORE THE EVENING of June 26, Edward Berner hardly knew the extent of his dreams. He did buy tickets on the Irish Sweepstakes, never sure whether they were legitimate or the counterfeit variety he'd read about. It made no difference since he never won. He also smiled a great deal at the handsome blond typist with the startling mammary development and caboose to match, and for a while she smiled back and came to his office to chat, but then the bachelor art director of black crew cut and narrow pants swung into the picture, and that was that. Ed did, however, score occasionally with a woman; never the woman he'd have selected if he'd had his choice. There was Viola, the secretary at his last agency, whom he'd convinced after moving to his current agency. She was thirty-four and divorced and running to fat, and she liked him. She wasn't bad, though nervous and irritated afterward; all eight times afterward. That last time, in a much-too-expensive room at an East Side hotel, she'd said, waspishly, that he was one of the smallest men that way that she'd ever experienced, and she admitted to experiencing more than a few. It hurt. He'd wanted to strike back by saying that Edith at her worst had more fire, more skill, than this much-experienced woman. But he didn't. How could he talk about his wife at a time like that? And then again, he was afraid she might point out something else about his physical makeup.

Not that he thought himself a bad looking man. He was thirty-eight and five-eleven and just under a hundred sixty pounds. He had dark brown hair—or what was left of it. He was balding; the scalp showing through in an uneven circle in back, the hairline receding deep above the forehead in front. But he wore his hair short, and often thought he could hide the baldness with a longer hairdo, if his hair hadn't been the kind that stuck up in back and at the sides when it grew over two inches. He had a large-featured face. His teeth were even, now that most in front were false. His nose wasn't really big; sort of long with a thickening at the end which made it look big. His ears *were* big; quite big. The rest of him was satisfactory, though he'd regretted his narrow build in younger days. Now he thought of himself as being slender in most places and not too soft in the gut.

So he had the dream of money, and the dream of women, and both were hopeless dreams because he never expected to get real money or the kind of woman who could transport him with delight and make cheating on Edith really worthwhile.

Sure, he'd dreamed as a kid of being a star for the Brooklyn Dodgers, and heavyweight champion of the world. In the Air Corps, he'd dreamed of being a fighter pilot, and ended up a Field Lighting man with a corporal's stripes. In college he'd dreamed of being a writer, and published three short stories in an N.Y.U. student magazine, the *Vox Vet Literary Supplement*. A great thrill, and one which had to last until the present, since he never published anything else, beside two letters in the *Times*. He became an advertising copywriter; not a successful one on big-billing packaged-goods accounts in giant agencies like J. Walter Thompson, Y.&R., B.B.D.&O. and Bates. He worked on small liquor and industrial accounts at agencies like Prior-Bailey-Stennis, total billing eight million. He made eleven thousand dollars a year, after sixteen years in the business. He was nowhere, and felt lucky to be there.

Dreams? The baseball star and heavyweight champion and novelist-writer and others all disappeared. Money and women remained, reduced, and what kind of dreamer reduces his dream? No kind. Edward Berner did not consider himself a dreamer; could not have told a TV panel show his dreams even for a two-week vacation in Hawaii. Until the night of June 26, when he understood that every dream he had could come true, and found he had so many the Druggishes took fifty hours to put him together so that he could realize them all.

The Druggishes weren't enormous; they only looked that way to a human since no human had ever seen a Japanese beetle his own size. The Druggishes weren't Japanese beetles, but it was the description Ed would have used if he'd been able to describe them. He couldn't, of course. It was not only part of the agreement by which he turned all those dreams he didn't know he had into reality, it was also a physical impossibility. The Druggishes wiped out his memory of them when they reassembled him.

It all happened because of Ed's desire to get out of the house, and Matty's desire to get out of going with Ed. Matty was five, and he knew enough about the power structure of his own little world to respect Mommy and not Daddy. Edith was caustic and critical and full of fun—the acidy kind of fun that made her say, "If the Ernest Hemingway of Green-Top Acres would deign to leave his latest epic and bring the garbage cans down to the road, the lucky sanitation men will again have the chance to serve a master of words." Ed had been trying to bat out a headline or two on Wylitt's Gin. Small space campaign in Paterson, New Jersey. Wylitt's was the eighth largest-selling gin in Paterson.

Ed brought down the garbage cans, and since it was still light and Matty had napped that afternoon, he suggested he take the child to the development's playground for a final half hour of swinging on swings and monkeying on monkey bars. Edith said fine. Matty said, "Naw. Better I sleep." Miri, Ed's ten-year-old daughter, glanced up from the TV set and said, "Don't look at *me,* Father. I wouldn't miss 'Dobie Gillis' for all the scarlet tanagers in Westchester." Which showed she was bright, all right, since Ed usually tried Matty first, then Miri with the pitch that she failed to take advantage of the lovely countryside and the beauties of nature and how about a little bird-watching expedition?

He laughed. So both kids were hip to Daddy. So they preferred sleep and television. He couldn't really blame them. His own father had bored him at age three.

But outside, walking around behind the garage and kicking at loose blacktop from the expanding hole in the driveway, he felt the empty ache of despair. His children loved him. The time he was sick Miri cried half the night. Matty would kiss him in the mornings, sometimes. They loved him as much as kids loved parents when they had no reason to be particularly aware of parents. But they didn't respect him. They would never respect him. He didn't respect himself. He was a nobody. Of course, lots of men right here in Green-Top Acres, northern Westchester, were nobodies. Very few somebodies lived this far from the city, this close to Putnam County, in houses costing, originally, between $17,800 and $20,500, depending on model and size of plot. But if the wife made him a somebody, the kids thought so too.

Edith made him a nobody. It was his own fault. He couldn't give her love. He avoided it as much as possible. It had settled down to a bi-monthly bout of convulsive release-seeking. He'd never loved her. He'd married her because he'd wanted a wife and home and sex. He got the wife and home, but his lack of love killed the sex. And it killed Edith's love. And so he was a nobody.

He'd tried hard to love her. That was where his dream, reduced though it was, hurt him. The blonde with the startling mammary development and caboose to match was what he wanted, for at least a month, and then he'd want someone else, and then someone else. Don Juan was, in his estimation, a fantastic hero.

And so there they were, he and Edith, friends of a sort, when Edith forgot to be crushed and hurt and bitter.

He lit a cigarette. He walked down the driveway, kicking loose pieces of blacktop to the sides. He saw his neighbor, Harry Amory, a massive, hairy man running to fat, but still quite a man. Ed added a little swagger to his walk. Harry was squatting near his station wagon in the driveway of the house to Ed's left, which was identical to Ed's own—the cheapest model: side-to-side split-level—and identical to the house on Ed's right and eight of ten in the two-hundred-house development. Harry said, "Ed, don't you ever buy these damned tubeless tires. One flat and they're dead." Ed said he wouldn't, though he had tubeless and liked them. Harry got up and went into his garage. His voice came out, deep and peremptory, "Gladys, get me a cold beer, huh?"

Ed went back to his own garage and got in the Chevy II. He took a ride, all the way across the Putnam County line and into the lakes region. He was going to turn back then, but he didn't. He couldn't. He'd come under the influence of the Druggishes just outside the town of Putnam Corners. They were up above somewhere and had their probe out and he drove onto the country road and the probe hit and Edward Berner was it.

He drove nearly two thousand miles without stopping. He was half dead with hunger, thirst and exhaustion when he staggered out of his car. It was night. He looked at the big hole in the ground and wondered why he'd come to this god-forsaken spot in New Mexico when he lived in Westchester County, New York, and had gone out for a ride that should have lasted no more than an hour and had lasted, instead, three days. He wanted to get back in his car and drive to a motel and sleep for a week, but he couldn't. That hole, something about that hole held him there.

He thought of a cigarette. He hadn't had one since leaving the house. He put his hand in his pocket; and that was when the man-sized Japanese beetle scuttled out of the hole and stood there on all six legs, its brown body offset by shimmering green wings set close about its back like a shell. It was about six feet long and three feet high and it had small, greenish-black eyes with fuzzy black feelers above them. There were other non-Japanese beetle features, such as a mouth that looked quite capable of devouring steak as well as leaves, and fingerlike appendages on the front pair of legs, eight per leg, and a metallic cloth sack under the body, held in place by two bands over the back, and a holster of sorts strapped to the chest. And other differences which Ed wasn't in condition to note at the moment. But a beetle still.

The beetle said, or seemed to say, since its mouth didn't move, "Ed, baby! Gladaseeya! C'mon in and meet the group!"

"My God," Ed said.

"Now that we've discussed religion, let's get down to politics and women." The beetle rubbed its feelers together gleefully. "I saw the President on television last night. There, that brings us to women."

Ed covered his ears against the wheezing guffaws, and discovered they came from *inside* his head. The beetle was *thinking* its speech and laughter.

"Look, dad," the beetle said, "let's kick a few tires. To coin a phrase, let's see the way the cookie crumbles. We've got only a few days to roll up the whole big ball of wax."

"Must you talk that way?" Ed murmured, knees trembling. He tried not to look at the huge insect.

"You don't dig? I mean to say, fellah, we've got limited time for the *ganz shmeer,* so the sooner the sooner."

"It's bad enough having to be here, but listening to this . . ." Ed rubbed his oily, stubbled face. "I can't stand that TV advertising talk even when *people* use it."

"But you *are* in advertising," the beetle said, its thought-tone subdued.

"Yes. And I've missed days—or is it a week?—coming here. Why did I come here?"

"No sweat, no sweat," the beetle muttered. "Only three days. Besides, you're too big for the job, or soon will be."

Ed looked at the beetle, and sat down on the sandy ground. His head whirled and his stomach boiled. "You made me come here, didn't you?"

"We put our ad in the *Times,* yes."

"Please, Mr. Beetle."

The beetle's thought-tone snapped, "The life form you refer to, in all its many varieties, is far more intelligent than you suppose. But calling a Druggish a beetle is not permitted!"

Ed nodded. "I'm sorry."

"Now, fellah, let's make that tea ceremony. We've got brainstorming to do."

Ed gagged, leaning politely away from the Druggish.

"Would you rather I said, Let's board the ship and discuss the situation with the Leadership Panel?"

"Much rather, thank you."

"It'll take some re-education," the Druggish muttered. "We used the two days of your trip to set up communicational patterns in keeping with your sectional, social and economic position. However, I'll transmit the change at once." The Druggish stood silently a moment, then said, "Now, if you'll rise, Mr. Berner."

Ed rose, and swayed dizzily. The Druggish came forward as if to help. Ed said, "I'm fine. Just lead the way."

The Druggish turned in a multi-legged shuffle. "I understand. We're repellent to you. But try to imagine how repellent a Druggish-sized Frink is to us."

Ed didn't ask what a Frink was. He watched as the Druggish disappeared into the hole; then came to the edge. After three or four feet of earth, there was a pimpled metal ramp, easy enough for a beetle to navigate, but steep for a human. The ramp went down some thirty-five feet into a lighted metal cave, or room . . . *or spaceship.* That last possibility was placed in his mind by the Druggish.

A spaceship had landed here two nights ago, shortly after beaming something down at Putnam Corners and catching Ed Berner. It had dug itself into the ground in a near-desert area and waited. Only when Ed Berner had approached had the hole opened and the Druggish emerged. And soon, Ed Berner would be free to return home, and the Druggishes will continue on to other planets.

"Really?" Ed asked, stepping into the hole, sitting down on the ramp and sliding slowly after the Druggish.

"Scout's honor, dad."

Ed was silent.

"Sorry, Mr. Berner. But yes, it's all true. The Leadership Panel will make you a proposition. Once you agree, work will begin. In a day or two, you'll be on your way home."

The ramp ended in a low-ceilinged, circular room, all shiny metal, bathed in a blue haze of soft, tinted lighting. Ed got up off the floor, bumped his head, and found he could stand if he stooped just a bit. The room was empty except for three additional Druggishes, sitting against the wall across from the ramp entrance. Ed knew they were sitting because their rear legs were folded. A moment later, he knew everything else. It was simply placed in his mind. He asked for food and drink. The three Druggishes were solicitous, but said their food and drink would disgust him.

"It's not necessary to eat or drink, Mr. Berner," the Leadership Panel said. (He felt certain all three spoke to him at once.) "Just give your consent to the project we proposed and we'll prepare you for it. During the preparation, you will be refreshed and sustained. On completion, you can feed yourself in your usual manner."

"Let me get this straight," Ed said, sitting down Indian fashion. The metal floor was terribly cold. "I'm to gather information for you. I don't have to write it down, or record it on any sort of machine, or film it. I just have to give my consent to have you prepare me to record it, whatever that means. In return for my consent, you'll make all my dreams come true."

"Yes. Unless we've misinterpreted use of the word 'dream' —legitimate hopes, wishes and aspirations, correct?"

Ed nodded. "How do I gather this information? And just what is it that I gather?"

"You gather by observing, experiencing, living—going on as you always have. As for what you gather, it's what your anthropologists gather when they live with primitive bush tribes. We, Mr. Berner, are anthropologists of sorts. To answer the unspoken questions in your mind, we want neither humans nor their planet. We do want information, detailed reports, material for text scripts, the facts of human existence."

"How do I give you these facts, pass on this information?"

"At regular intervals, we will return and contact you. We will . . . read your mind is the closest we can get to the process. Think of your brain as a fine recording device. At the moment you have no player for this recorder other than your mouth for speaking and hands for writing—primitive at best, and useless for us since they leave the memory cells and unconscious nearly untapped. But during your preparation in the tanks, your brain will be changed in such a way as to allow us to read it, in entirety. Your first report will be made immediately after preparation is terminated. That report will be the most complete, the most important by far. The information we'll get will form the basis for our understanding of American humanity. Subsequent reports, however, are necessary in order to update the information."

"It seems to me," Ed muttered, "you'd do better to raid a library and study history, science, the works."

"We did that too. Historical and scientific data, as well as what you call psychology and philosophy, were in our possession shortly after we landed. It is the specific quality of *humanity* which is the key to understanding everything available to us. If we were to give you the entire Druggish civilization in text scripts, recordings, motion pictures, and mind-pictures, you would still not understand us; not with your human mind. You would be absorbing dates and places and events from the human standpoint, when it was the Druggish who had lived it."

Ed nodded dazedly. He saw what they meant, but it didn't seem to make that much difference. And there was the question as to whether he would see and experience what they wanted him to see and experience. The office with its long boredoms and occasional tensions; home with Edith and the kids and television; a woman once in a while (and how would *that* help them?); the commuting to and from Grand Central fives times a week . . .

"All valuable to us," the Leadership Panel said. "All just what we want. But you needn't worry about it in any event. If you were aware of being a living collector of human experience, you'd become inhibited and do a bad job. So we will wipe out all memory of us—make you forget the Druggish completely."

"Fine," Ed whispered, shivering from the cold entering his anus and the cold emanating from his guts. "But why ask for my consent if you can do whatever you want and make me forget it was ever done?"

"We're civilized," the Druggishes replied. "Though you will live between 400 and 600 years when the Medical Assembly Panel completes its work, you will still not live long enough to learn what that means. Humanity is some hundreds of thousands of years removed from civilization and the actual, not stated, recognition of the worth of the individual."

In that, strangely, Ed agreed. "A jungle," he murmured. "A ripping, tearing place."

"A place of violence, both overt and covert," the Leadership Panel said. "And now, state your dreams."

The two days and nights of driving were too much. The huge beetles were too much. Ed wanted only to drink cool drinks and eat hot foods and sleep for a week. "Never mind my dreams. Just do what you have to do and let me go. Since I'll live forever and won't remember . . ." He waved his hand. "Go on."

"We neglected to instill belief. Now *believe.*"

A multitude of pictures flashed through Ed's mind, and while he couldn't recall a single one a moment later, their effect was electrifying. He knew that the Druggishes were a race a million times older than man; that their skills at everything were enormous; that they promised nothing they couldn't deliver. His dreams *would* come true!

Ed's mind was working now, feverishly, and he became crafty in an instant, though he wasn't sure he had to be. He remembered his irritation with stories, movies and TV shows on the Aladdin-Midas theme. There were always a limited number of wishes, and the protagonist always fouled up. At best, he returned to his previous dull existence with an unbelievable fondness for being stupid, plain and poor. Most of the time he destroyed himself with misused wealth or power. In many instances he was trapped into deadly errors by leaving out some little detail—such as forgetting to specify that a loved one coming back from the dead should be in a state of perfect health, or that the gift of turning everything to gold should be accompanied by the ability to suspend this power. Not that the Druggishes were promising such childish miracles; and not that Ed Berner would want them. He would be careful to ask for nothing that could lash back at him. He would be in complete control, at all times. But still, it was wise to pause a moment and remember those fairy tales and reduce the tremendous excitement sweeping over him.

He'd been overly excited the one other time a "dream" had been offered him: his rich Uncle Max taking him to Macy's and telling him he could choose anything in the whole store for his birthday. Of course, he'd been a child of eight, and Max would have laughed off a request for the twelve-thousand-dollar cabin cruiser, but even so he'd muffed the opportunity. He'd been afraid to believe that "anything" and had chosen a six-buck first baseman's glove and lost it three days later in a sandlot game near his Brooklyn home.

But now! Now he believed and the Druggishes were waiting! He stood up, and bumped his head on the low ceiling. He rubbed it and chuckled. "Slow," he said to them, and himself. "Slow, or I might bump more than my head."

"We will not allow you to make mistakes," the Leadership Panel said, and there seemed to be an impatient tone to the thought. "You are not haggling with an unfriendly and unwilling dispenser of black magic. If you wish, we can give you what we consider the best qualities . . ."

"No," Ed said. *"I'll* do the choosing." Hearing himself, he feared he sounded a little like the men in the stories asking for powers that eventually destroyed them. He paused a moment, and proceeded as calmly as he could.

"I want to look better than I look. Not different, really, or my life would change too much—no one would know me and how could I explain who I am? Just better—more attractive to women." He had another thought that went with that, but stopped and said, "Can you do it?"

"When we know *all* you want, we will know what can be done."

An answer like that would have struck Ed as hedging, but not when coming from the Druggishes. He cleared his throat. "We humans have an organ of, er, reproduction, men that is, and someone once said that mine . . . I wonder if . . ."

"It will be enlarged, Mr. Berner."

Here was the first of the pitfalls. "Enlarged within reason. *Sensibly* enlarged. Nothing extreme."

"Naturally. What good would a sexually incompetent observer be, anthropologically speaking?"

"I want great strength." Again he foresaw pitfalls. "Nothing that would make normal living impossible, such as hurting people when I didn't mean to. You understand? Strong. Stronger than any man on earth. But I want to walk normally, not spring off the ground with each step, and be able to pick up an egg without crushing it, and . . ."

"It is understood, Mr. Berner. Continue."

"You *sure* it's understood? And what if you forget such details? I mean, are you taking it all down?"

They answered him with weary patience. "The Medical Assembly Panel is tuned in."

"Long life. You said you'd give it to me. How many years did you say?"

"Four hundred to six hundred of your years. We can't be certain exactly how long you'll survive."

"Why not more? Can you give me more? I want all you can give me."

They seemed surprised. "You may find the four hundred insupportable. Have humans not yet learned how terrible ennui can be, boredom, experience revisited a thousand times?"

"We have," Ed replied quickly. "But I'll be something so vital, so wonderful, life could last forever and I'd enjoy it. Earth is big, at least to a human. I could live a hundred years in each country and not run out of things to do, to see, to enjoy. How much life can you give me?"

"Four hundred to six hundred years, at this Assembly. You can be Assembled again, if you so wish, perhaps three hundred years from now. That would give you another three hundred years, at the least. And then a final Assembly could give you perhaps a hundred to two hundred. You could total a minimum of seven hundred to eight hundred years that way, without reaching senility. Your maximum would be well over a thousand, though there you might reach an age equivalent to a hundred in untreated humans. Not very pleasant, physically."

"We'll worry about that when the time comes. I can always put a bullet through my brain."

The Panel answered swiftly. "Suicide is one freedom you are denied. We cannot allow a valuable recorder to destroy itself."

Ed wasn't sitting on the cold floor now, but a chill reached his vitals. "Even if I'm suffering from something like cancer?"

"You won't suffer from any of the killing diseases of your world. Unless the Medical Assembly Panel is very wrong—

and they haven't been, on any of the other twenty-six planets we've visited—you won't suffer from even minor ailments."

Ed rubbed his hands together. "Boy oh boy!" But he forced himself to think of all possibilities, and said, "If I were being tortured . . ."

"See to it you are never in a position to be tortured, Mr. Berner. Seek not leadership, power, excessive wealth. Live close to the way you currently live, though with more pleasure, of course. Then there will never be any reason to find yourself in a situation where you'll be important enough to torture, or to kill."

"Yes. That's what I figured anyway. But . . ." He tried to find a way around the lingering discomfort, and did. "I want to be unkillable. No one can kill me."

"That is not a legitimate hope or aspiration, Mr. Berner. We are not magicians from your storybooks. Everything alive, including the Druggish, can be killed. As was stated, you must try to live a life that will reduce the chances of death by violence."

The loopholes were showing up. The dangers were growing. He would have a thousand years of life to look forward to, and might die by a bullet, in an accident, in any one of the thousand senseless ways people died. And with so much more to lose than others! He began to sweat.

"Though, of course," the Panel said, "your powers of resistance and recuperation will be far superior to what they are now. Unless your body is torn apart, mangled so badly that the healing process is impossible, you will recover from much of what kills humans."

"A knife in the heart?" Ed asked, and held his breath for the answer.

"Unless the heart is removed, it will recover from any injury. The same is true of your other organs . . . or will be after Assembly."

"If I lose an arm . . ."

"You will not grow new limbs, since that is not inherent in your potential. But a limb pressed back in place, held there for a short while, will adhere and eventually heal. Humans can do that right now, you know."

"I heard something about it in the army. Fingers, I heard. Once an arm. But how could you . . . ?"

"We are in possession of several newly expired humans. We did them no injury. We merely appropriated what was already dead. Only that way could we know what we could and could not do with you."

The sweat trickled down Ed's sides. "You're sure now you can do what you say? Just what is this Assembly?"

"Finish your requests, Mr. Berner, and we will answer your question. And then, if you wish, you can leave this ship without submitting to Assembly, and with no memory, of course, of the Druggish. We are certain to find a willing subject, though we are now pressed for time, having chosen one so far from where we eventually landed. That was our one mistake on Earth, though a small one. On Eddlegurst, as the natives call it, we made a much more serious mistake. We chose as recorder a member of an inferior race, similar in every way to the dominant and intelligent race except for a mental aberration which didn't show up until we called for our second report. By that time, despite our Assembly, he had become a mindless hulk, feeding like a Zert. There was no written or mental record of these people on Eddlegurst, though they number in the millions, and we realized they exist unnoticed alongside the non-aberrants. Don't ask us how. We have not yet learned the answer, though our new recorder is dominant, intelligent and most willing to help. He just does not know the aberrants are on the same planet with him. He does not see them, hear them or feel them."

"Nothing like that here," Ed murmured, preoccupied with his own worries and growing tensions. What if the Druggishes made another big mistake, this time with him?

"We're not too sure of that," the Panel said. "You wouldn't know of it anyway, would you? Perhaps some element of your population, though seen and heard, fulfills the invisible race function. For a while we thought your blacks were that, but their situation is changing and other differences exist. However, after you make your first report, we will know a good deal more about Earth. Now if you've concluded your requests . . ."

"Not by a long shot! I want great mental power, tremendous intelligence, the ability to learn things in an instant, to create great works of art and understand secrets of nature and . . . *everything*."

"Your capacity to learn will be heightened, but the rest is beyond us. Your basic potential will continue to limit you, since we cannot create matching brain tissue; tissue sophisticated enough to carry on the thought processes of a mature, individualized creature; not even for our own people. And even if we could, we would not, for that would create a non-typical recorder—actually a non-human recorder—and your reports would be reduced in value."

It was greedy of him, Ed knew, but he felt acute disappointment. "Money," he said, a sullen note creeping into his voice. "I suppose you can't give me that too?"

"We can gather some by the time you emerge from the tanks, but it might create problems for you. Your medium of exchange is well regulated. If we remove it from the storage places, you might eventually be considered a criminal. If we duplicate it, you would certainly be considered a criminal. And it is unnecessary, since with your heightened intelligence and strength you should be able to increase your earnings considerably."

"But I'd still have to work for a living. I thought you could start me off with a hundred thousand and find out what was going to happen on the stock market, or at least pick a few winners at the track."

"Time, Mr. Berner, is too short for such frivolities. We have a full itinerary of planets to visit. You are receiving the greatest gifts any human has ever received, don't you understand that? Long life, freedom from disease, tremendous recuperative ability in case of injury, great physical strength, heightened mental power. We'll also give you qualities you consider important—increased attractiveness to females and enormous sexual capacity. If there are any other such minor adjustments you'd like made, state them. But *things*, Mr. Berner—money and ornaments and predictions to bring you things—these we will not waste precious time on."

They were right. The big dreams were already stated. But those "minor adjustments"—were there any more?

"Hurry, Mr. Berner. The treatment to our respiratory systems has only a limited effectiveness. When it wears off, we can no longer breathe your atmosphere and must leave Earth. This is not a sealed ship enclosing our own atmosphere, since we must be able to bring subjects aboard on each of the planets we visit, as we've brought you aboard. We have two days more, three at the most, and that long only because an ex-

ploratory visit requires far more time than subsequent stops
for reports. We've risked serious illness with an excessive
treatment for Earth's atmosphere. Retreatment without rest is
impossible; so even minutes may be valuable."

"Hair!" Ed said. "I want thick hair, dark, not gray. And
teeth. All my own teeth, but not crooked in front like they
were. White, even teeth. And . . . to get back to the mental
power, couldn't you give me some sort of *control* over people? Hypnotic, perhaps? Just an edge so I can swing things
my way?"

"The hair and teeth, certainly. The control over others?"
There was a pause. "The Medical Assembly Panel says some
minor adjustment may be possible, but no definite promise
can be made. We will try, Mr. Berner, but we will not endanger your humanity and therefore your value as a recorder."

"All right. Just try. Just give me an edge."

The three beetles rose, straightening their rear legs. "Is it
finished Mr. Berner?"

"Wait. I'm thinking." He rubbed his hands together and
squeezed his eyes shut and dredged his mind for a last wish
or two. "You sure there's no way to get me some money? A
few thousand to start off with?"

"No way safe for you, without destroying life. And we
cannot destroy life. The time has come for you to make your
decision, Mr. Berner. Do you go to Assembly, or do you
leave the ship? Answer now, Mr. Berner. We are not tamper-
ing with your natural reasoning powers. Answer."

Ed thought desperately. What could Superman do? "I
guess you can't make me fly?" he muttered, and laughed even
before the, "No, it is not inherent in your potential," came
into his mind.

What could Tarzan do? "How about special physical skills?
Climbing and swinging and jumping and . . . and swimming.
That's inherent in my potential. They say humans are descended from apes, and before that from sea creatures. Make
me an ape on land and a fish in water."

"It could be done. We would have to enlarge certain muscles, and in the case of radical improvement in ability to survive in water, make basic changes in your breathing appara-
tus. That would create deviation in your appearance from the

norm and reduce your attractiveness to females; perhaps even endanger your humanity and your usefulness as a recorder."

"Never mind," Ed muttered, and knew the time of bargaining was over. He was exhausted again. He was through thinking. He began to fear. "Now tell me what you're going to do."

They didn't tell him. They showed him. He followed them through a sliding section of wall into a room which was full of slim metal tanks, each large enough to hold a man upright. The pictures which came to his mind made him gasp. He would be taken apart, literally disassembled, and placed in the tanks and kept alive somehow. Then, when his parts had been improved to the point the Druggishes had promised, he would be reassembled and his brain "played" of its thirty-eight years of stored experience. One experience would be wiped from memory—that of meeting the Druggishes—and he would be sent back into the world of men.

He trembled. The Panel said, "Remember the truly wonderful compensation you'll receive, Mr. Berner. Remember, and answer."

He remembered. He had always considered himself a coward, but now his fear couldn't match his desire to be what the Druggishes could make him. He closed his eyes, shutting out the shiny tanks and the big beetles and everything but the dream of what he could be. "Do it. Do it now, fast, before I try to run."

"We cannot accept anything but a considered and logical answer."

"Do it!" he screamed. "You'll never get a logical answer from a man you're going to take apart and put back together again like a busted machine! Do it! Do it! Do it!"

There was no answer. His voice echoed in the metal chamber, and he followed it to its death in dim clangor among tanks and tubes. His organs would be put in those tanks. His heart and lungs and liver and all the rest would float in those tanks; float and rot and die in those tanks! Or the beetles would make mistakes and he'd emerge a scrambled horror!

He turned, beginning to run; and felt the incredibly cold and heavy air wash over him like a bucket of ice water thrown in his face. All at once he was still.

chapter 2

HE WAS LOST. That was the first thing he knew. He sat in his car and looked up the highway, stretching off into the flat, desert country. The sky was gray with approaching sunrise. No one had to tell him this wasn't Westchester or Putnam County, New York, but just where was it? And how had he got here?

He reached for cigarettes, lit one, inhaled deeply. He choked and threw the cigarette out the window with a disgusted shake of the head. Filthy taste!

"Now let's think it through," he said, and rubbed his face. And felt the heavy stubble of beard. He twisted the rear-view mirror down so he could look into it, and said. "Holy Cow." He hadn't shaved in a week, looked like! And his hair was so shaggy, it was barely recognizable as his own!

Once again he tried to think it through. He'd left the house Tuesday, June 24, and driven into Putnam County because Matty hadn't wanted to go to the playground and Miri wanted to watch "Dobie Gillis" and he just had to get out. He'd gone past Putnam Corners and turned onto the dirt road leading to the little lake and decided to head back home. And then . . .

"What the hell then?" he muttered. The next thing he remembered was looking down this highway.

He got out of the car. He was parked on a sandy shoulder, facing east if the evidence of an increasing glow in the sky ahead could be believed. His face was bearded and his clothing rumpled, but otherwise he felt fine.

In fact, he'd never felt finer. He stretched, and the singing exultation filled every part of his being. Lord, but it was great to be alive and young and strong and healthy!

He stopped in mid-stretch, hearing the tearing sound. His jacket had split up the back. Which didn't make sense since the suit was, if anything, loose on him.

He removed the jacket and examined it, and then felt the tightness of shirt and pants . . . and shorts. Everything seemed to have shrunk. "Or else I'm still a growing boy," he

25

said, and chuckled, and then felt himself. Something was wrong. He felt . . . bigger. Not taller or heavier, but thicker in the biceps and thighs, and especially down there in the shorts. He shook his head and laughed, and the sound of his laughter stopped him, it was so deep and booming.

He must've been drinking. He'd stopped at a bar and had a few and then a few more and blanked out. But he couldn't recall that first drink, or even stopping anywhere.

Wait a minute. An accident. He'd hit his head on the windshield and lost his memory and had just returned to himself. Amnesia! That had to be it!

But when he walked around the car, he failed to find a single dent that hadn't been there before. Maybe he'd slammed on the brakes and hit the windshield . . . though the glass wasn't shattered. Nor could he find a sore spot anywhere on his head or body.

But amnesia was the only answer, unless he'd begun losing his mind.

He took out cigarettes; then frowned at the pack, crumpled it and threw it away. He looked down at his hand, raised it to his eyes, stared at it. Strong-looking hand. Big, hard, thick-fingered hand.

"I've got to get home," he muttered. Too much about himself was strange. Not unpleasant, but strange. He moved to the door, and heard the hum of an approaching motor. The moving dot came over the horizon, growing rapidly into a battered pickup truck with two men in the cab. He stepped around his car, into the road, and waved, thinking to find out where he was, and as he did his shirt popped at the neck and right sleeve. He dropped his arm, remembering how he looked, but by then it was too late. The truck slowed, and pulled to a stop a little past his car. That was when he was sorry for another reason. The two men were hardly the sort he wanted to meet on a deserted road.

"Hey now," the driver said, pushing back a curl-brimmed cowboy hat from a dark, heavy face, "lookie there, Warner. That boy's been hittin' it up better'n we have."

"Yeh," the other said flatly, his upper lip high at the center, giving him an unpleasant, rabbity look. "You got a drink left in that jug of yourn, buddy-boy?"

Ed smiled dimly. "I was wondering, could you tell me where . . . which way to the nearest town?"

The driver opened his door and stepped down and came

around the front of the truck, swaggering and grinning. He was a big man, heavy around the shoulders and middle. He wore Levis and a checkered shirt and had a damp cigarette butt in the corner of his mouth. He read Ed's license plates, and turned to his friend. "New York. Fancy that."

"Tell him how to get to the big city, Pat."

"Why shore, Warner. You head east a thousand or so miles till you see the first telephone pole. Then you call Momma and ask for directions."

Warner found that amusing enough to grunt at. He too got out, looking up and down the highway. He was bare-headed, but otherwise dressed the same as Pat. He was smaller, thinner, meaner looking.

Ed kept the dim, placating smile on his lips. "Yes, well, I know I don't appear . . . the truth is I'm not feeling . . . I drive east, you say?" He moved back around his car, putting it between himself and the two men. "Thanks."

"You didn't answer Warner before, buddy-boy. He asked if'n you got a drink left in your jug."

Ed opened his door. "No, sorry. Thanks for the directions."

"Get away from the car," Warner said, and came quickly around Ed's Chevy. "You New York bums barrel through our neck of the woods and think you can do just about anything. Bum like you got no right here. Let's see your identification."

Ed's heart began thudding in his chest. Knowing himself, he knew he was terrified, yet he didn't *feel* terrified. Not the way he'd felt that time the three boys had jumped him outside the airfield in Marfa, Texas, and beaten and robbed him. He'd begged that time. He'd run. "You're not police," he said, and his voice didn't even sound frightened. "You just want me to take out my wallet. You want to rob me."

Warner was facing him from the front of the Chevy. Pat had circled around the rear and stood near the trunk. Ed was between them, back pressed to the door.

Pat looked up and down the road. The sun glinted over the horizon, accentuating the isolation. "When a man says that about another man in New Mexico, he'd better be ready to back it up. You don't look hardly able to back up the fact that you're alive, bum."

"And if he don't throw that wallet on the ground, fast, he won't be," Warner said.

They both moved toward Ed. He dropped his jacket and stood waiting. He thought of how afraid he should be, and didn't feel afraid.

Warner stopped first. He took a knife from his pocket and opened the blade. It was a good six inches long. Pat said, "Now you all won't need that, Warner. This bum's ready to fall down. Wait, I'll show you."

Ed turned to him. Pat took a long step forward, graceful for a man of his weight, and hit Ed high on the cheek with a quick right hand. Ed gasped, shocked as always by violence, but he didn't fall, or even stagger. Instead, his own hand shot out in sudden reflex action; a stiff-armed shove that caught Pat in the chest. It should have stopped his forward movement for a second. What it actually did was to make a soft, padded, crunching sound and send the big man spinning backward with a strangled, choking scream. Pat fell, curled on his side and vomited blood all over himself. He screamed again and fainted.

Ed caught movement from the corner of his eye, and turned as Warner danced in, knife sweeping low. The blade entered Ed's right side, above the belt, clear to the haft. It hurt terribly, and Ed groaned and lashed out in a hard, backhanded slap. Warner's nose and mouth mashed into red pulp and he dropped like a stone. He lay on his back, breath bubbling harshly.

Ed looked at them, and then down at himself. He too was bleeding, the red stain spreading slowly over his shirt, darkening his belt and trousers. Six inches of steel had entered his side; enough to kill him. But even as he watched, biting his lip, the stain stopped spreading and the pain subsided, and he felt as if he'd received nothing more than a scratch. Something must have deflected the blade.

He looked again at his assailants. He'd shoved one and backhanded the other . . . and they lay there, bleeding and gasping and half dead. He should have been amazed, and part of his mind knew this and was, but the other part, the part that handled his emotions, just nodded, satisfied.

He got into the car, raised his shirt and undershirt and looked at his side. There was a thin red line there. He touched it. Dry and crusted. He kneaded the flesh. The crusting flaked off, and a pale pencil-line scar was left.

He tucked in his clothes and drove onto the road. Let Warner and Pat live or die; it was all the same to him.

He went back in his mind to leaving the house, driving to Putnam Corners and finding himself at the side of the highway in New Mexico. New Mexico!

Amnesia. He'd lost his memory and ended up driving all the way here from New York. And the clout on the head that had blanked out the last week had also affected his ability to handle men like Pat and Warner. From a coward incapable of standing his ground even in a fair and equal fight, he'd become a man who could kill two thugs with his bare hands.

The reasoning didn't quite satisfy him. He felt too different in too many ways . . . ways that his amnesia theory wouldn't cover.

But whatever had happened, he felt wonderful; a feeling of strength, of bursting life force he'd never before experienced. "Please," he murmured prayerfully, increasing his speed to seventy, every reflex superbly alert, "please don't let it wear off."

He reached the outskirts of a small town two hours later. He stopped at a gas station and got out. Before the elderly attendant could do more than blink rheumy eyes at him, he said, "Been camping. Lost my gear. Any place I can wash up?"

The attendant pointed to a rest room around the side. "You want some gas?"

"Yes. Fill 'er up."

"Uh . . . you got any money, or did you lose that with your gear?"

Which was a damned good question. Ed took out his wallet and counted twenty-six dollars, plus thirty cents in his pocket. Hardly enough to get him back to New York. He waved the bills. "How about the loan of a razor?"

Fifteen minutes later, he was neater if not better dressed. He entered the phone booth near the highway and put in a collect call to Edith. She answered on the second ring. "It's me, Ed," he said.

"It's you." Her voice broke and he heard her crying. "It's you."

"Yes, well, something happened and I couldn't get in touch with you. I had a little accident . . ."

She gasped.

"Nothing serious," he said quickly. "But . . . I lost my memory, I guess. I'm in New Mexico. I need money to get home."

She stopped crying. "You're not in a hospital, are you, Ed? I want the truth. It's been five days. Five days without a word, Ed!"

"I'm sorry, honey. I don't know exactly what happened, but I'm not in a hospital. I haven't got a scratch, really. And the car seems to be okay too."

"Then why . . ." Her voice tightened. "All right. You come on home and then we'll talk. If you're not hurt . . . just come home. The police—I'll have to call them and say it's all right. Oh, they'll think I'm a beaut, they will! How much money will you need?"

"I don't know. Enough for gas and sandwiches and a night or two in hotels. A hundred. Better make it a hundred fifty. Not that I'll spend that much, but I'll feel better . . ."

"Did I hear a woman laughing? It *was* a woman, wasn't it, Ed?"

"What? A car went by, I think. A woman? What sort of . . ."

"All right. A car went by. You want me to send you a hundred fifty dollars, after I don't hear from you for five days. All right. Where shall I send the money?"

"I'll call again when I get to a hotel. It'll be in a little while. Wait there."

"What else have I been doing for the past five days but waiting here? I thought you were dead. Or . . . but you say you haven't a scratch and the car's all right and you have amnesia. And you're in New Mexico."

"Yes, that's what I say."

"I'm going to hang up now, Ed. You're not much better at lying than you are at writing."

Her voice was raging, and he didn't blame her for not believing him. At the same time, his own anger rose. "Just wait for my call."

"And what if I don't? What if I just take the kids and go away for a few days? Five days, for instance? What if I don't send the money?"

He thought it over, and then laughed. "Why then, I'll get it some other way. But you'll be damned sorry when I do get home."

"Oh, you're all right. No doubt about that. You're more than all right. You're drunk! You've been out on a five-day binge and you expect me . . ."

"I expect you to send me one hundred and fifty dollars, Edith."

"New Mexico," she said. "You lost your memory so you drove to New Mexico. Why not New Guinea? Or Newfoundland? Well, we'll wait till you get home. And then we'll see." She hung up.

He went back to the pumps and paid the attendant and asked about a hotel.

"No hotel, but a nice motel other side of town. Just stay on the highway about eight miles. Can't miss it."

He didn't miss it. He checked into a small, bright room—part of a long, barrackslike affair of twenty rooms—and called Edith. He gave her the address and told her to telegraph the money. The office in town would get it to him here. Then he emptied his wallet and pockets. He had twelve dollars and ten cents, after paying for this room.

He was hungry. As soon as he realized it, he felt he was starving! He would eat as much as he could hold: a steak and potatoes and salad and bread and beer.

He took off his shirt and examined it. He could wear it open at the neck, and roll up the sleeves, and hike up his pants to cover the dark bloodstain.

He decided to shower. If the telegraph money order arrived before he left, he'd buy a fresh shirt first thing. If not, he'd get something to eat no matter what anyone thought.

He stripped quickly and moved toward the bathroom door. But he stopped short, head turning to his reflection in the dresser mirror on his right. "Now wait a minute," he whispered, stunned, frightened . . . yet already beginning to smile. "Just one minute, here. Ed Berner never looked like that." The smile grew and he didn't care how it had happened and he brought up his arms, flexing the heavy muscles of his biceps. He took a breath, and the depth of his chest caused him to gasp and exhale again. He tensed the muscles of his legs, watching them stand out powerfully. That was when he noticed his genitals, and his laughter stopped and he stood in awe of himself.

He turned suddenly, closing his eyes and once again thinking back to Tuesday night and leaving the house and blanking out. Had he been this way Tuesday night? Had he somehow forgotten what he actually looked like? Had Ed Berner been a Greek god all his life without knowing it?

Impossible! His memories were memories of dissatisfaction with self, and who could be dissatisfied with a self like this?

Again he faced the mirror. He touched himself. When his eyes finally left the powerful muscles and powerful maleness, he looked at his face . . . and at his hair. The thinning in front had changed. It wasn't quite gone, but it was different. The hair fringing the widow's peak was no longer wispy and dying; it was thick, springy, vital, bushy.

He went on into the bathroom and fixed the shower to his usual hot blend, but when he got in, it didn't feel good. He raised the percentage of cold water, and then shut the hot entirely. He stood in an icy stream, waiting for it to become too much for him. It never did. His body sang, and he joined in with his voice.

He finished and jumped out and toweled. He followed every movement of his upper body in the small bathroom mirror. He admired this man. No, he *loved* this man! And this man was himself (though he didn't really accept it yet), and he had always despised himself.

He dressed and combed his hair, and then sat down at the edge of the bed. "Again," he said aloud, "let's think this out." He thought and reasoned and nothing explained what he was.

Edith would be the key. If she noticed nothing different, then he'd know he had always been this way; or was imagining he was this way.

That last thought frightened him. Could he have *dreamed* the changes in himself? He jerked his eyes to the mirror, and saw only his face, and except for the hair that didn't look too different. He jumped up, and the Ed Berner looking back at him was the Ed Berner he remembered from his life before this Tuesday.

With fumbling dread, he pulled off his shirt, pants and underwear. And smiled and knew it was no dream and knew he would no longer doubt himself.

He stopped at the office to tell the manager he expected a telegraph money order; then drove into town. It wasn't much of a town. Sunbaked and shabby. He explored the few streets and returned to the highway, which was the main drag, and parked in front of a place called Bill's Food Palace. He went inside and took a table near the door.

Three men sat at the short counter, talking to a girl. The girl was young and reasonably pretty, but it wasn't until she came around the counter to Ed's table that he saw why the men were so attentive. She was built. She was tall and curved and sure of herself. She walked with a sinuous, swinging grace that shouted, "Look at how desirable I am!" But the full-lipped pout and sullen glance said, "I'm much too good for you." He wished his pants were pressed. He wished he'd bought a new shirt.

"The counter's clean," she muttered.

"I'm sure it is," he said, smiling. "But I like elbow room, and service."

Her eyes flickered over him, contemptuous of his clothing. "*Big* man."

He looked up from the menu, still smiling. He caught her eyes, held them, said, "If you only knew."

The sullen look changed. She flushed. "What'll it be, mister?"

"I'll have the steak and potatoes. Salad too. And a bottle of beer."

She scribbled on a pad and walked back around the counter to a door. She opened it and said, "Bill, steak and potatoes."

"And salad," Ed called.

She looked at him. "And salad."

One of the men at the counter murmured, "Big spender too," and the other two laughed.

"None of that," the girl said sharply. "You let the customers be or I'll have Pete down from the station in half a sec."

Ed leaned back in his chair. Oh, he felt fine. This was his world. This girl was his girl, if he wanted it that way. And he wanted it that way. "A very big spender," he said. "How about you, sonny?"

The man who'd spoken turned around on his stool. He was short and broad and in his twenties. He looked unhappy. "If we wasn't in this here café . . ."

"I told you, none of that!" the girl said, leaning across the counter.

"Tell you what," Ed said, enjoying himself. There was no fear in him. He had lived his whole life with fear, all thirty-eight years, no matter where he had gone or what he had done. There'd been things to fear in working, and things to fear on vacations, and things to fear at home. There'd been much to fear on entering strange restaurants and looking at strange women whom other men might desire. And now he was sitting here in a strange restaurant and desiring a strange woman whom a young, heavy-set man with bulging forearms also desired. "Tell you what, sonny, you look pretty strong in the arms. Five dollars says you can't put me down in a hand wrestle."

The man got off the stool and walked toward Ed. His two friends whooped and one said, "He picked Chris Holbroke! Of all the men in the county, he picked the best. Oh, sweet seesaw!"

The girl said, "You shouldn't do that, mister. He's an ox."

"He made the bet," Chris Holbroke said, unsmiling. "You going to chicken out, mister?"

Ed took the five dollar bill from his wallet and put it on the table.

Chris Holbroke took five singles from a roll in his pocket and dropped them over Ed's five. Then he drew his chair into position, placed his elbow on the table and flexed his power-ful right hand. Low, so no one else could hear, he murmured, "I'm going to break your hand."

The fear tried to come alive. Thirty-eight years of self-con-tempt couldn't die in a day. But Ed remembered the two men on the road, and what he'd seen in the mirror, and he put his own elbow in position and grasped Chris Holbroke's hand. The kitchen door opened and a fat, middle-aged man joined the spectators. Ed said, "You ready?"

Chris Holbroke paled. He had put all his strength into what he considered a crushing hand-squeeze a second before.

After that it was easy. Ed squeezed once, pressed once, and Holbroke's knuckles hit the table. Holbroke gasped and massaged his hand. He bent low, trying to hide his pain; then got up and went out of the restaurant. "Next?" Ed said, won-dering if he were being childish in the joy he felt, but feeling it nonetheless.

The two men at the counter turned their backs. The cook said, "The new champ, well, well," and went back to his kitchen. The waitress smiled.

Ed ate his meal, calling for more bread three times. The

cook came out the last time, saying, "Hey, you're gonna hafta pay extra. Never seen a lean man put away ten, twelve slices of rye before. You do this all the time, mister?"

Ed shook his head. "Only when I've had a big breakfast."

The waitress thought that very funny. The two men at the counter paid for their soft drinks and got up to leave. Ed gave them a jaunty salute. One of them paused at the door and said, "You shouldn't push it, mister. Not in a place no one knows you. What if we was to wait outside to teach you a lesson?"

"I don't know. You do that. We'll find out."

But looking at them, he knew they were afraid. He seemed to *feel* their fear. He said, "Waitress, another beer please." The men left.

The waitress came with his beer and paused to write on her pad. He said, "You like beer?"

"Me? Sure."

"This one is for you."

"The big spender again, huh?" But she was smiling now. "I can't sit down with a customer, you know that." She patted her pale brown hair.

"Of course. The demands of all the other customers . . ." He waved his arm around the empty room.

She giggled, and sat down where Chris had been sitting, close to Ed. She made as if to move the chair back to its normal position, but he put his hand on her arm and said, "We'd better introduce ourselves."

Her name was Lois and she thought the name Ed a *strong* name. When he stroked her arm, she wet her lips and smiled and said, "I get off around seven, when Emmy comes on. I usually go on home . . ."

He said she was lovely and bent to kiss her hand, and felt the erotic thoughts come alive in her. She wanted him. He could walk out with this girl and take her to his room and make love to her.

He told her to ask her boss for a few hours off. She said no, it was impossible. He told her to say she wasn't feeling well and just had to lie down for an hour or two. She smiled then, eyes locked with his. "Go on, Lois. Go on, honey."

She wet her lips. "Don't know what's got into me, you just coming in here and all." She went back to the counter, and now her walk was an attempt at prudery, purity, the exact opposite of the heated thoughts in her brain.

She entered the kitchen. He heard the murmur of voices. Then she was back, shaking her head. "He said no. Can't you come around at seven?"

He nodded, but he wanted her now. Why should he wait? He wished he had the hundred and fifty dollars. He'd pay that cook for the inconvenience of losing his waitress for an afternoon. But all he had was six-eighty, after settling his bill and tipping Lois a dollar. He got up. "Let me talk to him."

"It won't do no good, Ed."

"I'll try anyway."

He went through the door, not knowing what he was going to do. He only knew that the fat man in the spotted white apron was preventing Lois from being his. For thirty-eight years, people had prevented the good things in life from being Ed Berner's. It had changed now. This man couldn't be allowed to change it back again, even for a few hours.

The cook turned from a range as Ed entered. "Hey, no one's allowed back here!"

Ed held out five dollars. "Lois says she's not feeling well."

The fat man went red. "Get your ass out of here! My waitress don't need a lawyer when she tries to goof off. I told her, if she's sick I'll get the doc right over and pay for it myself."

Ed put the five dollars away, examining his wallet carefully. "I'll pay for a replacement. Fifteen, twenty dollars. That's more than adequate, isn't it?"

"Don't change a thing," the cook muttered, but added quickly, "You only showed five."

"I'll have the rest in an hour or two."

"Out, out!" He stamped toward Ed, waving his arms.

Ed looked up. The fat man walked into that cold gaze, and stopped dead. Ed said, "I'm a doctor. She's not well. She needs a few hours' rest." He stared directly into the puffy blue eyes, and felt the man's growing fear.

"So you're a doctor. Even so, you couldn't've examined her. . . ."

"She's leaving now. When she comes back, she'll pay you the fifteen dollars. That's all right, isn't it?"

The fat man was whiter than his apron. He said, voice weak, "What sort of a way is this to act, mister? I mean, coming into my place . . ."

Ed stepped up close to him. He put his hand on the soft shoulder and tightened his grip. "That's all right now, isn't it?"

The fat man winced, and changed. "Yeah, sure, if she pays the fifteen dollars."

"She will. Just don't give her any trouble."

"Why should I do that?" Ed could smell the fear as if it were perspiration. "Ain't no one out there anyway. She'll be back before six, right?"

"I don't know."

"So then I'll get Emmy in early and pay her what Lois gives me. So it works out fair and square."

Ed dropped his hand. "Thank you."

"Well, sure, you're welcome."

Ed looked at him a moment longer, enjoying the feeling of power, of being able to make a man cringe before him. He felt ashamed, too, because this was being the bad guy, and soon the good guys would come to restore law and order and he would be punished.

Or would he? He had broken no laws. And he was stronger and braver than anyone.

He turned suddenly, caught by a wave of pure exultation. God, God, he could do what he wished in this world, this beautiful world full of beautiful women and good things to eat and, most of all, good *feelings* to reap. All the humiliations of the past were going to be reversed. He might even look up some of the perpetrators of those humiliations. . . .

Was he becoming something evil and dangerous?

But who was to judge? If a man found he could do almost anything he wanted, wouldn't he be insane not to gratify himself?

It was too early to think this way. Later, after he explored himself a bit more, he would think. He wouldn't kill anyone; not anyone who didn't try to kill him. He wouldn't rob anyone . . . though, in a sense, what he'd done to Chris, and to the fat cook, had been robbery, hadn't it?

Later, later. Now it was time for Lois.

She was back behind the counter, drawing two glasses of water. He nodded and said, "Let's go."

"You sure he said so?" She jerked her head at a table. A young couple sat there, reading the menu.

He took the glasses from her and put them down. He opened the door to the kitchen and said, "Customers waiting." He took Lois' arm and steered her to the front door. The young couple looked at them. The girl said, "Hey, Lois, what gives?"

Lois smiled faintly, and then Ed had her out the door. She stopped, pulling her arm free. "It's . . . it's not right, Ed. I don't know what you expect . . ." She peered at him, and the erotic thoughts were gone and doubt had taken their place. (Though how he knew this he couldn't say.)

"There's my car. There's the road. And here we are, with a few lovely hours to spend having laughs."

"Well . . ." She shrugged. "I can use a few laughs."

They drove out of town. She told him that laughs had been few and far between since her father died. "My mother's dating a character from Albuquerque; a super salesman, he thinks. He gives me a pain. And he's got her drinking more than ever. I hardly see her any more. Bet he doesn't marry her. . . ."

He made comforting, appropriate, agreeable comments, and felt a slight chill of distaste. But when he glanced at her, and saw the way the thin white skirt stuck damply to her full thigh, he forgot distaste.

He pulled off the road at the motel. She stopped in mid-sentence. "Hey, you said . . ."

"I've got a room here. Want to wash up after that heavy meal. Can't hold a girl's hand with steak fat all over mine. Can't kiss her either."

"Don't you worry none about that," she murmured, but smiled a little.

He drove up the gravel side-road and stopped in front of his room. "C'mon in."

"I'd better wait."

He was out of the car and around her side opening the door. "We'll be just a minute." He took her arm, leaned close, and murmured, "Prettiest girl I ever saw. And we've got millions in New York."

"Yeah, I bet."

"Prettiest, and sweetest."

"My, my, how the line goes on and on." But she got out and walked with him to the porch. He used his key. She said, "I really shouldn't." He opened the door and moved her inside, his hand on the small on her back. He closed the door.

"Always wondered what this place was like," she said, and blinked nervously around the room. "They charge much?"

He didn't answer. He came up behind her and kissed her neck and then her cheek. "Now you cut that out, Ed." He moved his hands up from her waist to the sweet swellings. "I said . . ." He turned her swiftly, his strength making her gasp, and plunged his mouth to the parted lips. He kissed her as if she were another good thing to devour, as indeed she was. He wanted to hum as he did it. He was so sure, so full of strength and joy in his strength. When he put both hands on her bottom and pulled her against him, he felt the erotic fire return to her thoughts. "Please," she whispered. "Oh, please, Ed."

He put his left arm under her knees and swept her up. He held her, and remembered trying to do the same to Viola, the divorcée from his last agency, and straining and staggering and being laughed at. He stood in the center of the room, holding this big, fine woman; holding her as if she were a five pound package. She looked at him, mouth going thick and slack. "Strong Daddy," she murmured. "Don't hurt baby."

She was his now. He brought her to the bed and lowered her slowly, without bending, testing the incredible strength in his arms and shoulders. He sat down beside her, and undressed her. She tried to stop him when he reached her tight pink pants, but he bent to her breasts, and soon she lay open to his eyes.

He began to move over her, fumbling at his clothing; then stopped. He stood up. She curled on her side, eyes questioning him. He stepped back and took off his shirt and then his undershirt. He stretched, and her eyes shone and she said, "The big spender's quite a man." She tried to make it funny, but her voice shook and he drank in the surprise and adulation. He removed the rest of his clothing. He wanted to look down at himself, but couldn't tear his eyes from her face. She was staring openly. "I don't know," she whispered. "I really don't know."

But it was fine. There was a moment's struggle, accompanied by the rich music of her moans. He enjoyed it immensely. And then he was reducing her to a palpitating object of service and pleasure, attaining manhood as he'd always dreamed of.

Afterward, she told him she loved him. "I know it's not supposed to happen so fast, Ed, but soon as you walked in . . ."

He assured her he'd be around a while, that he traveled this way often, that the chances of something "serious" developing were good. But it was the strong beat of his heart, the resurgent power of his passion, the smooth play of his muscles he loved.

She was surprised when he took her back in his arms a few minutes later. She'd been around, this sweet young thing, but he was something special. The third and fourth times she wept with pleasure. The fifth, sixth and seventh times she moaned and spittle drooled from the corners of her mouth. The eighth time she shook her head, lips puffy, face red, body wet with perspiration. "C'mon now," she said, voice hoarse. "You gonna kill yourself, sweetheart."

He took her, and she gasped for breath and lay still and looked at him with eyes vaguely worried. "What time is it?" she asked, but he wasn't about to check his wrist watch. Later, she got up and reached for her clothes. He said, "It's not an hour and a half since we came here. You're free for today."

"An hour and a half?" She stood beside the bed, shoulders slouched, breasts drooping.

"Yes." He drew her back to the bed.

She shook her head. "Enough's enough, as the man says. What's with you?"

He smiled. She struggled, but she was exhausted and he was full of strength and desire. And his desire enslaved her.

He experimented until it grew dark outside. She fell asleep as soon as he got out of bed. She lay on her back, the marks of their combat covering her body. He was satisfied now. Not drained, he didn't think he would ever be drained, but finished with the game, finished with Lois.

He showered and dressed. She was still lying there, mouth open, breathing heavily, body limp and de-sexed, at least to his cool eye. He moved to the door, and saw the telegram lying just inside on the floor. It must have been there since they came in, unless he'd failed to hear a knock at the door sometime in the past few hours.

He opened the envelope and took out a money order for

one hundred dollars. Edith had cut him fifty. She was showing her suspicion, and her continuing contempt for him as a
husband and a man.

He put the order in his wallet, and looked at Lois, and
thought of Edith. He had no real desire for Edith, but she
too would worship him before long; she too would lie flaccid
and de-sexed, beaten by sheer manhood. Then he would see
what to do with her, and with his life.

He got his torn jacket from the chair. He might need it
while traveling through the chill of the Western evening, but
he doubted it. He doubted he would ever again feel uncomfortably cold or uncomfortably warm again, in normal circumstances. What he was now seemed to preclude discomfort. Everything about him functioned magnificently. Why,
he could have taken Lois again, four or five or a dozen times,
if there had been any point to it!

He opened the door, but then he worried about Lois getting back to town and took the five dollar bill from his wallet
and put it on the night table. She stirred as he began to turn
away. He froze. He stood absolutely still, barely breathing,
beautifully balanced in mid-turn, enjoying this new test of his
physical perfection. Not a muscle quivered, though his position was awkward.

When he drove onto the highway, he automatically
reached for cigarettes, then remembered he no longer
smoked. He thought of a drink; natural enough to cap such a
session as he'd just had, but that too seemed unnecessary.

He would stop at the next town. He would cash his money
order and get a fresh suit of clothes and drive on. He realized
he wasn't allowing for a night's sleep, and thought it over,
and decided he didn't need sleep just yet. He would, eventually, but not tonight.

He pressed down on the accelerator. The Chevy picked up
speed. He leaned back, putting his right arm on the back of
the seat, steering comfortably with his left. Darkness intensified over the near-desert country. His lights tunneled the
roadway ahead. The world was still and beautiful.

He felt pleasure, such intense pleasure that, finally, he
couldn't contain himself, and put back his head and shouted
—a savage, piercing, roaring sound like no other ever heard.

chapter 3

HE SPENT only eighty of his hundred dollars getting back to
Westchester County, New York, and almost all of that for
gas and food (his appetite was simple, but enormous). He
never did spend a night in bed, though he caught four or five
hours' sleep at the side of the road. And he didn't bother
buying a suit, though he replaced his torn, blood-stained
shirt. His change in plan was the result of a growing desire to
be back among people who knew him; people who would in-
dicate, by their reactions, whether or not he was insane.

He pulled into his driveway at eleven p.m. of the first
Tuesday in July, and sat still a moment. It took that moment
for him to realize he was afraid; then he jumped out and
raised the fold-up garage door, angry at himself. What the
hell did he have to fear? No matter what Edith or anyone
else said, he knew what he was, even if he didn't know how
long he had been that way.

Or if you actually are that way, the inner voice of fear
said. *If you're not dreaming with a damaged brain.*

He put on the garage light, went back to his car and drove
inside. As he got out, the door to the playroom opened. He
and Edith looked at each other. "Hi," he said, a heavy pulse
sounding in his temples. "How're the kids?"

"Asleep."

He laughed briefly. "A good way to be. And you? You're
not asleep, are you?"

"I can see there's no need to ask how *you* are." Her eyes
went over him. He waited tensely. "You never looked better
in your life."

"Well, I feel . . ."

She backed abruptly, slamming the door on his words. He
turned to lock the garage. She hadn't seen anything different
about him. Of course, she'd been a good twenty feet away,
and the garage light was an inadequate 60-watt bulb in a high
ceiling, and she hadn't been *looking* for differences. . . .

She was sitting at the kitchen table, a magazine open before her, when he came in. He bent and kissed her cheek. She laughed sharply. "I suppose that's meant to make everything just fine. That's going to take the place of a logical explanation."

"No, this is." He pulled her up out of the chair and kissed her and ran his hands over her body. She struggled violently, making angry sounds under his lips. He didn't let go. He had no trouble holding her, and was pleased at how quickly, how easily, his passion came alive. He thought, *There's enough now even for Edith,* and smiled and raised his head.

"Let go!" she whispered. "This very minute! You . . . you have explaining to do! You have forgiveness to beg! You may very well never touch me again, or live in this house, or have the right to see your children. . . ."

"Shut up," he muttered, and gagged her with his lips and picked her up and carried her that way to the second floor and past the children's rooms to the master bedroom, and fell with her that way on the bed and didn't bother undressing her or himself.

She was outraged, and puzzled, when it was finished, but outrage was stronger. "Animal!" she whispered, getting up and stumbling over the mat in the dark. "With the door open and the children just a few feet . . ."

He reached out, grabbed her arm and brought her flying back to the bed with one tug. She began to shout, and he slapped her rump hard enough to cause pain. It was a nice rump, her most generous, most attractive feature, and he slapped it again. "I told you," he said, controlling laughter, "to shut up. Dear."

He began undressing her.

"No," she said, and grew still. "I mean it, Ed."

He tried working her dress up over her head. When she didn't help, he tore it up the back in one quick movement. She struck him as hard as she could, in the face. It stung, but the feeling could hardly be classified as pain. He ripped off her brassiere. She raked his cheek with her nails. That hurt, and he tore off her panties and slapped her rump again, bringing a cry this time. "Be nice," he said softly, and stroked her body and thought how good it felt and how wonderful it was to have fire enough for all the good bodies, all the women in the world. He laughed aloud, and the deep sound of it made her say, voice climbing, "Ed, you . . . what is it?"

"What is it?" He rolled away and got out of his clothing and came at her. "It's this, dear Edith. It's this." With that, he began her enslavement, her reduction to a thing of his pleasure and service, her development as the perfect wife. He worked on her with his passion, learning the art of love (as he had with Lois) even as he practiced it. She tried hard to retain her righteous anger, but a moment later he smiled at her heavy breathing and stifled moans of pleasure. And then her arms and legs locked about him and she said his name as he'd never heard her say it before, not even on their honeymoon. She told him that she'd feared for his life and loved him and he must promise never again to frighten her that way. "It's a new beginning for us, darling, isn't it?"

He didn't answer. He let his body do the answering, again and again. He wearied of her after the fifth time, rising as she wept with gratitude for her climax. He strode down the hall to the bathroom, feeling his strength and beauty. He showered and returned to the bedroom, still nude. The light was on and Edith was lying under the blankets. He stopped close beside her. Her eyes went over him, and she half sat up. "You're . . . you never looked . . . the size . . . and when did you . . ." She put her hands to her mouth and screamed softly. "You are my Ed, aren't you? I mean, of course, but your hair too. . . ." Her hand dropped and she screamed aloud and fell back in bed and lay still.

So he wasn't insane; he *had* changed during that trip to New Mexico. He would have to find out how, someday. But the important thing now was that the change was real.

Matty called out. Edith's scream had wakened him. Then Miri's voice asked what was going on. He went to the dresser and put on a pair of pajama bottoms. "It's all right, kids, Daddy's home."

Miri squealed and came running. He met her in the bedroom doorway and picked her up and laughed. He carried her into Matty's room as if she were three instead of ten. He sat down with her on Matty's bed and she squirmed free and put on the light. Suddenly, her joy was gone. She backed up a step. "What's the matter?" he asked, and turned from her and kissed his son, who blinked sleepily at him.

"I . . . don't know. You scare me."

"You mean my muscles, don't you?" He flexed his arm, still looking at the slender little boy with pale brown hair and his face.

Matty came awake. "Daddy, you got a bigger muscle than *anyone!*"

"Yes, that's it, I think," Miri said, still hesitating near the doorway.

"Well, I was away at a rest place in New Mexico and I exercised and ate spinach and salad and steak and drank four gallons of milk every day, and I grew bigger muscles. So why be scared?"

"*I'm* not scared," Matty shouted, sitting up and punching Ed in the shoulder. "I can hit hard, just like you."

"Sure you can." And he felt a pang for his boy, thin as he'd been, gentle and shy with outsiders as he'd been. But then he thought how he'd teach this child confidence, and give him the security of a supremely capable father, and money too before long, and he hugged him gently and turned to Miri. "You're not going to let your brother give me *all* the welcome-home kisses, are you?"

She came to him, but the fright remained in her face, and he felt it would be the same with all the adults and near-adults who knew him. At least for a while, until they convinced themselves he had always been this way. The five-year-olds and strangers would provide no such problems. Neither would they provide the satisfactions he was already planning. Just wait till he got to the office and Nick Bandson and Miss Carlsbad. Oh, just wait!

Edith came to the doorway, pale and disheveled. "I must have passed out. Perhaps too much . . ."

He put Matty back in bed and covered him. "Get back to sleep now, and you'll be strong as Daddy." Matty nodded somberly, and turned on his side and closed his eyes. Ed smiled to himself. He had never promised his children his own strength, intelligence, or skills. He had never thought them worth a child's desire. It was different now.

Miri said, "Daddy went to a rest place and ate and exercised and got more muscles." She said it questioningly.

Edith nodded, and blinked her eyes at Ed. "You . . . there was some sort of health program?"

"That's right." He didn't care whether they believed him or not. They would have to believe something, because he was here and he was the way he was. They would find their own explanations.

He went to Miri. She tried to slip away, but he picked her up again. "Now I'll tuck my *big* baby in."

She smiled a little. He kissed her cheek. She nestled against him. She was female, and his strength and beauty reached her. He knew this, as he seemed to know so many things now.

Later, he had Edith make him eggs and bacon. He had two servings, half a loaf of bread and a quart of milk. "You must've been starved," she said, looking at him across the kitchen table.

He wiped his mouth. She offered him her pack of cigarettes. "Gave them up," he said.

"You've given them up before."

"This time I mean it."

"Want some coffee?"

He hadn't had coffee, or tea, since New Mexico. He shook his head. "Gave that up too."

She wet her lips. "Ed, how did your hair . . . it *is* thicker, isn't it? Or am I imagining things?" She leaned forward and touched his head. She was getting used to him and beginning to doubt her memories of a week ago. "Did you really go to a health farm?"

He nodded. "I *was* in an accident, as I told you, and I did lose my memory. When I came to, I was in some sort of specialized rejuvenation center, a very expensive place which we ordinarily couldn't afford. Millionaires go there. The latest in hormones and gland treatments and so on. But I was an emergency. I was picked up right outside their gates. So they treated me and . . ." He smiled. "Here I am, better than ever. For free."

She withdrew her hand and shrugged helplessly. "It's so hard to . . . really, Ed, it's like nothing I ever heard of." But she was mild about it, defeated, unable to resist his smiling assurance.

She lit a cigarette. After a few puffs, she said, "Smile, Ed."

"Smile?"

"Your teeth . . ."

He smiled.

"They look so much more natural. They look almost real. Did they polish the caps?"

"Replaced them. New kind. Real enamel. Can't tell them from the type you grow." His smile broadened. "Remember how we used to wonder about movie stars who stayed young so long? The secret is health centers like this one. My bill would've been thousands and thousands of dollars, if I'd had the money."

Again she shook her head. Again he smiled. She said, "Upstairs, before. You never . . . well, not since that night on our honeymoon, and even then not *five* times in an hour or so. And you looked, you felt . . ."

"Hormone injections." He got up. "Hope it doesn't change."

Her own smile came then; a radiant smile. "I hope so too, Ed. You must be exhausted."

He was far from exhausted, but the time had come for a full night's sleep. "Yes. And there's work tomorrow. Same old schedule." He'd rarely said that without a sinking sensation, a feeling of dull depression, but there was no depression now. There would be no more defeats for Ed Berner. He stretched, and she watched and wet her lips and murmured, "I just can't remember ever . . ."

"How about a snack? I could go for some salad and rye bread."

She laughed.

While he ate, she told him she'd called the agency and said he was ill. "They'll never believe it, when they see you. I don't know what you can do."

He wiped the salad bowl clean with a last piece of bread. "Forget it. No problem." He poured another glass of milk, gulped it and belched stentoriously. "Pardon." But he wasn't embarrassed. Even his belch was strong.

He fell asleep a moment after getting into bed. Edith's hand was stroking his arm. He awoke at five-thirty, half an hour before his alarm was set to go off. Edith's hand was still stroking him, but no longer his arm. He laughed softly. Her hand jerked back and she reddened. "I'm sorry, Ed. I couldn't sleep. Did I wake you?"

He kept laughing, the strength singing in his body, culminating in the throb of passion. He pulled her to him. It was a very pleasant twenty minutes: setting-up exercises with a plus. The only irritant was her incessant talk of a "rebirth of love" and "the finding again of what brought us together years ago." He was ready to conquer the world, and she considered

him her personal stud. He could take what he wanted, become what he wanted, and she thought he would be satisfied
to go on much as he had before.

Showering, he began to consider various possibilities. He
could leave home and be free to pluck the whole big, ripe,
juicy world.

But Matty and Miri . . . and Edith herself, what would
she do if he walked away from her?

And did he *want* to do that? Was it necessary? He wasn't
going to marry any other woman. that was certain. It was *all*
of them, not one of them he wanted. So why not continue to
have his home and children and conjugal comforts?

As for the other triumphs—the emotional and financial
conquests—if a family couldn't help, neither could it deter.

He asked Edith for a bowl of hot cereal, and ate a pound
of farmer cheese and half a loaf of bread too. She drove him
to the station, Wednesday being one of her shopping days.
He said, "We sure could use a second car."

She nodded. He'd been saying that for years.

"I think I'll get one next week."

Her head jerked to him. "And what will we use for
money?" she asked, in a return to her old, sharp tone.

"Oh, I've got a few ideas." He flicked his eyes at her and
smiled. "Trust me, huh? Things are going to be different."

She nodded again, but he felt she didn't believe him. She
couldn't know how far the changes in Ed Berner went. Actually, he wasn't sure himself how far they went, but he knew
he was *more* than he'd been, better in every way, and that
had to mean more money.

Edith left him off a block from the station, to avoid the
morning crush of cars. As he reached the tracks and cross-
over gate, Harry Amory's Olds station wagon swung to a
halt beside him. Harry got out the door on the other side,
and Gladys, his wife, slid across the seat to take the wheel.
She was half undressed, as usual, with an open raincoat
thrown over her nightclothes. Gladys was a tall, hefty blonde
with a large, warm face; one of the most attractive women in
the area, in Ed's opinion. Harry was big and rough and, by
admission, too hot-tempered for his own good, especially
when it came to "characters giving Glad the eye." Which was
why, normally, Ed turned away from temptation and gave his
attention, and greetings, to Harry. He'd barely exchanged a
word with Gladys in the past six months.

But now he stepped to the car, leaned in the passenger's front window and said, "Hey, Gladys, how're things?"

She had one hand on the wheel, one hand on the gearshift and her fine long legs were stretched to the brake and gas. Her nightgown was white and sheer and up around mid-thigh, and that open raincoat did nothing to protect her from his eyes. He almost reached out to stroke those firm pillars of flesh.

"Gee, Ed, fine. . . ." One hand pulled the raincoat together, but the moment she let go, it fell apart again. Ed smiled and looked and let her see him looking. She colored delicately.

"Why don't you and Harry come over to the house this Saturday night? We'll barbecue a few steaks and have a few laughs."

"Ask Harry, why don't you?" Again her hand tugged at the raincoat, but he felt her pleasure at his admiration, her stirring, awakening excitement.

Harry's heavy hand came down on Ed's shoulder. "Ask me what? And why don't we let Gladys get back to the kids. Or don't you approve of that procedure, Ed?"

Ed remained leaning on the window. He turned his head. Harry was smiling, but it wasn't too friendly a smile.

"I was just saying you and Gladys should come to the house this Saturday night for a barbecue. Steaks and ribs and some laughs."

"You mean hamburgers and hot dogs and yawns." Harry's smile was almost gone. "That's what happened the last time, didn't it? That's what happens at every area barbecue."

Ed chuckled easily. "I give my solemn word we'll have prime porterhouse, as much as you can eat."

"You're on, buddy. It'll cost you fifty bucks if it costs a dime. And don't forget, I drink the best brandy, when I can get it."

"You'll get it." Harry's hand still lay heavy on his shoulder, but he turned back to Gladys. She had the raincoat buttoned now, and he concentrated on her wide gray eyes. "What about your preferences, Gladys?"

She shrugged, smiling. "Just as long as I get away from the kids a few hours. I used to like a little caviar, before Harry changed my tastes."

"Oh, sure," Harry said, pushing in beside Ed. "Her old man bought her eight, ten ounces of Romanoff every day."

"Not my father, but some of the men I dated . . ."

They were beginning to quarrel. Ed didn't particularly mind that, but he said, "Whoa. Keep this marriage together until Saturday. I'd hate to have the date canceled by divorce."

"You're funny this morning, Ed," Harry said, voice rumbling on the edge of anger. "Very funny."

Gladys giggled. "What happened to you the past week, Ed? Edith was walking around with a long face and we heard . . ."

"Emergency trip to New Mexico. Business. Did myself quite a lot of good. That's the reason for our celebration Saturday." He held her eyes an instant. "I'm looking forward to it."

"You sure are looking forward to something," Harry growled.

Gladys was flushing again. "Harry! Can't you ever learn to kid around like other men?"

Harry said, "C'mon, Ed. The train's due any minute."

Ed stepped away from the car. He smiled and waved, not taking his eyes off Gladys. She returned his wave, and began pulling into the road, and glanced back at him. They'd been neighbors for six years, and she'd never given him a second glance; especially not one so weighted with interest. It was also weighted with confusion, but he expected that now, from everyone. Soon the confusion would go and Ed Berner would be accepted for what he was—the greatest; Number One; the man who had it all!

He turned, slapping Harry on the back. The big man stumbled forward, then turned, glaring. "You presume too much, neighbor. What the hell's got into you?"

"Me? Nothing, Harry. I feel chipper. . . ."

"Just remember, not everyone feels chipper in the morning." His eyes were moving over Ed, puzzled, trying to learn something. "If I were to haul off and whack *your* back that way, you wouldn't recover for a month!"

Ed walked past him, smiling. Harry was big all right, about six-two and well over two hundred pounds. Big and broad and soft and out of condition. How had he ever respected, actually feared, this hunk of blubber?

But he didn't want to spark Harry's much vaunted temper. He wanted the Amorys at his home this Saturday. He wanted Gladys where he could get his hands on her. "You mean a *year*, Harry. I'm just not in your fighting class."

Harry grumbled under his breath and fell in beside him and they walked across the tracks and up the cinder path to the platform. Harry asked about New Mexico, and Ed made up answers, and Harry said, "We'd better stop here, if we want to make the smoker."

"Gave it up, Harry. See you Saturday." He left the big man, sensing the worry, the loss of prestige Harry felt in their relationship, the confused anger. All of which made him feel very good.

Prior-Bailey-Stennis had the third floor in a new building on Third Avenue, five blocks from Grand Central Station. It was a comfortable enough little agency, if not what Ed had dreamed of when entering the business. Men made out well there. Men like Nick Bandson, Ed's group head. Bandson's salary was twenty thousand or better. He'd come from Young & Rubicam, out of McCann-Erickson, and used this background as a knife to carve himself a solid position at P.B.S. His contempt for the men under him was carefully nurtured, and publicized, so that none of them could ever become strong enough to hurt him, or even to leave his aegis. His three writers constituted the largest and best-billed group in the agency. They handled all the Wylitt Beverage Company account, two million of the total eight-million-dollar agency billing. They also handled a million in industrial accounts.

Ed wrote just about all the liquor ads, as well as the speeches for Wylitt's executives. But nothing he did escaped the minor changes that transformed *his* ads and speeches into Nick Bandson's ads and speeches. Only when Bandson was on vacation did Ed get anything through on his own. P.B.S. management might have cared about this situation, had they known. They'd not learned of it in four years. Bandson was their boy, and Ed Berner was a docile nonentity—a "loser" in trade parlance.

Ed checked in with the receptionist, who said, "Good morning, Mr. Berner. You certainly look well for someone just out of the hospital."

"Don't I though," he answered coolly. "Want my doctor's name?"

She was a sour little maiden of forty-plus, chosen for her frigid dislike of people as the perfect human time clock. No one had ever been known to get her to change a late arrival, early leaving or extended lunch hour. She was treated with delicate courtesy, because she *had* been known to make those who incurred her displeasure even later than they were, no small thing since P.B.S. examined time sheets and attendance records when handing out raises. Ed was sure he'd received that end of the stick more than once, though he'd always been exceedingly humble in her presence.

She jotted down a number next to his name. He came around to her side of the desk and read it. "Five *to* nine, dear," he said. "Not five after."

"Did I put down five after? I'll change it when I go over the sheets this evening."

"Change it now."

She looked up at him, shocked. "You do your job, Mr. Berner, and I'll . . ."

"Change it now. I no longer trust you, Miss Carlsbad."

"You no longer . . ." she echoed dimly.

"Change it now, or I'll go directly to Mr. Stennis."

She paled and bent to the sheet. She crossed out the entry and wrote in another. Her rigid body and clenched left hand promised him a multitude of created and enlarged latenesses.

"Thank you. I'll want to see my time sheets each Friday from now on, before you hand them in."

She went from white to red. "I'm not required to do that, Mr. Berner."

He bent over the desk, his face just inches from hers. When she tried to draw back, he followed her, maintaining the inches-apart position. He heard someone enter the waiting room, and murmured, "My position here is going to change very shortly, Miss Carlsbad. I'm going to be very interested in the attendance reports and time sheets. If necessary, I'll bring the situation to the attention of Mr. Stennis. We want a totally objective person in charge here. There have been complaints. I won't go into details, but it would be to your interest to begin cultivating a more pliable and pleasant attitude. Times change, Miss Carlsbad. Companies change. Those who know how to change with them survive. Those who don't . . ." He straightened, and found himself looking at the stout shape and bovine face of Paul Stennis. "A matter of some importance, Mr. Stennis," he said gravely.

Mr. Stennis rechewed some portion of his breakfast, rather like a cud. "What exactly . . ."

Ed said, "But not important enough to burden your ears," and gave Miss Carlsbad a knowing look. She smiled pathetically, placatingly, and he could feel her neck bending before him. At the same time, he received an impression of irritation from Stennis.

"There was something I wanted to ask you, Mr. Stennis. Could we make it now?"

Stennis said, "Ed, you were out four full days."

"Five," Ed said. "But I did come back." He grinned.

Stennis smiled vaguely, annoyance giving way to confusion. "You feeling better?"

"I was never ill."

Stennis blinked, and looked at Miss Carlsbad. "Wasn't Mr. Berner listed as ill?"

Her answer was immediate. "Yes. His wife called in. She said he was ill. I took the call myself." The neck was rising.

"She had to say something," Ed said, and walked through the door into the hallway. Stennis hesitated, shocked, then trundled after him. Ed led the way to Stennis' office and entered. He took the chair beside Stennis' big desk before the president of P.B.S. had hung up his straw hat. As soon as Stennis was seated, Ed leaned forward. "I was in New Mexico, Mr. Stennis. I'd been offered a job, a good one, and decided to try it out immediately. They liked me, I liked them, and so I'm being absolutely honest. They offered me thirteen thousand, Mr. Stennis. I want fifteen. Match the thirteen and I'll stay. If not, forgive me my little deception."

Stennis swallowed his cud. "Raises come through group heads, Ed. When did Nick last put you in for one?"

"He never put me in for one. I'm still doing all the work, and he's still making all the dough."

Stennis started, and Ed gave him a way out by chuckling. Stennis also chuckled, in a strained, nervous manner. "You wouldn't want Nick to hear that, would you, Ed?"

"By all means. The truth will out."

"Well, we'll forget your opinion of Nick. I never knew a writer who liked his group head. You haven't had a raise in several years?"

"More than four years."

"You're making eleven thousand, correct?"

"Yes. And I should be making fifteen."

"You're asking, however, for thirteen."

"I am."

"I keep close tabs on my writers, Ed. To be frank, you haven't exactly been a ball of fire."

"How would you know, Mr. Stennis, since you must judge me through Nick? And Nick colors everything with his own delicate . . ."

"No more of that, Ed. I don't know if you deserve two thousand at this time."

Ed leaned back, crossing his legs. He looked at Stennis, smiling naturally, and said, "I'm worth all you could pay me, Paul. If you'll allow your own instincts to take over, instincts that built this business without the help of slicksters like Nick Bandson, you'll know I'm right." He waited, *pushing* his confidence and worth upon Stennis, willing the man to recognize it and value it; and in a moment felt the truth take hold. He relaxed. "But whatever your decision, I've liked working for P.B.S. I think I'm going to move quickly from now on, and I'd like to do it here. But here or somewhere else, I'll move." He rose.

Stennis said, "Sit down, Ed." He went through the executive-decision act: fingertips together, lips pursed, forehead wrinkled. After a while, he stood up. "We'll put that two thousand through, as of the pay period after next. I hope you'll justify my opinion of you."

Ed shook his hand. "Your opinion of me is going to grow considerably, Paul. Thanks."

He went down the hall, his feeling of triumph fizzing out almost before it began. Two thousand dollars more a year. Edith would flip. But what did it mean, really? Twenty or twenty-five dollars a week additional take-home pay. A few hundred a year more in savings. A second car, perhaps. Great for the old Ed Berner. But what the new Ed Berner wanted was two thousand dollars in his hand right now; and to make that two thousand grow to ten, to twenty, and then to enough money to keep him free the rest of his life. It would have to be plenty, because the way he felt now, he was going to live forever!

He reached his office, and cautioned himself. It was one thing to be strong, and to feel his power with women, and another to be able to amass a fortune. What if he lost this job? What could he do with his strength, dig better ditches than the other laborers?

This needed thinking out. He'd bet Chris Holbroke, in that New Mexico restaurant, that he was the stronger man. Holbroke had taken the bet because Ed didn't look particularly powerful. Yet he was. In that lay a way of making money. Holbroke had bet five dollars. If he could find someone to bet five hundred, or five thousand . . .

He knew no one who gambled at that level.

There was always Las Vegas. Maybe one big bet. But that meant dealing with professionals, which could lead to violence of a sort that frightened him. The strongest man could be defeated, and killed, by a bullet.

He had too much to live for. There had to be some way to make big money fast, and stay healthy.

Paul Stennis had given him a two thousand dollar raise, a minute after saying he held Edward Berner in no high esteem. Ed had looked into Stennis' eyes and willed his worth to be known, and it had become known. He was strong in mind as well as body.

He sat down and looked at his desk and the work waiting to be done. How deadly dull it all seemed, now that there were so many exciting possibilities. With money, he could travel everywhere, seeing and doing, experiencing and loving. Oh, the varied loving that waited!

In fact, he could turn his new skills, his incredible powers of loving, to financial advantage. There were rich women who paid men to be their lovers, weren't there? He'd seen some of the aging "maidens," widows and divorcées, and their youthful paramours, in Miami that year he and Edith had driven down. He'd read of them cavorting in the posh nightclubs and restaurants of New York, in the gambling rooms of Las Vegas, in all the vacation spots frequented by the rich. There were novels full of them. Movies too. And what gigolo of fact or fiction could possibly compete with Edward Berner for rendering service with satisfaction guaranteed? Being a professional lover was the one way of combining business with life's greatest pleasure!

He grinned; and then the grin weakened as he thought of the type of woman who would have to buy a lover; women older and even less attractive than Edith. He'd have to court whoever paid the tab. Youth and beauty would no longer be the standards by which he would choose a female; bank account, real estate and listed securities would be the criteria. Quick, natural hunger, the wonderful chemistry that took place when a man eyed a new and attractive woman, the spur-of-the-moment impulse toward a lovely and desirable girl, all that would have to give way to a calculated plan of action that would bed him down with crones.

He winced, and shook his head. His sexual gifts were not to be wasted, not to be prostituted. He would take no woman who didn't arouse his full desire.

He grinned again. And he would take every woman— young or old, single or married, initially willing or unwilling —that he did desire! Every damned one of them!

He had an instant of shame. The old Ed Berner had feared society and its morality, and shame was the sign of that fear. But shame died quickly as he sensed its basis. There was plenty of reason to let other people think he was moral, since society could punish wild ones, but no reason to go on fooling himself.

That cleared the air, but it didn't present him with any immediate way to wealth. He could grow here. He was certain of that now. A year or two and he'd have Nick Bandson's job. Another few years and he'd be high in management. Thirty, forty, even fifty thousand a year was a distinct possibility.

But the time wasted locked in this office. Time that could be spent singing in the sun, bathing in the seas, tasting the foods and pleasures of the world, reading and sleeping and lazing and loving. *Living,* and not wasting a single precious moment!

"Well, dad, you put something over on the old guy, didn't you?"

Ed looked up. Nick Bandson leaned in the doorway. He was young and lean and beautifully dressed, always beautifully dressed in tight-fitting suits of Brooks Brothers genre. "Two grand, without your group head's recommendation. Not playing the game, fellah, but congratulations anyway. Let's hope you can justify it."

Ed looked at him. Bandson frowned. "You still sick, Ed?"

Ed remembered the years of quiet persecution. He wanted to drag this rotten man inside and make him scream a little. The wanting was so strong he feared it and turned in his chair.

"What's this?" Bandson murmured in what Ed used to think of as his "dangerous" voice: soft, breathy, full of quick insult and anger. "My booze man's getting too big for his bottles? He thinks he can kick the boss and get away with it? I'd turn around and make a curtsy, Ed, if I were you."

Ed said, "C'mon in and close the door."

"Be glad to." The door closed. "Though it might be better if I busted you in a gym. These walls stain too easily." He laughed and came up close behind Ed. "You're not forgetting I'm six years strong at karate, are you, Edward?" The flat of his hand cracked down on the desk top, making the ashtray and jar of pencils rattle.

Ed faced him again. The satisfaction of destroying Nick was very important; it was one of the good things he had promised himself.

"Well, Edward. What's your pleasure?" He leaned forward, much as Ed had done with Miss Carlsbad, one hand braced on the desk, the other on his hip. Ed sighed. How to hurt him without killing him, and without getting into trouble, that was the problem. He solved it quickly, using Nick's own vaunted methods of combat.

Palm up, he swung his right hand in a judo chop hard into the elbow of the arm bracing Nick on the desk. There was a brittle sound; Nick shrieked and collapsed; his chin hit the desk and he slid to the floor. He stayed unconscious long enough for Ed to rush into the hall, shouting there'd been a freak accident.

Nick was very good about the whole thing. Ed carried him to the elevator and then two blocks through the street to a doctor's office. In the street, Nick began describing what would happen once his arm healed and he applied every day of those six years of karate to Ed's fragile body. Ed suggested Nick allow his intelligence to operate. "I'm carrying you now, and I'm not even breathing hard. I could throw you to the other side of the street without half trying. I could kill you by merely tightening my arms, right here and now." He gave a gentle sample, and Nick grunted. "Be very careful what you say about me from now on. Be careful even what you *think* about me. You're among the few people I really hate, Bandson. If I could get away with it, I'd murder you today."

Nick stared at him, believed him and grew very still. Ed left him in the doctor's office and started back toward P.B.S. But his sense of inner satisfaction was high, it was a clear summer day, the girls were out in their tight, bright dresses. He didn't want a drink and he didn't want a smoke. He went to a cafeteria and ate three sandwiches. And thought: *How can I get money fast without endangering my life or freedom?*

He could go into show business: *The Incredible Berner, Strongest Man on Earth.* But he winced at the thought. He would become a totally known quantity, and a cheapened one. Advertising was a far better business for his purposes. He could probably become middleweight champion of the world, but why bother? Again, he would become something cheaper than he was, and it would take as long as rising to the presidency of P.B.S. What he wanted was to challenge some top professional for a private bet—if he could raise enough money to make the bet worthwhile. But what top professional would take such a risk?

He bought another sandwich and devoured it thoughtfully. He remembered ways of making money from movies, novels, TV and radio plays, newspaper stories and club car talk. None were fast enough for him; or if they were, entailed considerable danger. He wanted to make money, be safe, and also stay out of the limelight. That last was important, though he didn't know why. Fame had never seemed repellent to him before, when he'd had no chance to achieve it. Now it brought quick distaste to mind.

He sipped his third glass of milk, and decided that whatever had happened to change him, the change itself was somewhat less than a total success. He was strong enough and smart enough to succeed in just about anything over a period of years—certainly in his own business—but that one special skill, that touch of genius needed to come up with the totally new, was missing. It was his strength he would have to rely on; that and the hunches he got about people's thoughts, and the not-yet-fully-proven ability to influence those thoughts to some degree.

A lovely colored girl sat down at a nearby table. He watched her legs cross, and enjoyed two inches of tan thigh exposed by her stylishly short skirt. When she glanced at him, he smiled. She looked away, but soon her eyes were back.

So many wonderful women to experience. And that, when he came right down to it, was the most important thing in the world to him. Next to life itself.

He checked his watch. He had to get back to the office. He couldn't afford to throw away his job; not yet. He needed time. Time to seek out new people, perhaps dangerous people, with money to risk and the habit of risking it. He didn't know where they were, or how to find them. He cautioned himself to patience. This was only his first day back.

He returned to the office. Stennis came by as he was reading the print order for a 30-sheet poster on the blended whisky. "Bad business, Nick's accident. We need an acting group head. Think you can handle it?"

"Of course."

Stennis nodded and left. Ed called Edith and gave her the news. There was some pleasure in hearing her excitement.

A good-looking new girl came by his door. She glanced at him, and he waved, and she smiled. He called her in and introduced himself. She wasn't more than eighteen or nineteen, and the old-enough-to-be-your-father feeling attacked him. But then they talked and he looked at her—very lean in the legs and waist and neck and face, very fine-boned and very delicate; and very full in the breasts and buttocks. He warmed and his conversation warmed and she dropped her eyes several times and laughed low in her throat and wet her lips. He wanted her, and after a while knew that she wanted him. Not that she had at first. He'd done a lot of looking and thinking and pressing with his thoughts before the knowledge came that she could be his. When she bent to look out the window behind his desk, he turned in his chair and ran his hand up under her dress, watching the doorway at the same time. He stroked her backside through thin panties. She froze a moment; then jerked away, shocked. He was rather shocked himself, at his audacity, his incredible confidence. He said, "Let's have lunch later this week."

She stared at him a long moment, color rising in a hot wave from her neck to her face, continuing clear to where dark hair dipped in a soft wave over her forehead. He met her gaze, smiling. Finally, she nodded. "But you shouldn't ever . . . do that again."

He murmured something about being carried away by her beauty, and knew she was a virgin, and knew she wouldn't be one for long. "How old are you, Beth?"

"Eighteen, Mr. Berner."

"I think I've established a relationship that calls for first names, don't you?" He laughed.

The color came again, but fainter.

"All right, Ed. But you have to promise . . ."

"I'll promise only to admire you, and want you, and try to make you want me."

He walked her to the door, slipping his arm around her waist and giving her a gentle squeeze. Her breath came quickly. She turned up her delicate face and said, "I don't know what's got into me. I never in all my life . . ."

He was elated. But once she had gone his thoughts returned to money. He needed a good apartment in the city. He needed time to spend in that apartment, and luxuries to put in that apartment. How could Casanova have operated if he'd had to waste eleven hours a day at work and on the train?

He wrote half a dozen lines for the 30-sheet poster, and made sure they were good ones. Then, acting as his own group head, he spent several hours choosing the very best and working on a rough layout in keeping with the national campaign. It might be a long time before he was free of this office.

chapter 4

AT THE DINNER TABLE Wednesday night, he underwent further scrutiny by his wife and daughter. Changes in his hair and teeth and facial expression were touched on. (Matty was content to talk about crises and combat in day camp, even though no one was listening.)

"And you eat like . . . like three men!" Edith exclaimed as he finished his eighth slice of bread.

He nodded. He thought how nice it would be if they stopped talking and let him turn on the television. He liked watching the seven o'clock news with dinner, but Edith didn't allow it, as she didn't allow reading at the table. She was right, of course, but still . . .

He thought of everyone being quiet and the television being on, and asked for dessert. No one commented on his appetite this time, even though he cut himself a huge wedge of pie. No one spoke at all. Matty had sunk into a daydream, head propped on hand, little weasel face smiling quietly. Miri was playing with her dessert. Edith was staring at the TV set as if it puzzled her. Ed put the rest of the blueberry pie on his plate, poured the last of a quart of milk and said, "Let's see the news, dear."

Edith got up and turned on the television. Ed ate and enjoyed both pie and news. Then he took a small cigar from his pocket. He'd bought it in Grand Central, wanting to see if it would be more palatable than cigarettes. He lit up, puffed warily, and smiled. Not bad! But when he tried to inhale a little fragrant smoke, he choked like a kid with his first butt. So he puffed, and thought that life at home was going to be a lot quieter, a lot more pleasant, from now on.

Edith put Matty to bed at seven-thirty, and a complaining Miri at eight-thirty. Her warm glances and secretive smiles showed Ed what she wanted. It was all right with him. He didn't think he would sleep tonight; just wasn't tired. But if he'd had his way, he'd have spent the night next door, with Gladys.

He began thinking of Saturday night. Edith hadn't been too pleased when he told her about the barbecue. She wasn't overly fond of Gladys; but then again she wasn't overly fond of any attractive woman. He wondered whether she'd be susceptible to a suggestion of sleepiness after a few stiff drinks. He was sure Harry would. The big man was a sleeper on the train, conking out as soon as he hit the seat. After four or five brandy coolers, Harry might wander inside and sit down and doze off. That would leave Ed and Gladys alone. . . .

Edith went up to help Miri prepare for bed, and Ed stepped outside to sample the sweet evening air. It was dark now, the stars emerging clearer each moment; a profusion of glittering pinpoints that claimed his attention, suddenly and completely. Of course he'd looked at the stars before, but he had never felt what he now felt about them. It wasn't anything specific, but it was strong. His chest contracted and he was full of wonder, longing and fear.

He shook his head, and walked around the front of the house to the driveway. He saw another point of light, the master bedroom window in the Amory house. And Gladys walked by, nude to the waist, hands raised to her hair. It was only a quick glimpse, and he hadn't really seen more than her back and shoulders, but the raging fire came and shook him like a dog shakes a rabbit. He began to walk down there. If Harry was home and got in his way . . .

He stopped. Of course Harry was home, and of course he'd get in his way! He couldn't go around breaking into people's homes. He'd end up in jail if he didn't watch out.

He returned to the house. Edith was in the kitchen. He looked at her, lean and rather stringy, with faded brown hair worn too long for her thin face. Her legs, however, were still good, and her rear was surprisingly full. He would concentrate on those features . . . or on Gladys.

Edith wept in his arms that night. At first she wept with the newly discovered joy of physical love. Later, she wept with pain as he abused her, driven to satisfy a craving which was stronger now than when he'd started two hours before.

He left her exhausted and ashamed. He was a little ashamed himself, and more than a little disgusted. When there wasn't even the motive of novelty, of discovery of a new woman, when there was a history of years of resentment, of growing dislike, a sexual *tour de force* seemed almost indecent.

And yet, she was his wife and therefore his conjugal partner.

But he felt that she shouldn't be his wife. He felt she was the last woman in the world who should be his wife.

He washed, and ate a sandwich and a large can of beans. When he returned to the bedroom, she was asleep, one hand over her eyes, her cheeks streaked with tears.

He dressed, went down to the garage and drove toward Putnam County. He passed through Putnam Corners and continued along black country roads until he saw the blue neon glare of the Montrecell Roadhouse. He'd never stopped there. It was much too raucous a place, as anyone could determine by driving by with car windows open. He stopped there now, pulling into the dark parking lot in back. He wanted a beer or two. He wanted to see what went on inside. He was no longer afraid of the raucousness. Besides, he had a long night to kill.

He was disappointed at first. What went on was men and women laughing, drinking and dancing to the noise of a three-piece band and, occasionally, shouting at each other. But the shouts rarely led to blows, and when they did the owner, positioned at one end of the bar and distinguished by a maroon cummerbund and white jacket, nodded at the bartender who then revealed his talents as a skilled bouncer. Ed had the opportunity to observe all this in his first hour, sitting at the bar and drinking beer. There were several good-looking women in the dining room-ballroom area, and one glanced at him invitingly as soon as she got on the dance floor. She was tall and red-haired and theatrical, every inch a "piece." Her escort was a short, thick-set man who chewed a long cigar and danced surprisingly well. He caught the direction of the redhead's eyes after a while; then he too looked at Ed. His look was a cold command to turn away. Ed didn't turn away. He was thinking of money, not women. He was again mulling over the problem of how to make a pile, quickly. When the thick-set man said, "Now what are you looking for?" Ed was surprised. He focused his eyes. The thick-set man was taller than he'd seemed from a distance. He was only an inch shorter than Ed, and twice as broad. He was no longer young, but looked capable of taking on anyone in the place, including the bartender who was drifting over.

Ed considered playing the part of the mild-mannered but persistent suitor who miraculously trounces the heavy; but he couldn't work up any malice against the thick-set man and the idea lost its appeal. Besides, the man was very well dressed in a flashy, Broadway manner and wore a glittering diamond pinkie ring and what looked like diamond cuff links. If appearances weren't deceiving, he had money; lots of it.

"I asked you a question," the quiet voice said. "What are you looking for?"

"A poker game," Ed replied, smiling.

"Well she ain't it, is she?"

"Not unless the game has changed considerably since I last played."

The small, cold eyes blinked. "Do I know you?"

"No. But you should, if you like poker."

The man was losing his anger. "Yeah, yeah. Go drink your beer and keep your eyes away from my friend."

"How about your friend's eyes?"

The anger returned. "Whad'you mean by that?"

"I mean we'd both be happier playing poker."

The man stepped forward, his big chest touching Ed's arm.

"Now don't give me trouble, mister. Don't make me do something I'll be sorry for. That broad's my pleasure for this week. I'm on vacation. I'm paying the bills and collecting the sugar."

"Understood, and unopposed."

"Then all right." He turned and stalked back to his table. The redhead loo ed past him at Ed. He sat down, leaned toward her and spoke. She answered with gestures. He walked around beh'nd her chair and pulled it. She got up, face pale. They exchanged seats. The redhead's back was now to Ed. The thick-set man glared. Ed grinned.

The owner came over. "Good evening. I'm John Montrecell."

"I thought Montrecell was a geographical item, like Monticello or Catskill."

The owner smiled. He was small, suave and well preserved. "Mr. Gordon is the wrong man to have as an enemy. If you want a girl, I can introduce you to half a dozen. You want a sure thing, I can introduce you to that too."

"No thanks. What's so special about Mr. Gordon as an enemy?"

"You saw him. What you didn't see is his friend who drives him around and is sitting at another table, off there behind the partition. The friend is armed. Mr. Gordon is from the Bronx. He does something there which isn't legal. Bookmaking, probably. But whatever it is, it isn't what you and I and honest people do. That kind of man isn't safe. No telling what he'll do in anger."

Ed thanked him for the warning. John Montrecell said to have a beer on him, and ambled away. The band played. Mr. Gordon danced with the redhead. She looked at Ed. Ed turned to the bar. He sipped his free beer, and tried to figure out how to get Mr. Gordon into a card game. He had thirty dollars in his wallet, but Mr. Gordon didn't have to know that. Mr. Gordon could think he had three hundred, or three thousand.

He was still searching for a way to that card game when someone tapped him lightly on the shoulder. It was a neat young man, very Ivy League except for his shoes, which were practically dancing slippers, long and delicate and extremely sharp-toed. "Hi, I'm Dick Nelson."

"Pleased to make your acquaintance."

Dick Nelson smiled. "That's good. I'm a friend of Mr.

Gordon's. He said you were interested in a poker game. We're staying at a house over near Lake Osibo. Know where that is?"

Ed nodded. He'd seen the signs leading to the private lake and its private community.

"It's one o'clock now. In half an hour, Mr. Gordon's leaving. We'll play poker, if you want."

"Just the three of us?"

"Just the two of you. I don't gamble." He smiled, showing beautiful white teeth. He was an altogether beautiful young man, except for his shoes and a bulge in the left side of his jacket. Ed wondered if, with time, other unbeautiful things would emerge about Dick Nelson, and he had a moment of doubt. How could he be sure Mr. Gordon would allow him to win, or leave with his winnings? And *would* he win?

"You changed your mind?"

"No. How do I find Gordon's place?"

"Just follow us."

Ed said all right. Dick Nelson went back into the ballroom and out of sight behind the partition on the left. Ed beckoned the bartender. He bought a deck of cards for a dollar, put it in his pocket and nursed his beer. He was beginning to feel hungry, but was unwilling to spend any more of his money, now that it was his poker stake.

At one-thirty, the gentle tap on his shoulder came again. Mr. Gordon and the spectacular redhead were just walking out the front door. Dick Nelson and a less spectacular blonde faced Ed. "Let's go," Dick Nelson said.

Ed got off the stool and followed them to the parking lot. Mr. Gordon and the redhead were entering the back of a Lincoln Continental sedan. Dick Nelson and his blonde got in the front seat. Ed walked past them, and heard the Lincoln start. He ran to his Chevy. The Lincoln was backing away from the wire fence as he fumbled for his ignition key. It was moving toward the road as he started up. It turned left and out of sight as he backed from the fence.

He raced to the road and turned. The Lincoln's taillights were already dwindling in the distance. He got the Chevy into third and put the gas pedal to the floorboard. And held it there, despite the next three turns. He was doing eighty when he came up behind the Lincoln. The Lincoln slowed, and Ed touched his brakes. The Lincoln turned suddenly, screeching into a narrow side road. Ed slammed on his brakes and followed, the Chevy rocking dangerously on two wheels. When it steadied, he put the gas pedal back to the floorboard. The Lincoln was doing seventy on this narrow dirt road. Ed more than matched it, inching closer and closer to the big car as they skidded around turns and bounced along straightaways, their headlights flailing the roadside shrubbery. He was practically touching the Lincoln's bumper when its blinker light went on to signal a right turn. He flicked his headlights in response, and stayed close. He was grinning, perspiring, enjoying the action, absolutely confident of his ability to react quickly enough to avoid a serious accident.

The Lincoln didn't turn. It began to slow. It slowed little by little, until Ed's speedometer showed a bare twenty miles an hour. Then the blinker went on again, and it turned right and crawled up a steep driveway to a circular blacktop clearing. Ed was still only inches behind when it stopped. He cut lights and ignition and got out. Dick Nelson was already moving toward him. "Say," Ed said, "you drive with guts, Dick."

The beautiful young man stopped. Ed couldn't make out his face in the darkness, but he heard quick breathing. "Yeah," Nelson finally said.

Gordon and the two girls were out now. Gordon murmured to the redhead. She said, "But I'm hungry. I thought I'd make us all . . ."

"That's what you thought, all right," Gordon interrupted.

Nelson laughed, turning from Ed. "You too, Tina. Hit the sack."

The blonde trotted up a path between dense evergreens. Ed couldn't see a house, but knew it must be nearby. He could smell the freshness of the lake. The redhead said, "If I'd've known what a grouch you was . . ."

Gordon stepped forward. She began to run, but not quickly enough. Gordon's foot caught her in the backside, and she stumbled forward and fell. Nelson laughed again. The redhead rose, crying, and went up the path, brushing at her knees. Gordon said, "Okay, mister, let's play poker. I hope you make it worth my while, after all the trouble you caused."

Ed couldn't see where he'd caused any trouble, but said, "Sure thing. My name's Ed."

"My name's Mister Gordon."

Dick Nelson laughed and laughed. Ed followed Gordon and Nelson up the path through the trees. It was very dark at one point, and the thought came to him that he could smash Nelson down from behind and then his boss, and take whatever they had. But he didn't, and the path turned, and they were at the rear entrance of a large fieldstone and shingle house. Through thinning trees on the left, Ed could see the lake. It was black and quiet this cloudy weekday evening. There were no other houses nearby, as far as he could tell, and he began to feel very much alone. But then he reminded himself that Nelson and Gordon were also very much alone, and he followed them into a lighted kitchen.

Gordon took off his jacket, tie and cuff links and rolled up the sleeves of his white shirt. Nelson picked up the clothing and jewelry and left the room. Gordon sat down at the kitchen table. "Dick's getting the cards."

Ed sat down and tossed his deck on the table. "No need for that. Bought this at the roadhouse."

Gordon looked at him. "You asked *me* to play, mister."

"So I did. That's an unopened deck."

Gordon picked up the pack. He turned it this way and that, and slit the stamp with his thumbnail. He took out the cards, discarded the jokers and shuffled expertly. "Five card draw. No openers. Ten and fifty. Dollars, that is." His eyes watched Ed.

"Fine. You deal first."

Gordon dealt smoothly. Ed's hand was a pair of sixes, a ten, a jack and a king. He decided against keeping the king, and threw out three. Gordon began to hum. He discarded two, and smiled. "That's three for you, right, mister?"

"Right."

Gordon dealt the three, and gave himself two. Ed watched carefully, to make sure he wasn't being cheated. He examined his cards. He'd picked up another pair—eights. He looked at Gordon. The thick-set man smiled again. "You going to put some money on the table, mister?"

Ed returned the smile, and thought how good he felt because he had two pair. He thought this as hard as he could, and saw Gordon's smile change. He took out his wallet and slipped two tens from inside. He tossed them on the table. "Just to start with, Mr. Gordon."

Gordon looked at his cards. Ed stared at him, and felt that

the thick-set man was worried. "With no openers, you can fold up for free. It'll save you twenty dollars."

Gordon took a thick sheaf of bills, held by a money clip, from his pocket. He removed a twenty and dropped it over Ed's two tens. "Any time I won't stay in for a lousy twenty, that'll be the day. What you got?"

Ed showed his two pair, and held his breath. Gordon tossed his cards face down on the table.

The next hand, Ed had a single pair—queens. He drew a third queen, and felt that Gordon wasn't happy enough for a man with a pat hand. He said, "Just have to see that full house, Mr. Gordon. What's your bet?"

Gordon muttered, "You sure it's not a straight or a flush?" But he bet only twenty, and threw his cards away when he saw Ed's queens.

The third hand was being dealt when Nelson returned with an opened deck of cards. He shrugged and drew up a chair to the left and behind Gordon. Gordon said, "Get back, Dick. You make me nervous." Nelson shoved his chair further back.

"Let's set a ten dollar minimum per game," Ed said.

"Why? You unhappy about my betting? I made you waste a hand yet?"

"No, but I might make you waste a few. I'm a cautious player."

"You won't make me waste nothing," Gordon muttered. He lit a cigarette and jerked his head at Nelson. "Get an ashtray." Nelson went to the counter and got an ashtray.

Ed had nothing that hand. He saved his two highest cards, and Gordon drew three, which showed he might be settling down to play instead of trying to frighten his opponent. Ed ended up with a pair of tens. Gordon bet twenty dollars. Ed examined his hand, but moved his mind toward Gordon, trying to feel something from the man. And he felt elation. He could almost see three cards; pictures. He tossed in his hand. "Not this time."

"What? I played two lousy . . ."

"You play your way, and I play my way. You want to set a ten dollar minimum?"

Gordon rose and glared across the table. Dick Nelson hunched forward. He still wore his jacket, and it still had its bulge. Gordon sat down again. "Twenty dollar minimum, cheapskate."

Ed shrugged. He was sweating, but felt he had learned two valuable lessons. One, that he had a tremendous edge over any and all opponents in a card game. Two, that he should never again gamble with this type of man.

He played a pat hand, even though he had a single pair—fours. He leaned back and smiled as Gordon frowned over his cards. He thought how great it was to have a heart flush. Gordon threw in his cards, muttering disgustedly. Ed threw in his own, face down. Gordon reached for Ed's cards. Ed put his hand over Gordon's. "You didn't pay to see them, Mr. Gordon."

Gordon jerked back his hand. Dick Nelson said, "Let's see them anyway, Frank."

Gordon told Nelson what he could do with himself. Nelson got up. Gordon said, "Sit down. I didn't tell you to leave, did I?"

Nelson sat down, flushing. He glared at Ed. Ed said, "And I didn't tell you to stay, Dick. Why hate *me?*"

Nelson bit his lip and looked away. He was no longer a beautiful young man. He was now a murderous young man.

Ed won all of Gordon's cash in the next hour, losing only one hand, and that almost deliberately. He'd picked up an image of aces from Gordon, but wasn't sure how many. Since he had three nines, he covered Gordon's fifty dollar bet. Gordon had three aces.

Gordon turned to Nelson. "Give me my checkbook."

Ed stacked his cash, rolled it and put it in his pocket. He stood up. "No thanks, Mr. Gordon. I don't know you and you don't know me. Let's call it a night."

"After you took six hundred dollars off me? You're kidding."

"Six hundred, or just six. What's the difference?"

Gordon also stood up. He hadn't looked pleasant all evening, but he did now. "This is the difference. I'm *telling* you to accept a check."

Ed shook his head. "Sorry."

"You'll be very sorry. . . ."

"You do a lot of threatening," Ed said sharply. He was sick of these animals. True, he'd won their money, but they didn't know he had an edge. They had no right to badger him this way. "I'll play as long as you have cash, not a hand more."

Gordon glared. Ed wasn't sure what was going to happen.

There was hesitancy in the man's mind, but it could go either way. And Ed knew Gordon had gone the way of violence before.

"Go ask Syl and Tina for their cash. And add your own."

Nelson left the room. Gordon sat down. "You pushed me into this game, mister. And I got a feeling you're playing an angle."

"If you mean cheating, you're wrong. And you know it."

"Do I? You win too much. Too damned much."

Ed went to the sink and drank a glass of water. He looked at the refrigerator. "Mind if I get something to eat? I missed dinner."

Gordon stared at him.

Ed found a large broiled chicken and three tomatoes. He devoured them at the counter, used a dish towel as a napkin and returned to the table. Gordon was still staring.

Nelson returned. Gordon said, "This guy just ate our snack. The whole chicken. Took him half a minute."

Nelson said, "Charge him six hundred bucks. I'll collect."

Gordon smiled. "It's an idea, for later. How much you got?"

"Two hundred."

"Okay. I'll win the six hundred back. But the next time I come up to the country for a week, I gotta take more than two grand."

He lost the two hundred in nine hands, Ed allowing him a few wins to keep down his pressure and suspicion. When Ed rose a second time, Gordon stayed seated. "Get the flashlight, Dick. Show him to his car."

"No thanks. We got here without flashlights."

"You mean you don't trust Dick here? Why, he's just a boy, not yet twenty-four years old. Get the flashlight, Dick."

Dick went to a drawer near the sink. Ed turned and went through the door. Gordon shouted, "You think that lousy eight hundred bothers me? Montrecell will cash anything I write. Anything! I've spent . . ."

Ed was running now, and left the voice behind. When he reached the blacktop circle, he glanced back. Footsteps were pounding from the house. He opened the door of the Chevy. A flashlight beam swung around a turn in the path and stabbed at him. He slammed the door and found his key. Before he could use it, a shot sounded. It wasn't very loud—just a sharp crack—but he froze. Dick Nelson came panting up to the door. "Get out. You and our money."

Ed reached for the door. Dick danced back, grinning. "If you got ideas, mister, you better forget them. If you've seen things in movies, you better remember funerals in real life. 'Cause I'll use this gun."

"Sure you will," Ed said. He opened the door slowly and got out. "You'll risk the electric chair for eight hundred dollars. Gordon too, for a lousy eight hundred."

"And you'll risk a bullet in the head for it." He was the beautiful young man again, grinning his beautiful white grin.

"Why not put the gun away? I'll fight you for the money."

Nelson shrieked laughter, bending over and kicking at the road. But his gun stayed steady. "Oh, that's the best yet! He'll fight me for it! Now call me a yellow bastard." He laughed a little longer. "Okay, give back the money you stole."

"I won."

"You stole. That's why I might have to shoot you."

"No one'll believe that, especially coming from you and Gordon."

"The money. The money. I'm going to hurt you if you don't give back the money."

Ed put his hand in his right trouser pocket and closed it over the thick wad of bills. It was his stake for freedom, but he could always get a new stake. No reason to risk his life; his wonderful, wonderful life. No reason to give up too easily either. "I threw it away on the path."

"The money," Nelson said softly, and reached into his jacket pocket with his left hand and took something out. He switched the something to his right and the gun to his left. "The money, mister." He came forward with cautious, resilient steps. "You might not get up if I hit you with this."

Ed saw it then; a thick section of leather tubing. A blackjack. A weighted bludgeon that could easily crush a skull.

He was afraid. At the same time, he remembered the two men on the highway in New Mexico, and said, "Honestly, I threw it . . ."

Nelson leaped forward, swinging the blackjack. Ed jerked up his left arm, more quickly than any other man could. The blackjack struck his wrist, breaking it. He fell to his knees, then over on his side, and lay still.

"I told you," Nelson said. "You hear me, mister?"

Ed didn't move.

"Was that your head that broke," Nelson muttered, "or your arm? If it was your head . . ." He put the blackjack away and stood rubbing his face. Then he bent and slid his hand into Ed's pocket. Ed punched him above the ear. Nelson dropped over him. Ed got up, shoving Nelson aside. He saw the gun on the blacktop and kicked it into the brush. His left wrist radiated pain. He bound it with his handkerchief, and it felt better. Probably a simple fracture, already set in place. He would have it put in a cast at the hospital in town. They would ask questions, and he'd better have an answer ready—something like slipping in the bathtub.

A question came to mind for which he had no answer. *Was Nelson alive?* He'd hit him hard; much harder than he'd hit either of the two men in New Mexico. Nelson was lying just a few feet away, absolutely still. Was he breathing? Was he bleeding there in the dark?

Ed didn't bend down to see. He moved toward his car; then stopped. He felt that Nelson had absorbed a double dose of punishment, half of which belonged to Gordon. And Gordon sat back there in the house, thinking he had made a fool of Ed. It wasn't enough that he should come out here and find Nelson. Not nearly enough. Ed hated him now, and that hate had to find an outlet. Ed also wanted Gordon to know with whom he was dealing. Gordon had to fear Ed so that he wouldn't consider coming after him, or bringing in the police. Gordon had to accept what had happened as Nick Bandson had accepted his broken elbow.

He went back up the path to the house and through the back door into the kitchen. Gordon was in the middle of the room, laughing and pulling the redhead toward him. She looked upset, and was saying, ". . . get mixed up in anything rough. You paid me, sure . . ." She saw Ed and stopped.

Gordon turned. Ed said, "Poor Dick. He was running to catch up with me and tripped and fell. Hit his head on the blacktop. Made a nasty sound. He's hurt. Better get him to a doctor."

Gordon's eyes went to Ed's hands, then to his pockets. He was looking for the gun. Ed said, "He dropped his flashlight and something else. I couldn't find them in the dark."

The redhead said, "You don't have to stick around, mister. If Dick got hurt it's his own . . ."

"Shut up, Syl," Gordon murmured. His eyes still questioned Ed for the gun. "Dick never fell. This guy did something to him."

"I don't like people calling me a liar," Ed said.

"Mister," Syl said, shaking her head behind Gordon's back, "go on home now."

Gordon suddenly smiled, convinced that Ed was unarmed. He turned casually and slapped Syl's face. "I hate a talky whore, don't you, mister?"

"Call me Ed."

Syl backed to the wall, holding her face.

"Okay, Ed." Gordon came forward, looking happy. "You made yourself an evening, didn't you? Got yourself a poker game and won eight hundred dollars and flipped my whore and put my boy away. Quite an evening. Now it's going to end."

Ed nodded. "It is indeed. Don't you wonder why I came back here without Dick's gun?"

Gordon was crouching now, fists clenched. "I never look a gift horse in the mouth. You're a square, so you came back."

"That's the wrong answer. I came back because I wanted to say goodnight. To you, and to Syl."

The redhead looked at him. He smiled. Gordon swung a massive right hand. Ed caught it in his open left, and squeezed. Gordon said, "God, God!" and dropped to his knees. Ed let go. Gordon rocked from side to side, his mashed right hand held out before him. Ed reached down and took him by the chin and tilted up his face. "Does it hurt, Mr. Gordon?"

"Yes," Gordon whispered.

Ed tightened his fingers on Gordon's chin. Gordon grew very still. Ed put his other hand on top of Gordon's head. "A strong man like you, Mr. Gordon, must've broken walnuts in his hands."

Gordon barely breathed.

"I break walnuts too, Mr. Gordon. Sometimes I squeeze too hard and the nut is ruined. Messy."

Gordon whispered, "I got no beef. You won fair. I was just kidding."

Ed straightened and walked to Syl. "That's one way of saying goodnight. I can think of other ways, nicer ways."

She smiled slightly, still holding her face. He took her hand away and stroked her cheek, red from Gordon's slap.

She murmured, "Can you get me to the train? There's one to the city at six."

"Sure. And that gives us a few hours to say goodnight."

"Wait while I get my things."

Gordon was getting up. He stumbled to the table and sank into a chair, his back to Ed. Ed went to the refrigerator and took out a half-empty bottle of milk. He rummaged in the cupboards and found a loaf of white bread, short a few slices. He ate the loaf and drank the milk and was still thirsty. He tried a bottle of cherry pop—a flavor he'd always liked—but it sickened him with its unnatural sweetness. He drank water instead. When he turned, Gordon jerked his eyes away.

"And I never put on a pound," Ed said.

Gordon's mashed right hand lay on the table. He nodded, looking at it.

"You a heavy eater, Mr. Gordon?"

Gordon cleared his throat. "Yes."

"Maybe you don't get enough exercise."

"Maybe."

"Though you tried to get some tonight."

Gordon's smile was ghastly.

Sylvia entered the kitchen, straining to carry a large piece of blue airplane luggage. Ed hurried over and took it from her. She smiled her thanks, glanced at Gordon's back and murmured, "Tina's coming too. With Dick hurt, she don't want to hang around. Besides, we don't owe them a thing. We had to hand over a hundred each when Frank was losing to you. That's almost half of what we got."

The blonde entered with a smaller, lighter valise. Ed took that too, and suddenly realized he was using his left hand; the hand with the broken wrist. And he'd used it to crush Gordon's hand! He put down the bag, untied the handkerchief and moved the wrist. Still a little sore, but definitely not broken. He'd either made a mistake, or . . .

He remembered the knife wound in New Mexico. It had healed immediately, the scab flaking off under his fingers. Could his broken wrist have knit in these past fifteen minutes?

He was sure it had, even though it was impossible. Lots of things about him were impossible.

Ed picked up the bag and smiled at Tina. She was three inches shorter than the redhead, considerably younger, and showed a spectacular rear development as she walked toward the door.

She presented no problem. Three wouldn't be a crowd in this instance. It might even be fun.

The girls were grateful for his help, very impressed (after seeing Dick crawling up the path, mumbling nonsense), and quite willing to express their gratitude and respect, just as long as they caught the six o'clock train to Manhattan. He promised they would, and drove to the little motel off Route 9, not far from the Harmon station. The manager, when awakened, was too sleepy to bother checking how many people were in the car outside, or whether more than two were going to use the cabin. Besides, it had only one double bed, so if anyone was going to save the two bucks for a cot, he'd have to sleep on the floor.

The manager was wrong. No one slept on the floor. No one slept at all, and the girls missed their six o'clock train. They didn't complain. They caught the seven-ten, and gave Ed their telephone numbers, and made him promise to call soon. Syl went so far as to say there would "hardly ever" be a charge, "maybe something for dinner, you know." Tina was almost in tears, but her business sense was stronger than Syl's. She did, however, run back to the between-car area to tell Ed that she'd "flipped" at the threesome idea and would be willing to halve her usual fee for that particular procedure. Her eyes glowed as she said this, though he wasn't sure if it was for Syl or himself.

After the train pulled out, he threw the numbers away. It was the non-professionals he wanted, the women who had never thought of Ed Berner as an exciting male; such as Ruth Trisk of the dark hair and solemn smile whom he had loved throughout his four years of high school and who had given him one kiss in all that time, the night before she became engaged to a wholesale butcher from Staten Island. She lived in Manhattan now, he'd heard, and could be found in the telephone directory under the name Andrew Artis. She had two children, religious scruples, a basically cool approach to men. Not at all the type for an affair. But who knew what would happen if the new Ed Berner came calling? The pitying rejections, the reluctant dates in movies and ice cream parlors, the lost years of youth might be erased from his memory.

It was Gladys Amory he wanted; and the others who would surrender against their wills, feeling they had too much to lose, fighting as hard as they could, making their capitulations the dearer, the sweeter, because it was not at all certain they *would* capitulate.

And there was the erotic aspect, growing ever more important to him; he who had never dared hope, or try, for anything beyond a quick release from desire. Syl and Tina hadn't been very surprised by his experiments. He *wanted* surprise; and shock and tears and resistance and, most of all, the climax of exploding passion. Innocence and Purity could best provide him with what he wanted. Innocence and Purity could best satisfy the savage need for converting disinterest to sexual bondage. Just thinking of certain women that way made his hands sweat.

He didn't go home. He phoned instead. Edith answered, half asleep. She hadn't even known he wasn't lying beside her. "The alarm didn't go off. Didn't you set it? Where are you, Ed? You're . . ." She came fully awake. "You're not leaving me again? You wouldn't, not after all we've come to mean to each other!"

He explained that he wasn't sleeping well lately and had gone out for a ride and the Chevy had broken down. "Fuel pump, so I had to get it fixed. Now I've just got time to catch the seven-forty out of Harmon."

"Ed, Ed," she whispered, "what's happening to you? These wild stories . . ."

He told her, very firmly, to stop the melodrama. He said he'd see her at dinner, and to please make shrimp, lobster or a good swordfish steak.

"You never liked seafood."

"I do now. Make a lot." His mouth watered as he hung up.

He experienced the luxury of a shave in a first-class barber shop, glancing in the mirror at the well-dressed, well-spoken men who came to spend seven and eight dollars for a trim shave, manicure and shine. He saw the valet service sign, and had his jacket pressed.

Listening to the soft talk, inhaling the rich aroma of hair cream, after-shave lotion and good talc, he also experienced a moment of distaste for last night's sordid events. No more professionals for him, men or women. This was his world from now on. Money without violence. Money come by honestly. Money which gave a man a soft voice and hearty laugh and calm, assured way with people. Money which made the world one beautiful cushion on which to recline.

On leaving the barber shop, he went to a hotel coffee shop and sat at the counter and had six poached eggs on six pieces of toast, three bowls of oatmeal and three containers of milk. The elderly counterman said he hadn't seen anyone eat a breakfast like that since leaving the farm, and with a misty smile gave Ed a jelly donut on the house. Ed washed it down with a fourth container of milk.

He walked toward the office at ten-thirty, and didn't hurry. He had spent close to ten dollars, and didn't worry. So what if he was more than an hour late? So what if his bank account was a fragile eleven hundred dollars? He had the nucleus of a fortune in his pocket.

Poker was a good game. Rich men played poker. He had to meet rich men.

He was thinking of how to do this when he came into the reception room. Miss Carlsbad tightened her lips and picked up her pen. He said, "Good morning. Had to do some research before coming to the office. I started at eight forty-five."

"What corroboration . . ."

"Eight forty-five, dear."

She tried to fight him, but he thought how he would soon be in a position to control her salary, her very job, and she bent her head and wrote 8:45 in neat numerals next to his name. He went on to his office, picked up the phone and asked the operator for Beth Hammermill, the delicate eighteen-year-old he'd met yesterday. When she answered, he asked if she was free for lunch. She murmured, "Well, I'm not sure . . ." He said he'd made reservations at the Cheval Blanc, and began to explain that it was one of New York's fine restaurants. She surprised him. She interrupted to say she loved the Cheval, and had he ever tried the San Marino? They arranged to meet at twelve-fifteen in front of the building. He recalled that she'd worn a simple but very finely styled dress the day before. It *could* have been expensive.

He wondered exactly who she was.

chapter 5

BETH HAMMERMILL was the only child of Roscoe Francis Hammermill, partner in an eighty-million-dollar agency that, like most, bore three other names, none of which represented a current owner. She was well educated, well brought up, accustomed to the best things in life, including gentle and preferential treatment. She told him this and everything else he wanted to know as they sat side by side at a wall table in the rear room of the Cheval Blanc, his hand under the table and under her dress. She talked about her childhood, her schooling, her vacations in Easthampton, her decision to learn the advertising business by working the next two summers as a copy secretary. Her father knew Stennis. Her father knew just about everyone in the business. She would work at Bates next summer; Y.&R. or B.&B. the summer after.

"I go to Easthampton weekends," she said, puffing at a cigarette, looking nervously around the room. His fingers stroked the silky, virginal flesh of her inner thigh. "We have a home there. Right on the beach. It's beautiful this time of . . ." His fingers dared further. "Ed, don't," she whispered, but he smiled into her eyes, and virginal or not her thoughts were aflame and she leaned toward him. "Do . . . do you care for me?"

The waiter came with their order. The tablecloth was long enough to protect them from curious eyes, and he kept his right hand where it was and raised his wine glass with the other. "Very much," he said. He sipped the wine, and shuddered. Disgusting stuff! And yet, he had always liked wine. He pushed it away.

She bent her head, staring into her glass. The waiter spooned out a fragrant beef stew. Beth's head stayed down and her shame was intense and her desire was more intense.

"Ah, perfect," Ed said.

The waiter smiled. "Thank you, m'sieur."

Ed nodded, though his compliment hadn't been for the food. Beth Hammermill knew what his compliment was for.

Beth Hammermill, whose father was worth ten million or more. Beth Hammermill, who was going to introduce him to her father and her uncle Grant and their friends, all rich, all addicted (she'd informed him after casual questioning) to an evening's poker on the porch facing the sea during the long, cool, pleasant summer nights at Easthampton.

He withdrew his hand. She ate with eyes down. He enjoyed his meal, though it wasn't nearly enough for him. He had two desserts, and was still hungry. Beth said she had to get back to the office.

"Not today, sweet."

"But I have work . . ."

"You're working for me this afternoon. We have research to do. I'll call in for both of us."

She shook her head, eyes locked with his, frightened. He said he'd be right back and went to the phone booth in front. He called Miss Carlsbad. "Have to research further today," he said. "Anyone calls, say I'll be at the Forty-second Street Library. I'm taking a secretary to transcribe my notes. Miss Hammermill."

Miss Carlsbad asked when they'd be back.

"Certainly tomorrow morning," he said, and laughed.

She was silent a moment; then tittered humbly.

He took Beth Hammermill to the Larington Hotel, and deposited her in the coffee shop while he registered at the desk as Mr. and Mrs. Blake. The room had one big bed and air conditioning and a television set. They didn't need the television set.

Three hours later, when he put her in a cab for Penn Station, she said, "I'll see if we have room next weekend. Are you sure you want to come to Easthampton, Ed? I could meet you in Manhattan. . . ."

He was very sure he wanted to come to Easthampton. He'd have tried for this weekend, if he hadn't wanted to keep that barbecue date with the Amorys. He would bring his eight hundred dollars with him. Table stakes were what he wanted. Big table stakes!

He had two sandwiches and three glasses of orange juice at a stand in Grand Central. An hour and a half later, when Edith served the huge swordfish steaks, he ate his and half of hers and a whole pot of mashed potatoes. He went out on the back lawn with the kids and played circus, swinging them around. Matty brought out a ball and Ed taught him to catch. Miri already knew how to catch. She'd learned in gym. She also showed him how she could broad jump. He watched her and said, "That's pretty good."

"You oughta see Mr. O'Seeny! Wow!"

"Bet Daddy can jump better," Matty said.

Miri laughed. "Mr. O'Seeny was an Olympic champion."

Ed said, "That so?" and put the cigar he was about to light back in his shirt pocket. "Well, let's see now." He squatted, swung his arms, jumped as hard as he could. He sailed through the air, landing at least twenty-five feet from where he'd started. His forward motion was so strong he fell forward on his hands and knees when he landed. He looked back, feeling sure he'd broken every world's record. Matty screamed, "That's good! That's good! It's like flying! I want Eli to see! It's like flying!" He raced off to get his friend from next door, Eli Amory, six years old, big and husky, who took after his father, and had oppressed Matty with his father's physical strength ever since they'd been able to communicate.

Ed turned to Miri. She was upset. "What's the matter, honey? Didn't I do as well as Mr. O'Seeny?"

"You did better," she said quietly. "Much better. Much, much . . ." She frowned, already losing her fear, her discomfort; already forgetting why it was she had felt fear and discomfort. "Were you an athlete in college, Dad?"

"No. But I could have been, don't you think?"

She smiled. "Yes. Boy, could you show Mr. O'Seeny and the others a few things!" The smiled weakened. "You never jumped before. I remember once you couldn't run fast at that picnic the development gave, was it two years ago, when I was still little?"

"Three years ago." He'd finished last in the Father's Day Sprints. He'd done poorly in the Father-Child Potato Bag Race. He'd wandered away before the softball game had begun. He'd avoided the next three area picnics. Now he was sorry this year's was already over. "Any more picnics this summer?"

"I don't know. I'll find out from Kathy. Her daddy's the representative or something for the committee or something. Would you go? Would you take me?"

"Any picnic you dig up, I'll go and I'll take you. And we'll win every prize given."

Her smile was beatific. "We will! I'll find out! Oh, *boy!*"

Matty's shrill piping approached, drowned out every second word by Eli Amory's deeper tones.

"He did so! A hundred feet, I bet! You'll see!"

"Aw, even *my* father can't jump more'n five, six feet. The record . . . we can look up the record and I'll bet it isn't . . ."

"Hi," Ed said, and turned his back on the kids and crouched and leaped through the air. Miri clapped her hands. Matty screamed, "See? See? A hundred feet. Like flying! Your daddy can't do that! No one's daddy can do that! And I'm going to jump like that when I grow up. You'll jump like your daddy and I'll jump like my daddy and I'll jump more . . ."

Eli cut the tirade short the only way he could. "Gee. No one jumps like that, Mr. Berner. That's great."

Matty nodded rapidly. "That's great. Great. It's great, isn't it, Daddy?"

"Oh, not too bad, for a hot summer night after a long day's work."

"Gee."

Ed laughed, at the children and at himself. He was full of pride, and aware of it, and amused by it. And then saddened by it. If only he'd been this way when it counted, back in Brooklyn when he was a kid; a frightened, meek, defeated kid. If only the power had been his when he'd gone to high school. What couldn't he have done on the football field, the basketball court, the baseball diamond! What couldn't his life have been with a beautiful body and tremendous strength and a mind always a step ahead of others' and the courage that all this brought. Ruth Trisk would have been his; and not for dates in movies and ice cream parlors, but for long sessions on the couch in her living room, where he'd heard the wholesale butcher spent his evenings. And longer sessions in her frilly little bed in her pink and white bedroom where no boy had ever been. And all the other girls. . . .

He turned away from the children and lit his cigar and puffed. He'd been cheated, robbed, marred by failure. He'd come too late to joy and strength and success. There could never be any making up of the lost years.

But his bitterness fled as suddenly as it had come. He felt that the lost years were not the enormous portion of his life they appeared to be; that he would have time enough to wipe them out, if not in the next thirty-eight years, then in the fifty following them. And as incredible as this seemed, he knew it was so and grinned and rubbed his hands together and chewed his cigar. He faced the kids and said, "Let's play circus. This time you'll be the trapeze artists and I'll be your assistant."

He swung them up in the air; actually threw them up and caught them, sure of his strength and ability. They screamed in fear and delight, and after a while trusted him implicitly. Eli's mother called him, and he didn't want to go home. Ed caught him up, put him on his shoulders, said, "Have to deliver our guest in style." He trotted around the house and down the driveway and across the Amorys' lawn to where Gladys stood at the door. "Here he is," he said, and swung the child down in one easy movement. "Your pride and joy."

"My *big* pride and joy," she murmured, as if not wanting someone inside to hear. "And not so much pride, and not so much joy." She raised her voice. "Get on inside, Eli, and make sure you wash tonight."

"Mr. Berner threw us up in the air, way up, like we was on a trapeze, and he caught us and he jumps better than anyone, anyone in the whole world! Like flying, honest, Ma!"

She stared at him. "Go on inside."

Eli ran past her, and began shouting to someone, either his sister or Harry, about the fun and games at Mr. Berner's house.

"That's one of the few times he's admired anyone but his father and the baseball star of the moment." Her eyes went to his arms, exposed by the short-sleeved sport shirt. "You've certainly gotten into shape, Ed."

"Always had the potential," he murmured. "Never bothered much. Past few months, I decided to work out a little."

"You should've done it before." She was murmuring too. "Looks nice. I mean . . . wish Harry would work out a little."

"Doesn't he?"

"No, never. I told him . . ." She caught his smile, and her color rose. "You cut it out now, neighbor." She touched her hair.

She was wearing a yellow housedress, modest enough, but nothing was really modest on a woman as big and bountiful as Gladys Amory. Her fair skin was pink and moist; her lips full, and red enough even without lipstick. She was beginning to breathe quickly.

"Well, doesn't he?" he repeated.

She turned as if to go. He took her arm. She glanced into the house and then past him. "What if someone was to see?" She was trying to smile, trying to sound jovial and kidding, but she didn't quite succeed.

"You haven't answered my question, Glad."

"I don't understand it." Her eyes fell.

He squeezed her arm and thought how much he wanted her and how wonderful it would be if he were to take her in his arms and touch her and make love to her. He thought it through, in specifics; the undressing and caressing and violent action. Her color grew more pronounced, her breathing heavier.

"Big man like Harry," he murmured, "always falling asleep on the train . . ."

"He's wide awake enough at home."

"Oh?"

"Wide awake enough," she repeated, her eyes coming to his as if forced to, her lips trembling slightly. He held those pale gray eyes transfixed. "But . . . you know how marriage is."

"It shouldn't be that way for you. You're the best-looking woman in this whole damned place. The best-looking woman I know. I can't wait for Saturday night."

She moved her arm a little, and he let go. She raised her voice, laughing, trying to shake off the thoughts he'd put in her mind, the thoughts she'd begun putting into his. "Saturday night will be a wing-ding, all right. Barbecue and drinks and a fifty-foot walk home. Like wow, dad."

"Like wow," he repeated softly. "Just you be ready, Glad. I've waited almost six years for Saturday night. Just you think of it, and be ready to take advantage of it. It's going to be the beginning of something neither of us ever . . ."

Harry shouted, "Hey, Glad, what's holding you? It's time for 'Atomic Quiz.' You'll miss the first contestant."

"Coming!" She backed through the door, her eyes locked with Ed's. "Wouldn't want to miss 'Atomic Quiz.' Harry's favorite."

"Certainly not. But the bomb goes off this Saturday night."

"First contestant. Oh boy."

"You'll win a prize this Saturday."

"Big prize or little prize?"

"The biggest."

She began to close the door, smiling, her eyes glittering. "Bragging or complaining?"

"Promising, Glad. Promising, sweet."

The door closed further. "And we murder the rest of the gang, right?"

He leaned toward the narrowing opening. "No, just put them to sleep. I know how."

"I'll *bet* you know how, Ed."

He was delighted. She was playing the game with him, right along with him, every single step of the way. Her fire matched his. He hadn't expected this. He put out his hand and held the door open. "Wear something black."

"Dress?"

"You know. To set off that wonderful white skin and blond hair."

"Not a dress." She grinned at him. "What else could it be?"

"It could be . . ."

"A coat. A jacket. Don't tell me. I'll figure it out by Saturday night."

"Will you wear them?"

"Them? The mystery thickens."

"Glad!" Harry bellowed.

"And if I do wear them," she whispered, "how will you know?"

His hand went through the door and cupped her chin. Her smile was gone. They looked at each other; then he dropped his hand and went back up his driveway. Music reached him from the house on the other side. He looked there. Phyllis Blaylock was sitting out front, a transistor radio in her lap. She waved and looked away. He wondered if she'd seen anything unusual in his conversation with Gladys. He'd touched her arm, and cupped her chin in his hand. A neighbor could do that; just being friendly, just kidding around.

Perhaps he had better pay some attention to Phyllis too, in the way of preventative medicine. He could plant some hunger in her mind. . . .

The thought repelled him. She was lean and stringy; sour of face and shrill of voice. She was, he realized, very much like Edith, though a few years older.

It was getting dark. She hadn't seen anything. And even if she had, there'd been nothing to see. And even if there had, he could handle whatever questions were asked, whatever situation developed, whatever might threaten him.

That last thought, and its resultant feeling of power, ended the matter. One flick of his finger and Harry Amory would go beddy-bye. One flick of his finger and *anyone* would go beddy-bye.

He walked around back and found he was swaggering and didn't correct it. Who had a better right to swagger?

He played with the kids until Edith called them in. Then he opened a folding chair and smoked another cigar and looked at the stars. His thoughts of Gladys drifted away. He sat with head tilted back, eyes moving from point to point of brightness. More emerged with each passing moment, each deepening shade of darkness. He grew still. His cigar went out. He began to think of reasons for being the way he was.

How *had* he become this powerful being, this beautiful man? An accident didn't explain it. Nothing explained it. Except perhaps what he'd told Edith and the kids: some sort of hospital where they rejuvenated wealthy people. But he would have remembered that, wouldn't he?

Amnesia afterward. That would explain his not knowing. But how could they have increased his muscles, and his genitals? And in just three days. The hair and teeth, maybe . . . but what about his hunches, and being able to push his thoughts across to others, and his healing so fast, and his limitless sexual strength?

Nothing explained what he was, and he stopped thinking of it. He lit his cigar, telling himself he would go back to New Mexico some day, perhaps on vacation in August, certainly next year or the year after. He would go alone, and search out the answer. Further west along that highway, someone might recognize him. They'd say he'd been here or there and had done this or that, and it would be explained.

But what could explain it? What?

He went into the house. He watched television until Edith said, "Ed, honey, let's go to bed," and then he went to bed. At twelve he left her and came downstairs and watched television until the late movie finished. He made three sandwiches and washed them down with a quart of orange juice.

He played solitaire, and read last Sunday's *Times*, and switched to a magazine. He finished the magazine and just sat. The world slept and he was wide awake. Why? What sort of change was this? What sense did it make? A man had to sleep when everyone else slept, didn't he? He thought of going upstairs and lying down and closing his eyes. But he didn't do it. There was no weariness in him. He was as alert as if he'd awakened from ten hours of sleep an hour ago.

He went outside into the mild summer night; into the stillness and the darkness. The sky was an enormous black bell pressing down on him, made even blacker, it seemed, by its myriad specks of brightness. Pressing, pressing, reducing the miracle that was Ed Berner, mocking him, threatening him; and he quickly re-entered the house, to get away from it. He walked into the living room, and then the kitchen, and then the dining room. He didn't know what to do with himself. Finally, he went down to the playroom and the bookshelves and looked at titles. There were books from college and books he'd bought from book clubs and the encyclopedias he'd bought for the kids (barely opened), and old books Edith had brought from her mother's house after the old lady died, and some books he couldn't place at all. Books which he and Edith had talked of reading and complained they'd never had time to read. Now he had time.

He chose *Don Quixote,* which he had read in college because he'd been forced to and which he would now read because he wanted to. He sat at the kitchen table and read quickly, very quickly, with intense pleasure, and finished half the book before six, when he went upstairs to wash. He woke Edith at six-thirty and asked for breakfast. "Sleep good, honey?" she murmured slyly. She thought she had worn him out. She didn't know how ridiculous that was. She didn't know that a length of time equal to half a waking day had passed since he'd touched her, and that he'd lived another life during that time, and that he was full of the wisdom, pain and laughter of a country, a people and an age she knew nothing about.

He felt he alone had time enough to know *all* the countries, peoples and ages in books. Why, he could read everything, every single word ever written, if he wanted to! The time he had! The enormous time he had!

Later, when he thought of it, he couldn't logically explain

this feeling of endless time. After all, some insomniacs skipped sleep a night or two a week and didn't gain that much more reading or living time. But still, the feeling persisted that his life had just begun. The same feeling he'd had when bemoaning his youth. The feeling that made days and months and even years very small items in the life of Edward Berner.

Carl Weston called him for lunch. He often ate with Carl, an old friend from his first agency. Carl listened in shocked silence as Ed told him he was too busy with his new job as acting group head ("It'll be made permanent soon, and the money will go up again"), and Ed got great satisfaction from his murmured, "Well, congrats, kid. Never thought we'd make it." Carl *wouldn't* make it. Carl was a carbon copy of the old Ed Berner; a loser from point one. Ed said he'd get back to Carl next week, but knew he wouldn't. He didn't need commiseration from a fellow loser any more. He was a winner now. He had money and girls to make; satisfaction to find. He had the world by the nuts!

He called Beth, expecting eagerness and excitement. He was surprised. When he asked if she'd been thinking of him, she said, "Yes. A good deal. I'm not sorry for what happened last time, Ed, but I don't want it to happen again."

"You don't want . . ."

"Not the excesses."

"Excesses is a word you use in relation to drinking, or emotional exhibitions, or other negative things. You don't use it in relation to love."

"What we had wasn't love. Not . . . after a while."

"You're still a child in some ways," he said sharply; then fought his annoyance with quick laughter. "Erotic experimentation is part of love—the most wonderful part."

"I may be a child in *many* ways, but my instincts have always been effective in protecting me, in guiding me. They tell me that I'm not built the way you are. They tell me I was used against my will. You're a very strong man, Ed, and not just physically. You changed my thinking. As soon as I was away from you, I was upset by what happened. Badly upset. I don't want to be used any more, Ed. I want to make my own decisions, as I'm able to now, over the phone."

He felt shock, almost fear, at hearing his secret expressed so clearly. "And what decisions would you make, free of my mental strength, as you call it? Not to see me any more?"

"I don't know."

"Do you want me to hang up now, and never call again?"

"I don't know."

He told himself he *would* have hung up, if it hadn't been for the weekend at Easthampton. What did he need this child for, with a world of women waiting? "Well then . . ."

"I do want to see you again," she murmured. "Even though I found out you're married. But you've got to promise me not to . . . to force me into excesses."

"That word again. And a new one—force."

"Please, Ed, be honest with me. You know what I mean. Let me be myself. I'm not saying you shouldn't . . . love me, but do it naturally, with some thought for my limits."

He said all right and that he was jammed and that he'd see her for lunch. The Cheval again.

"Don't be angry with me," she whispered. "You're my first man. I feel like a fool, but you awakened me and I . . . care for you."

He said he wasn't angry and he cared for her too, and was suddenly very anxious to hang up, very anxious to escape the feeling coming over him. He didn't like himself. "Got to go," he said. "Heavy schedule."

"You're not worried about me, Ed, are you?"

"Worried? I just have work . . ."

"About my expecting more than knowing you, being with you occasionally, and eventually parting with a cool so-long."

He chuckled, not knowing what else to do.

"Because even if you wanted to leave your family, which is ridiculous, and marry me, which is even more ridiculous, I wouldn't. I couldn't take what you'd do to me."

He kept his tone light. "Most women would sell their souls for what I'd do to you."

"Perhaps. Some, certainly. But I'm low voltage. I like holding hands a long time before getting into bed. And sleeping once in a while. And feeling I'd . . . but this is where my lack of experience might betray me. I like feeling I'd satisfied my man, drained him, wrecked his usefulness as a dissemina-tor of sperm, at least for a while. Every woman wants that feeling, Ed. I'm sure of it."

"You're sure of it," he said, mocking gently. But he liked

what she was saying, and the way she said it. He liked Beth Hammermill.

"Without the experience, I'm sure of it," she answered firmly. "Normal women, that is."

"Normal women. And now we'll spend a few months defining our terms."

She sighed. "You're right. But that's how I feel. Am I living in a dream world, a child's world?"

He could have shaken her then, and turned it to his own advantage when they next met, but he said, "No. I'll remember your . . . what did you call them? Limits?"

"Yes. Thank you, Ed. And I'll remember your needs."

He smiled, and they said goodbye. It would be the Larington Hotel again, for just an hour this time, and with much less action.

As it turned out, there was no action at all. Paul Stennis came in at eleven, to say the client had called. "Sy Roverstein has decided he doesn't like our new magazine ads. With time so short, he wants changes that amount to a whole new campaign. I wish Nick were here."

"I'll handle it," Ed said.

"You've never had to deal with Sy. He's getting powerful up at Wylitt. He's not just ad manager now; he's also district something-or-other, and he thinks in terms of new, new, new. I have a hunch he'd like to take the account away from us so he could say he brought it to a better agency. He's a real cocker-knocker, y'know? An ex-salesman. Boor, really, and loud as hell. How can you handle him when you've never even met him?"

"I met him once, at a client meeting, when Nick was out ill. I can handle him, Paul, so relax. When do we see him?"

"We're going over now. It'll last through lunch, so cancel anything else."

Ed canceled Beth. She was hurt. He explained that business was business. She said, "You sound like my father."

"Don't you like your father?"

"Like him? I don't even know him. If he had less money, I might be able to say I *love* him."

He smiled, thinking she would get to love her father after all, if the poker games worked out. Then he went to the washroom to freshen up. Looking in the mirror, he decided he would buy two or three good new suits, as soon as the money came in. After next weekend, probably. And that second car; a little sports model, like the MG, or perhaps the Triumph; certainly not the used car he'd always planned on. And an apartment in town.

But first things first. Mr. Sy Roverstein had a rendezvous with destiny; Ed Berner's destiny. He could be the first step in a ladder of success, if success in advertising became necessary. And whether it would become necessary or not, changing Mr. Roverstein from tiger to lapdog would be fun.

He walked into Stennis' office. "Let's go, Paul. We've got a campaign to sell."

"You sell Roverstein," Stennis muttered dispiritedly, "and you'll sell Dennison Motors next week."

Ed said, "Now *that's* an idea."

Stennis laughed and got his hat. Dennison Motors was pressing hard on the heels of Chrysler, and billed over eighteen million dollars. P.B.S. was going through the motions of pitching Dennison, now that the automobile company had decided to leave its old agency, but it was a hopeless game. What big car account would come to a small, heavily-industrial agency with under eight million in total business? So Stennis laughed, and Ed joined him, but they didn't laugh for the same reasons. Ed had just seen the way to big money in advertising, quickly . . . if he had to stay in advertising. And it might not be bad staying in advertising as a new-business specialist with a cut of the profits. It could lead to a hundred grand and more. It could happen in the next year or two.

But *could* he swing an ad manager hard enough to his way of thinking to carry over into management meetings and board of director meetings and chairman of the board decisions?

Mr. Roverstein would help answer that question.

They entered the Park Avenue offices of the Wylitt Beverage Company at ten to twelve, and were shown directly to the main conference room, where Sy Roverstein and three other men waited. They all looked alike to Ed, though in reality they differed in many ways. It was the age bracket, between fifty and sixty; the weight range, from plump to heavy; the facial expressions, all self-importantly grim.

The magazine campaign for the blended whisky, as well as for the gin, the vodka and the two bourbons, was pinned to a cork wall at the far end of the room. Sy Roverstein—the only totally bald man present—said, "Hello, Paul." He barely flicked his eyes at Ed. "Where's Nick Bandson?"

"Ill. Ed Berner here is the acting group head. Ed, Sy Roverstein."

"We've met," Ed said, and leaned across the table, hand outstretched. "Nice seeing you again, Sy."

Roverstein was startled. He didn't remember Ed, or appreciate the familiarity of his greeting, but he took his hand. Ed gave him a firm grip, and thought how lucky it was for Wylitt Beverages that a truly creative, instinctively *right* ad man had been brought into the meeting. From Roverstein he got an impression of change—from displeasure to watchful interest.

He was introduced to the three others, only one of them important: Fuller Wylitt, Jr., son of the founder of Wylitt Beverages and chairman of the board. A break, his being here!

Stennis sat down facing the four men across the long, wide table. Ed took the chair beside him. Stennis said, "Sy, I understand you're not quite satisfied with our blended whisky campaign. That surprised me. I thought we were finalized. At this late date . . ."

"Not just Wylitt's Special Reserve. Wylitt's Gin and Vodka and . . ." He waved his hand at the cork pinup wall. "You can see for yourself. Mr. Wylitt and I . . ."

"Pardon me," Ed said, and turned to Stennis. "Paul, they've got the unrevised copy there. What happened to our new lines?"

There'd been no new lines. Stennis blinked, and paled. His eyes told Ed to shut up, that there wasn't time to play games, that they had to get the current campaign through as is. At the same time, Ed knew Stennis had no real hope of changing these unchangeable client minds.

"New lines?" Roverstein turned to Wylitt. "Never saw them, Fuller."

Ed got up and walked to the cork wall and the layouts. He took a pencil and small white pad from his pocket. "I'm terribly sorry, gentlemen. There's been a mixup somewhere. I don't blame you for being dissatisfied with the lines as they are."

"Lines *and* layouts," Roverstein said. "The visuals are totally . . ."

"Of course. The layouts don't fit the lines. But they *will,* when you hear the new lines." It was almost impossible to make their deadline and go into new art. He smiled back at the table. Stennis looked ready to faint. "It's heartening to know that our client sees things as we do; that we both arrived at the same conclusion, independently of each other." He looked at Wylitt, and thought how bright a man Wylitt was, and how brilliant an ad man Ed Berner was, and how sharply sales would climb once the new campaign was put into effect.

Roverstein began to speak. Wylitt murmured, "Let Ed go on, Sy. The art never bothered me. It's the lines. I want to hear the new ones."

"Not new, Mr. Wylitt," Ed said, distinguishing, by his lack of first-name familiarity, between the chairman and his ad manager. "Improved. It would be foolish to throw away a carefully-thought-out campaign. It's to our advantage to hone it, polish it, bring it in on target so that Wylitt's products *say* more to the consumer than any others in the industry." He turned his eyes on Roverstein. "I believe it was Sy who expounded that theory at the all-brands meeting last year. Sy is known at P.B.S. as the exponent of careful revision before allowing an ad bearing the Wylitt logo to see print." And he thought how well he remembered Roverstein's words, and how Roverstein had been impressed with Ed Berner's demeanor at that unremembered meeting, and how Roverstein and Ed Berner, together, could make Wylitt's liquor sales climb and bring honor and money to Sy Roverstein.

Roverstein smiled. "Didn't think anyone paid much attention to the ad manager at those agency meetings, Ed."

"We'd better, Sy. We'd better."

Roverstein laughed. Stennis began to regain his color. One of the other men said, "I'd like to see the art stay, Sy. A change here and there in the headlines, a word or two in the copy—the right word or two, of course—and we'll have a real campaign."

"Let me read you those right words, gentlemen," Ed said, and turned to the cardboard-mounted water-color layouts. He looked down at the blank pad, then up at the first ad. "Instead of the rather prosaic, 'Wylitt Is Good Taste In Whisky,' we insert one vital word and get . . ." he faced them, " 'Wylitt Is *Your* Good Taste In Whiskey.' " He gave Roverstein a grin and thought how terrific the line now was, and Roverstein slapped the table.

"That's it! That's the way to go. The direct personal approach, treating the consumer not as a vague mass but as an individual."

"Person to person advertising," Ed said, nodding.

"From Wylitt," Wylitt pontificated, "to you, Mr. Consumer."

"The P.B.S. approach exactly," Stennis said, "whenever we've had clients aware enough to accept it. Exciting advertising. Not really an innovation . . ."

"We don't innovate," Roverstein said, frowning.

"Certainly not," Stennis said, and turned quickly to Ed.

"Never," Ed said sternly. "As Paul has often stated, and Sy too, newness for the sake of newness, innovation for its own sake, is product suicide. But *improvement,* daring based on a sound platform of tested copy and art, *that's* great advertising. And that's what we now have."

He turned back to the cork board, laughing inside. How easy it was! As easy as getting a woman. As easy as defeating a man in a hand wrestle or fist fight. As easy as winning at poker.

Stennis said nothing as they rode down in the elevator two hours later. There were other people present. Nor did he speak in the cab, only looked out the window and hummed tunelessly. But once they reached P.B.S., and even before they had entered his office, the words came, and they were exactly what Ed wanted to hear.

"Wonderful job, Ed! You can *sell!* Not only that, your extemporaneous creative ability is amazing! We've got to start thinking of you as something more than a copywriter. Of course, you're a group head, but even that . . ."

"Take me along on the Dennison Motors pitch, Paul."

"Dennison? Certainly. But I'm thinking in terms of what we can actually bring into the agency. A new toy account, over a million . . ."

"We're going to get Dennison, Paul. Give me all the copy and art help I need next week, and we'll land eighteen million."

Stennis stopped near his desk and stared at him. Ed gave him hope, and then belief. Stennis wet his lips. "I can't go over my copy chief's head, but Hal will certainly . . ."

"I've got to run my own exploratory, Paul. Hal Brower's a swell guy, but he'll slow me down."

"Maybe you *should* slow down," Stennis muttered, dropping into his chair. "After all . . ."

"I can do it, Paul. Eighteen million. More than twice as much billing in one account as we now have in the entire agency." He paused. "And when I do it, I want to be creative director."

Stennis looked shocked, and then embarrassed. Ed was feeding him enthusiasm and belief, but he couldn't go this fast. "Have you been nipping at the Wylitt's Special Reserve?"

"There hasn't been a creative director here since Verrinson left."

"I handle . . ."

"The agency's going to grow, and it needs a creative director; for prestige, if no other reason. And there's another very good reason. I want to coordinate art and copy for our new business campaign. We can grow faster than any agency in history. Faster than Papert-Koenig-Lois, and B.&B., and J. Walter in its heyday."

Stennis blinked his eyes. "Come now, Ed."

Ed turned to the door, letting him off the hook. "We'll talk again, next Friday, after we've landed Dennison. We'll talk edibles, so to speak."

"Edibles?"

"Turkey, not peanuts."

Stennis laughed. Ed walked out. He went through the reception room, merely waving his hand as Miss Carlsbad began to ask where he was going. He was beyond the Miss Carlsbads now. On the street, he caught himself swaggering and looked in a shop window, and changed his walk. He was beyond swaggering, too. He walked quickly, evenly, with a feeling of growing power. It might be fun to stay in advertising. The right position could give him enormous money. And prestige.

He could run P.B.S. He could be master of everyone there —over a hundred people. He, Ed Berner, the loser just a week ago! There was something to be said for that, just as there was something to be said for making a pile at gambling and trotting all over the world. Wealth gained at gambling brought no power; just freedom. Wealth gained in business brought sufficient freedom for much of what he wanted to do . . . and power.

To have people under him. To be their boss. To have them fear him, respect him, obey him.

It was something to consider. He considered it thoroughly as he ate an enormous meal at the Automat. Then he went shopping for tomorrow night's barbecue. He walked to First Avenue and a fine meat market. He bought four aged porterhouse steaks, the very best quality and cut. He went to a little gourmet shop on Madison Avenue and bought a large jar of first-grade Russian caviar. Next door was a liquor shop. He took the manager's recommendation in brandy—a cognac of venerable name and year. He had spent far too much for a backyard barbecue, and tried to think what else would please Gladys.

He returned to the office, knowing what else would please Gladys. He didn't have to buy that. He *was* that.

He dumped his packages on Miss Carlsbad's desk and told her to refrigerate the steaks in one of the water cooler compartments. "I'll pick everything up at four-thirty. Right?"

Miss Carlsbad said, "Of course, Mr. Berner," and smiled ingratiatingly.

He gave her a nod.

chapter 6

SATURDAY AT TEN, Edith began complaining about the heat. At noon, even the kids mentioned it. Ed had heard a radio report of temperatures in the mid-nineties and humidity up in the impossible eighties, but he just didn't feel it. He cut the grass, handling the mower with fingertip ease, enjoying himself. Across the driveway, Harry Amory leaned against his mower, mopping his face. Harry looked pale and exhausted, his belly bulging out over his striped Bermuda shorts, his T-shirt dark with sweat. "A killer," he called. "Ninety-three already. It'll hit ninety-eight, maybe a hundred, by four o'clock. So why'd we complain of the snow?"

Ed chuckled and ran his mower closer to the driveway. Harry's face showed surprise as he looked Ed over. Ed was wearing tan chinos and a long-sleeved shirt. He felt great, just great, but a little hungry. He wished he'd stuck a sandwich in his back pocket.

Harry grabbed his mower as if it were a deadly enemy and

began cutting grass. Five minutes later, with two-thirds of his lawn still uncut, he gave up. Ed called, "Anything wrong, Harry?"

Harry said something about his mower not working correctly, and pushed it into the garage. Ed was starting on his slope when Gladys came out the front door. She wore short shorts, matching blue-and-gray print halter, and high heels. Her blond hair was blonder than usual—freshly rinsed, he guessed—and set in a neat bouffant. She looked his way immediately, and waved. He cut the engine and walked over. They smiled at each other from a distance, and then from close up. She said, "Harry's inside, lying down. Thought he was going to faint. How can you take the heat, Ed, and look so cool?"

"Conditioning, I guess."

"I'm starting to wonder about that conditioning of yours. I don't seem to remember your being in such great shape before." She was still smiling, her eyes going over him. "Your hair . . ."

"I think this is the first time you ever really looked at me," he said, his own smile easy on his lips. He felt . . . happy. Happy being here with her and knowing he was going to be with her tonight.

"That could be, neighbor."

His eyes went to her legs. Long, long legs, pale and smooth and full in the thigh. Muscled legs, yet very feminine. And those short shorts cut up high, showing the crease and curve of her buttocks.

"Hey," she murmured, "I'm up here, neighbor."

His eyes went up her, slowly, past the warm curve of belly, over the rich swell of breast, to the big, pretty face and wide gray eyes. "No you're not," he said. "You're all over. You're perfect all over."

He expected some withdrawal then, but her thoughts reached him and he knew there would be no withdrawal. She had been waiting for this; waiting for years without knowing it. She had been hungry for this, without ever admitting it to herself. Now that it was coming closer, she was reaching for it. He felt he could put his hands on her, right out here, and she wouldn't withdraw. She felt it too, because she turned and said, "See you tonight, neighbor." Her voice was full of wanting. Her thoughts said, "Make it happen, Ed. Please make it happen."

He watched her walk away. When she reached the door, he said, "It's going to be hot tonight. Tell Harry shorts are in order. I'll be wearing them. You wear them too."

She turned her head. He was looking at her bottom. She said, "And those black things, the mystery items?"

"There'll be other times. I'm sure of it, aren't you?"

She shook her head. "I'm not sure of anything." She went inside.

It didn't take much doing. Gladys and Harry came over at nine. Matty was already asleep and Miri was spending the night with a friend up on the hill. Gladys said her six-year-old was playing baby-sitter to her four-year-old, and had instructions to go to sleep in half an hour. "We told him to come right up here in case anything bothered him. That's one advantage of going to a next-door neighbor's." She smiled at Edith, and the two women moved away to chat. They both wore shorts, yet the difference was enormous. It was as if Edith were fully clothed and Gladys were nearly nude. Ed stopped looking at Gladys and her skin-tight shorts-and-halter outfit; the same she'd worn this afternoon. He turned to Harry.

"Another advantage of going to *this* next-door neighbor's is that he keeps his promise." He picked up the bottle of cognac. "Satisfied?"

Harry examined the label. He nodded, surprised.

"And porterhouse, the best." He raised his voice, "And Romanoff caviar. Ten ounces."

Gladys turned, smiling. "Thank you, neighbor."

Edith's eyes dropped to Gladys' shorts. She looked disapproving, and annoyed. The disapproval was for what Gladys showed; her own shorts were of Bermuda length, and full. The annoyance was a continuation of what she'd expressed when Ed brought home thirty dollars' worth of delicacies for a simple barbecue. And perhaps she sensed something.

Ed returned his attention to Harry. "Okay?"

"A-okay," Harry said, and moved to the back door. "Can we get outside? It's cooler there, now that the sun's down." He looked wrung out, burdened by his weight, drained of all energy. Which made Ed rub his hands together and say, "Everyone'll appreciate a nice brandy cooler, my own recipe."

Edith said to make hers a gin and tonic, very light on the gin. Gladys said that would suit her too. Ed said, "Which leaves all that beautiful cognac for us, Harry. A shame, isn't it?"

Harry chuckled through the screen door and went around to the beach chairs. Ed heard a creak and a sigh. He walked into the kitchen, where Edith was complaining of the lack of counter space. "Outside, ladies. Tonight, *I* do all the work. Just relax and try to keep Harry awake."

Edith gave him a sour look. Gladys went to the door. Edith said, "You'll mess everything up."

Ed gave her little pat. "Go on now, honey. Have some fun. I know it's been hot, but try to relax." The second pat did the trick. She murmured, "I don't know why we had to have them. We see them every day. I wish they were on their way home." She kissed his cheek and leaned against him. He nodded, winked, said, "All things come to an end. Be patient."

He wasn't very patient himself. He mixed two powerful drinks, using three shots of liquor in each, pouring them into tall glasses with ice and mixer. He made a normal drink for Gladys, and put no liquor at all in his own, just a little Coke for color. He brought the glasses out back, where the stand-light cast a soft yellow glow. He made sure everyone got the right drink, and raised his glass. "To bigger and better fun."

Gladys smiled. "Cheers."

Edith sipped.

Harry drank in thirsty gulps, finishing the ten-ounce mixture in short order. "Aaah! Nothing like really good brandy."

Ed drank a little soda water, and nodded. "Mmmm. I agree, buddy." He got up. "How about another? They're not too potent."

Harry said another was fine.

Ed said to Edith, "Let's show them a husband and wife chug-a-lug."

Edith protested, but Ed went over and urged her and kidded her and said the drinks were weak and they'd stop anyway after two or three. He sang, "Here's to Edith, she's true blue . . ." and she drank down the mixture, after which she sang for him and he drank down his pop.

"What about Gladys?" Edith asked.

Gladys said, "No, please. I haven't been feeling too well today. Stomach. I'll just stick with this."

"Then we'll have all the fun," Ed said. "Hey! I forgot your caviar. C'mon in and tell me how you like it." He turned and walked to the door, hoping Edith or Harry wouldn't say anything to stop her. He entered the kitchen and took out the caviar. He was prying off the lid when Gladys came in, holding her drink.

He took the glass from her hand and set it down. He put his arm around her shoulders and pulled her into the living room, where there was less chance of their being surprised. He heard Edith laugh at something Harry said, and then both of them laughing. "What did you put in their drinks?" Gladys murmured, her voice weak.

"Enough. One more and they'll sleep a while." He drew her gently toward him, wanting to prolong this first sweet moment.

Her bare legs brushed his bare legs. He sighed.

"How can you be sure?" she said, and her head went down on his shoulder and her lips touched his neck.

"I can." He couldn't tell her about using his mind. "Trust me, my wonderful Glad."

He kissed her, and their bodies came together. He intended to caress her a little, excite her a little, and then let go. But she began to move, and she wouldn't end the kiss, and her hand went to him and opened him up. And then she dropped to her knees and he was beyond stopping. She rose again, her shorts falling about her ankles, and said, "I knew you'd be something special. I knew it!"

She did it all, right there, with him leaning up against the wall. He listened to the voices out back, but wasn't sure he could have stopped her even if Harry and Edith had both come in. She rode him, and continued on after he'd finished; continued until she rolled her head back and clenched her teeth and screamed deep in her throat; a wild sound; a sound of agony and exaltation. Then she pushed away from him and went to the stairs. "You wonderful bastard. You better be strong tonight."

"I am. I'm very strong. There's no end to my strength."

She went up the stairs, head hanging. "I'll make you ashamed of lying like that."

He brought out fresh drinks for Harry and Edith, and a fresh soda for himself. He said Gladys was visiting the little girls' room, and raised his glass. "Here's to all of us, we're true blue," and drank down the pop as if it were pop.

"That's quite a man you got there," Harry said, thick of tongue.

Edith giggled. "If you but knew."

Ed shushed her, and she giggled some more. Harry said, "Well, here's an end to troubles," and began to drink. He paused for breath once, said, "Whoosh!" and finished his drink. He dropped his glass, bent for it, almost fell out of his chair. "Now you, 'Dith."

She was already drinking. She paused several times, and finished as Gladys came out of the house with a tray of caviar hors d'oeuvres.

"Tha's wha' we need, baby, food."

She brought Harry the tray. He took two crackers, stuffed them into his mouth and made a face. "Faw, crappy stuff. Where's them steaks, Berner?"

Ed said, "Got the charcoal grill around the side, ready to go. Didn't want to add to the heat."

"Good thinking," Harry mumbled. "Good thinking, ole man."

"While I'm grilling the steaks, I'll have another drink. Join me?"

Harry nodded. "Catch ole Harry turning down twenny-year-ole bran'y. Jus' catch me!"

Edith drained her glass of a random drop. Ed looked at Gladys and moved his head toward the house. He said, "Edith, tell Harry that joke you told me three, four weeks ago. The one about the Arabian and the belly dancer."

"Can't do that," Edith said, and giggled. "Not decent. Y'see, there was this 'Rabian prince coming to New York. His fav'rite belly dancer . . ."

Ed walked back to the door. "Give me a hand, will you, Gladys?"

"Sure, neighbor."

They went inside. He took the steaks out of the refrigerator. She stood leaning against the counter, taking tiny bites of a caviar-covered cracker. He mixed two powerful drinks and gave them to her.

"Steak will help sober them up," she said, still leaning back, long legs crossed at the ankles.

"They'll never get to the steak."

"Then why make four?"

"I eat a lot. I do everything a lot."

"Don't brag, neighbor. No man can satisfy my type of woman."

"What type of woman is that?"

She turned and went to the door. "I don't know. Maybe nympho. Maybe nuts. I've always wanted and wanted, and held back. But you pressed the right button, neighbor. You won't get away easy." She glanced over her shoulder to see what effect her words had had on him. He was smiling. "You'll beg me to let you alone, neighbor." He laughed. She put the glasses on the dining room table and came back to the kitchen. She grabbed him. "I mean it, neighbor!" And kissed him and started moving.

He shoved her back. She tried to grab him again, but he poked her with one finger and she gasped and held her stomach. "That hurt, neighbor."

"Go on about your business, neighbor. I'll call you when I want you."

She swayed toward him; then shook herself, as if fighting a drug, and turned and left with the drinks.

He seasoned the steaks, smiling to himself. He was triumphing again; a double triumph this time: over Harry and the world of big, beefy men he'd envied and feared. Over Gladys and the lush, desirable females who'd been beyond him.

Gladys the beautiful, the violent, the insatiable, the truly erotic. Or would she fail to live up to her previews, once they found themselves alone with unlimited time?

He didn't think so. He thought she was the one woman he wanted more than any other woman at this moment. It was quite a compliment, if she but knew it.

He ate four rolls and drank a quart of milk to hold him until the steaks were ready. He carried the big slabs of meat out on a platter, past Harry, Edith and Gladys. Edith was still trying to tell her story.

"Wait . . . the Arab di'nt say that. He said . . . wait . . ."

Harry was leaning back, eyes half closed.

Gladys said, "Ummm. Looks good enough to eat." She wasn't looking at the steaks.

He laughed all the way to the grill. He placed the meat over the glowing charcoal and returned to his company. Harry was sitting up, trying to light a cigarette. Edith had finished her story and was staring into her empty glass. Harry finally got his light, and said, "Those were real drinks, hey?" He let down the beach chair's back until he was stretched out at full length. "Real drinks." He coughed and threw his cigarette away. Gladys got up and stepped on it.

Ed looked at Edith. "You aren't feeling too well, are you, honey?" and thought how sick and headachy she was and how she just had to lie down for a moment and how it was understood that the Amorys would go home as soon as she went inside.

"Terrible," she muttered. "Jus' terrible."

"Here, let me help you." He went to her and helped her out of the chair. She stumbled. He caught her in his arms and carried her to the house. As he passed Gladys, she made a gleeful child's face.

After putting Edith to bed, he mixed another brandy cooler and brought it outside. Harry seemed asleep, but Gladys shook her head and said, "Harry, time for food."

Harry's eyes opened. "Yeah, yeah. Bring me to it." He struggled into a sitting position. Ed put the glass in his hand. Harry drank. Some of the liquid slopped over his chin. He wiped at it with the hand holding the glass, spilling more brandy and soda on his pants. He finished what remained and lay down again, heavily. "Uh-boy," he muttered.

Ed went to the grill and fixed the steaks. Another ten minutes would see them ready. His mouth watered as he returned to his guests. Harry's eyes were closed again. Ed said, "Harry, let's wash up before eating."

"Wash up? Yeah. Let's." He didn't open his eyes and didn't move.

Ed pulled him out of the chair. Harry said, "Hey, c'mon now, fellah, cut it out."

"Sure, fellah. This way." He put his arm around Harry's waist and half dragged him across the grass. Gladys leaned back in her chair, legs stretched out before her. " 'Bye, Harry," she murmured, and looked at Ed. "Hurry back, dear."

Harry's head lolled. "Yeah," he muttered. "Yeah." But at the door he suddenly jerked free, fell to his hands and knees, and scrambled erect. "Goddam it, you lemme alone. Who the hell you think you are, scrawny shrimp bast . . ." He swung wildly at Ed.

Gladys got up, frightened. Ed said, "C'mon now, Harry. We're going to wash for dinner."

Harry called Ed several choice names and swung again. Ed tapped Harry on the side of the head, caught him as he fell and carried him into the house. He brought Harry down to the couch in the playroom and dumped him there. Harry wouldn't need any mental suggestion. Harry was good for the night.

Gladys was with him as he walked around the house to the grill. She watched as he put three huge steaks on one platter and a single steak on another. "You're bragging again," she murmured. "I don't know if I can eat one of those monsters, and I'm as big an eater as they come, when I want to be. No one can eat *three*."

He carried the platters back to the yellow glow of light and placed them on the circular redwood table which held four settings. He sat down and began to eat. He finished one steak before she'd barely started hers, and got up and went into the house. He brought out two loaves of bread and two quarts of beer. She watched as he ate, and ate faster herself, and drank the beer he poured. She said, mouth full, "You make me so *hungry!*" and he realized that watching her, his own enormous appetite was increased. He was half through his third steak when she pulled her chair around the table beside his and began cutting pieces off his steak. They ate together, stuffing their mouths full of meat and bread, washing it down with gulps of beer. She belched once, and covered her mouth and looked at him. He pulled her hand away and kissed her, their lips greasy, their hands groping for each other despite the grease and charred meat. They returned to eating, stretching the remaining meat with more and more bread, and when the meat was gone, folding slices of rye in two and dipping them in the blood and fat. Gladys finally stopped, took a last sip of beer, and then sat watching him. "In a minute," he said, and started on the last of the bread, wiping both platters clean. Her hands came to him. He continued to eat and drink, and she caressed him. When he finished eating, he was half undressed and wholly ready. He said, "Right here is fine. The strip of woods protects us from the people in back, and the hedging and sloping ground protects us from the Greskins on the north."

"If it didn't," she said, "we'd be in trouble right now."

He laughed, looking down at his nudity. "Turn off the pole lamp."

She went to the pole and threw the switch. Darkness swallowed them. When his eyes adjusted he saw her stooping, then straightening. She came toward him, and there was no cloth to interrupt the whiteness of her body.

He stood up, stripping his sport shirt over his head. He met her, and she was still tall in her high heels. He asked her to keep them on as he wanted her to be his height, his match, his equal. "God and goddess," he murmured. "A mating to shake the earth and create legends."

"Let's hope not," she answered, and laughter caught them. Still laughing, they fell to the cool grass.

She was more than her preview had promised. She was more than any woman had a right to be. She was, in fact, his equal. When his inventiveness flagged, hers took over, and when exhaustion caught her, his strength carried them both.

The night was changing, growing lighter, and still she wouldn't stop. She twisted into him, gasping; and he calmed her and quieted her and said, "Gently, gently, before we say goodnight." They were gentle for the first time that evening. They ended with soft touches and a brushing of lips, and stood up and found their clothing. Gladys walked quickly around the house.

He sighed. She'd been fine, with great staying power. Fine and strong . . . and gross.

A good deal of the excitement he'd felt for her was gone now; gone forever. Of course, he would want to see her again. But the time when he would actually avoid her was already shaping up.

He sighed again. It was sad, this lessening of appetite. Not that he'd ever run out of appetite for women; fresh women; not the way he was now. But still, it was sad.

He went upstairs, undressed and washed and got in beside Edith. The clock-radio read four A.M. He closed his eyes and slept. He didn't sleep for long, but he dreamed enough for a ten-hour night. They were dreams of glory . . . but each time he triumphed he had to run, to hide, to leave his triumph. Something menaced him.

Sunday wasn't very pleasant around the house. First, Edith woke him, her head wrapped in a damp cloth which smelled of cologne, her face drawn and pale. "Harry's in the playroom," she said. "I went down and there he was, stretched out on the couch. Send him home this instant."

By the time he dressed and went downstairs, Harry was sitting up, head in hands. He wasn't any more pleasant than Edith. "What'd you do," he muttered, "fill that cognac bottle with rubbing alcohol? I never got this sick on good brandy before."

Ed chuckled. "We'll have some breakfast and you'll be a new man."

Harry rose and swallowed uncertainly. "I've got a home of my own, and it's right next door." He turned toward the garage.

Ed saw him out; then went back inside. Edith was in the dining room, sipping black coffee, the pot on a stone holder. "Some party," Ed said, sitting down across the table.

"Yes," she said grimly. "Some party. What time did Harry go to sleep?"

"I wasn't in condition to notice. Just before Gladys went home, I guess."

She kept sipping. "Did he eat with you?"

"I don't think so. No, I guess not."

"You don't think. You guess."

"No, he didn't eat with us." He got up. "Speaking of eating." He went to the kitchen.

"So you and Gladys ate the steaks?"

"You know my appetite."

"You bet I do." The bitterness increased. "Appetite for more than steak."

He took out milk, rolls and cheese, and brought them to the dining room. He went back to the kitchen for a glass, plate and silverware.

"I wish you'd never gone to that . . . that rest home or hospital or whatever it was. I wish you were . . ." She stopped and poured fresh coffee.

He sat down. "You wish I were the way I was before? You wish we were as idyllically matched as we were before?"

She set down her cup with a clatter. "It was better! Now you're . . . you're . . ."

"Now I'm happy." He bit into a roll. "Doesn't that mean anything to you?" He really wanted to know, and probed her mind. He read guilt, fear, anger and confusion, but above all a vast self-pity. She was no longer sure of the man she'd married. She preferred the old order, loveless though it had been.

She would trade love for her previous position of dominance and power.

She began a fresh tirade, but he'd had enough. He beamed a strong thought— one which made silence her goal.

As he was finishing his third roll, Miri returned from her friend's house with, "Great news! They're having a picnic over at Kowaskel Park. It's a fireman's benefit and starts at twelve, and there're races for fathers and races for kids and prizes and you'll take me, won't you, Dad?"

He said he certainly would. "Go outside and find your brother. Tell him he can invite Eli Amory. And you can bring your best friend."

"Tina? Oh boy!"

"I thought it was Kathy."

"Oh, her. I like Tina better."

He grinned. It would be Mary in another two weeks, and then Kathy again and then Tina, and then someone else. The "best friend" changed often at the age of ten. He rubbed his hands together, feeling very young himself. It would be great fun to be the hero of the Fireman's Benefit Picnic.

It was a hot day, only slightly less uncomfortable than Saturday. He ran the hundred-yard dash against a field of eleven, and came in ten yards ahead of his nearest rival without straining. He ran the mile immediately afterward, defeating five younger men, being careful not to win by too great a margin. He won the potato-sack race; and with Miri the three-legged race. Then he entered the chickenfight, hopping on one leg with arms folded, bumping into his opponents. He defeated eighteen men, and called it a day.

Matty was hysterical with pride; Eli silent with envy.

Miri kept turning to Tina with a cool, superior air (though her eyes glittered), saying, "He doesn't like to show off, but if he really tried . . ."

Edith sat at a table at the edge of the athletic field, sipping a Coke and pretending to read a magazine. Between events, Ed returned to the table to use the towel, and she would glance up and murmur some caustic little comment, as, "Through playing yet, little boy?" He was having too much fun to care. He was living a dream.

After the last event, she rose and said, "Want me to take

the children home? That fat brunette who followed you around the field is waiting. Has she told you her name yet? It's Louise Haverston. She's a widow. And there's a cheap blonde who kept watching you through binoculars. Binoculars yet! She should be easy."

He wiped his face with the towel and grinned. The brunette was plump, not fat, and quite pretty. The blonde was sexy, not cheap, and well worth a second glance. Both had been around when he'd competed, and the brunette had shown interest with her eyes and gay applause. He was glad to learn her name.

They went home. He ate a huge snack, took his copy of *Don Quixote* outside and read for two hours. They went to the Stone Mill for dinner, and then to the drive-in movie. The show seemed insipid to him, but the kids were hypnotized and Edith enjoyed the music and dancing. He closed his eyes to the screen, thinking of the busy week coming up. He had to get Stennis to approve his heading a creative group for new-business pitches. He had to find a small apartment, and a whole new wardrobe. He wanted to choose a car this week, and buy it next week. And he would pay for everything with the weekend at Easthampton. Also, there were several women. . . .

"You're half asleep, aren't you?"

He looked at Edith. "What?"

She nodded, pleased. "You'll probably be sick tomorrow."

He closed his eyes again.

"Don't say I didn't warn you."

He kept his eyes, and his mouth, shut. While she slept tonight, he would finish the last few pages of *Don Quixote* and start on another exciting experience. He wondered if *Moby Dick* would bore him as it had in college.

It didn't. He read from midnight, when he left Edith sleeping, until five-thirty, when he finished the massive tome. He was reading faster and faster, with clearer visualization and greater pleasure. He started Will Durant's *Our Asiatic Heritage* (one of five Durant volumes they'd gotten from the Book-of-the-Month Club, and never had time to read). It gave him his first non-pleasurable experience in reading; he hated to leave the fascinating sweep of history and the cloistered hours of night for the growing day. He retained some of this feeling even as he boarded the train for the city and the triumphs he knew lay ahead.

So many ways to live, he mused, writing an idea for the car pitch on the little pad he carried in his breast pocket. So many pleasures to enjoy. The thrill of having a woman. The physical well-being and ego-satisfaction of athletic prowess. The economically-rewarding, luxury-creating conquests of business. The emotional gratification of striking down an old enemy, or an armed criminal assailant. The quiet hours of living other lives and other times; of gaining knowledge, depth and perception through books. So many good things to gather. So much richness in life.

He'd had none of them before; hadn't even known some existed. Now he had them all.

He remembered his dreams of two nights ago; something had threatened him, something unseen and unknown. His next thought was of New Mexico and the still unanswered question of what had happened to him there.

It bothered him for a moment, until he got another ad idea and wrote it down on his pad. Besides, what difference did it make that he didn't know how he'd become something special, as long as he remained something special?

It was inconceivable that he would change.

chapter 7

THE THIRD WEEK of Ed Berner's rebirth was a largely success-ful run for the money. It had its disappointments, but they weren't totally unexpected and didn't change his plans too drastically. They merely proved what he'd already begun to suspect—that he couldn't count on Instant Money—and they didn't come until the weekend.

Before that, he convinced Stennis that small or not, P.B.S. had a chance to land Dennison Motors, if Ed Berner were put in charge of a creative group. He got two writers, two artists, and immediate respect from an entire agency which had largely ignored him. He put his staff to work on four of his own campaign ideas, and accepted two more from them. He also managed—after much mental pressure—to get an ex-pense account of the type allowed only top executives. This was, ostensibly, to help him prepare for big client meetings.

He used it to buy good food and cigars, four suits at Brooks Brothers, several pieces of fine luggage. It would soon help defray the cost of the studio apartment just four blocks from the office (he would take possession next week) and the pale blue Triumph sports car he'd chosen at a showroom uptown (delivery in two weeks).

He took Beth to lunch Monday and Tuesday, and both times they spent less than an hour eating and almost two hours in the Larington. He was careful not to exceed her "limits," and found she was learning the art of love quickly within those limits. Also, he enjoyed her talk of a world he was not yet a part of. A world of education for education's sake and not for jobs. A world of money so long established that it ignored income and concentrated on finding purpose in life. He listened to her, and began to respect her, and was sure she could survive quite happily, without losing any of her intellectual enthusiasm, as a secretary, or middle-class housewife, as well as a career woman or society matron. She was beautifully balanced, and the man who married her would be lucky. The *normal* man who would need a beautifully balanced wife. As for himself, he needed the whole wide world of men, women and things. They didn't know it, but he was married to them all; could use them all!

He read Tuesday night.

On Wednesday, he went around to the secretarial pool, tucked into a corner near the art department, and said hello to the handsome blond typist with startling mammary development and caboose to match; a girl he'd admired on first coming to P.B.S. She'd shown some interest, but then had begun dating the unmarried art director with crew cut and sophisticated leer. Her name was Anise and she said, "Hey, Ed, long time no see," and "Whatcha been doing?" and "I been hearing things 'bout you lately."

He said he'd tell her all about himself at lunch. She said sorry, she was meeting Phil, her art director. He told her Phil wouldn't be available this noon; he was working through lunch on a rush project.

"How would you know?" she asked, bridling a little.

He gave her warm, soothing, flattering thoughts. "He works for me, honey. He's in my new-business group."

Her limpid blue eyes widened. "And he never said a word!"

So the art director remembered Ed's early interest in his blond special.

Ed gave her more thoughts; erotic thoughts this time. He built on her growing respect and created a growing warmth. He arranged to meet her at the San Marino, and then called a hotel near the restaurant and reserved a double.

She was even better looking without clothing, and had no limits; at least none that became discernible in two hours. She held his hand all the way back in the cab, shaking her head and murmuring, "Oh brother, what a man." He was pleased, but already bored.

For the second night in a row, he needed no sleep and read until morning.

Thursday, he took his eleven-o'clock snack at the Automat and looked for the pretty Negro girl. He found her, and sat at her table, and talked to her. His thoughts said he was intensely interested in equality for all, as well as in her as a woman. They left the Automat because she had to get back to the Thirty-Eighth Street residential hotel where she worked as a switchboard operator. He walked with her, and wanted her, and made her want him.

A tenant on the third floor was in Europe, she said as they approached the hotel entrance. She had the key because she fed his collection of tropical fish.

He said he loved tropical fish. Could he see them?

He saw them . . . an hour later, on the way out. The girl, Billy, had forgotten to feed them and had to go back. He kissed her at the door, held her close, heard her breath pick up speed again. "Aren't you something," she said, stroking his head. "And they tell those stories about Negro men."

But she was already very late and her replacement would be angry, so they arranged to meet tomorrow.

He slept heavily Thursday night

Friday, he and Billy ate lunch in the apartment with the tropical fish, and broke a bed slat, and laughed a lot. They also discussed the worth of the individual, and Ed found he had much to say, not all of it encouraging or to Billy's liking. But he said it anyway, and felt better for it.

When he returned to the office, there was a message from Gladys. She would call back at three-thirty. He stayed at his desk, and told her when she called they certainly *would* see each other again.

"I thought you'd be breaking down my door," she murmured. "I wanted to break *yours* down."

"Maybe you did."

She laughed. "Can we meet in the city? I'm sure I can get in tomorrow for shopping, or Sunday to visit a friend."

He explained that he was going away on business, but they'd make it next week. "One of those dark little lanes up in Putnam County. Your big station wagon should be comfortable enough."

She agreed with alacrity. "Why not tonight, neighbor?"

Her enthusiasm was contagious, but his new two-suiter stood packed in the corner, his car was in the garage down the street, his eight-hundred-dollar stake made a heavy lump in his pocket. He was driving to Easthampton with Beth after work. "That business trip, remember?"

"Sure it's business?" She laughed. "What did Edith have to say about it?"

"No trouble at all." Which wasn't quite the truth. Edith had begun to raise the roof last night, when he'd broken the news. He'd cut her short by using mental pressure, and left her docile if not delighted. "She understands that money comes first."

"You kid me not?"

She wanted confidences, and he wanted to get off the phone. "Next Wednesday or Thursday, Gladys. 'Bye."

It was a pleasant trip to Easthampton. Beth said dinner was served quite late weekends at her home, and he was hungry, so they stopped at a roadside restaurant and spent an hour eating and talking; he eating and she talking. He enjoyed listening to her, both in the restaurant and during the three-hour drive. She had read widely, and thought deeply. As long as they stayed off the topic of their personal relationship, she was gay and animated. The one time they touched on themselves, she grew quiet; then said she had little hope they would know each other a year from now. "I know you must consider me ancient," he said, reaching out and stroking her thigh, "but I'll last longer than *that*." She didn't smile. She said, "*I* won't. Besides, I'll be going back to school in September. You're not one for a letter romance, Mr. Berner." He said they'd see, and felt saddened, because she was right.

But then they were in the Hamptons, and she directed him, and they reached the big old house on the dunes overlooking the Atlantic. It was actually outside Easthampton, near Amagansett, in a rugged and isolated section of shore line. He commented on this.

"Yes, Dad likes solitude in his surroundings, but he fills the house with guests every weekend. We've got twelve bedrooms and twelve baths in that old monstrosity, not counting the servant couple's room. Every bed is occupied, in some instances by two."

"How about your bed?"

She smiled. "You stay out of my bed, Mr. Berner. This is home for me, at least during the summer. My daddy thinks I'm a good girl."

"And your mommy?"

"She's remarried. Daddy stayed single, and I stayed with him. He's liberal enough, but not with me. He once threatened to ruin an account executive from Bates who became a little too attentive during a weekend. He could do it, too."

Ed chuckled, but decided right then and there that poker would be his sole entertainment, as well as occupation, this weekend. Unless, of course, the opportunity arose with someone not a daughter of Roscoe Francis Hammermill.

At eight-forty, as he was getting settled into his second-floor room, there was a knock on the door and Beth called, "Put your trunks on, Ed. We've got time for a swim before it's really dark."

He'd never been much of a swimmer, even in sunshine-filled lakes and pools, and walking to the window he could see enormous breakers smashing onto a shore shadowed by dusk. He considered pleading exhaustion after the long drive; then realized he was full of energy and actually in need of a way to work off some. Besides, what did the new Ed Berner have to fear from *any* physical enterprise?

The sun had disappeared into the sea by the time they came padding through the sand, each carrying a huge bath towel. Ed's old trunks felt dangerously tight, but they must have looked all right because Beth said, "I've never had eyes for anything but the Atlantic that first dip of the weekend, but you're quite an exciting bit of nature yourself, Mr. Berner."

He grinned at her. "The Atlantic could never make me stop looking at you. Not for a second." Which wasn't quite true, even though she was lovely in a yellow, modified bikini. The dark, roaring water was beginning to hold great promise of pleasure, offering an opportunity to use his body to its limit, to test his endurance.

Beth dropped her towel and hugged herself. "It's always ten or more degrees cooler here than inland. And it's later than I thought. Maybe we shouldn't try swimming. We *could* get in trouble."

He placed his towel beside hers and straightened and looked out over the surging immensity. "Last one in," he murmured, and began to move forward.

She reached for his hand. He didn't want anyone's hand; not now. "Race you," he said, and left her behind and ran into the surf and was hit by a small wave and felt a sudden chill, and almost remembered another sudden chill. He stopped and tried to capture that memory, but it wasn't there. He heard Beth laughing close behind him, and moved forward again, the water up to his waist. Another wave hit him, and then he heard Beth shouting and saw something coming; a monstrous black shadow about fifty yards out, building high and thick, beginning to show white on top. Beth was retreating, calling, "Careful, Ed! They're rough this time of . . ."

He faced forward, and the wave was towering over him, and he knew he should dive under it; knew it was foolish to subject himself to the lashing, crushing weight of water. But he wanted to defy it, and he did.

The wave crashed down. He was choked, blinded, deafened. Any other man would have been sent tumbling and scrambling and gasping for air; but he dug his toes into shifting sand and leaned forward, arms outstretched, fighting the power of the sea. He staggered a little, and stroked a little at the peak of the surge, but when the water receded he was still standing there.

He looked back. Beth seemed frozen, half turned to him. She said, "That's quite a trick." He laughed his exultation and threw himself forward and began to swim. She called something about it being too dark, but he kept going. He settled into a breath for every two strokes, and realized he didn't have to bother breathing so often. He stroked ten times before his next breath, then twenty, then thirty, and finally decided on a breath for every twenty-four strokes. He was so involved with stroking and kicking and counting that he forgot Beth and the shore and everything but the pleasure of his body slicing cleanly, smoothly through the water. He felt he was swimming faster than any human ever had before; felt he could keep going indefinitely, perhaps all the way to Europe! But sometime later the pleasure diminished and he found he was breathing every ten or twelve strokes, and he also became aware of hunger. He hadn't eaten in more than three hours. It was a long time between meals for the new Ed Berner.

And with that he knew the earlier feeling of endless energy was false. The only way he could keep going indefinitely was if he carried a supply of food with him; a huge supply. He was chained to his intake of energy. It was a limiting factor, and one he would have to remember.

With that, he stopped swimming and turned toward shore, or toward where he thought the shore would be. He saw no shore. He saw nothing but water; dark, rolling, endless water. The first twinge of fear dug into him as darkness thickened. The sky was losing all traces of gray. There was no way of telling where the sun had set—where west lay. The night was deepening.

He began to swim, but stopped after a few strokes. How could he know he wasn't going further out, increasing his danger with every stroke?

The sea was empty and endless. He was alone in the empty, endless sea.

He panicked and began to flounder and swallowed some water. He heard his voice gurgle as he tried to shout with water filling his mouth.

It couldn't end like this! It was too stupid! He had strength enough to keep going, strength enough to get back to shore, if only he could find where shore lay. He was stronger than anyone, had more to live for than anyone; it just couldn't end out here!

The bitterness of death mixed with the taste of salt, and he opened his mouth to gasp for air he didn't need and to utter a scream for help that no one could hear. He thrashed more and more wildly. He began to throw his life away.

Something happened. A calm descended on him. He turned over on his back and floated and breathed normally. Thought returned. He couldn't believe he had effected this change himself, and looked on with surprise and gratitude. At the same time he considered the fact that he might very well die.

He didn't think of Edith or the children for more than a moment. His insurance was adequate. Besides, life had a way of taking its own tragic or triumphant paths, no matter how much or little a man left his family. For himself, he felt a deep and aching regret, because he was losing so much more than an ordinary life. *If only I'd died before New Mexico,* he thought. *If only I were losing less than this sweet, sweet life; this life which could run on forever . . .*

His thoughts stopped there, as if he weren't allowed to think of death. He lay on his back, arms outstretched, rising and falling on the cold body of the sea. He rocked in a black limbo. Finally, he closed his eyes and half slept.

He was wide awake the instant the change came. His senses tuned in on an approaching presence and he began to swim toward it. After a while he paused to look around. A star lay low in the sky. It seemed to rock; or was that because he and the sea rocked?

He thought of the North Star and reckoning the points of the compass by it. He kept watching the star until he heard the voice and knew it wasn't a star but a light in a boat. The voice was a man's, followed by a woman's. The woman was Beth.

He swam, and called out. The boat was suddenly there; a pontoon affair with a bench seat across twin shells, as used by lifeguards at the city's beaches. Beth saw him. She stopped shouting and dropped her head and sat still. The man leaned down. "Grab my hand and get up in the seat. I'll hold onto the boat. . . ."

"Stay there," Ed said. "I'm okay. Just lead me back to shore." He was already ashamed of having caused trouble.

Beth raised her head. "But you must be exhausted. You can't . . ."

He swam ten swift strokes away from the boat, turned over on his back, kicked himself some distance, turned face down again, jackknifed under the water, came up blowing and returned to the boat. "Can we go now?"

The man took one oar, Beth the other, and they rowed. Ed followed, swimming easily on Beth's side. Whenever he glanced up, her face, a pale oval in the darkness, looked down at him. They went on and on, and Ed wondered that he'd swum and drifted this far.

He didn't see the shore, but Beth called down that he should get away from the boat. They were coming in and the waves might slam him against the pontoons. He swam off in a diagonal; and then his hands scraped bottom and he stumbled erect. He went over to where Beth and the man were struggling to pull the boat out of the surf. He grabbed a crossbar and turned to the shore and walked. The boat was beached a moment later.

He stood there and rubbed his hands together and felt the water trickling down his face. "Thanks for saving my life."

The man—a teen-aged boy, Ed saw now—laughed and said, "The way you were swimming, I don't think you needed us." He looked at Beth. "You okay?"

She was hugging herself, shivering. "Me? Don't be silly!"

The boy shrugged.

Beth put her hand on his arm. "I'm sorry, Leroy. Thank you. Thank you so very much." To Ed: "Leroy lives in town. Dad lets him swim here. If he hadn't come by just when he did, I'd have lost fifteen minutes, maybe more, getting someone from the house to help me with the boat."

"I'm Mr. Hammermill's favorite delivery boy," Leroy said, smiling. "That's 'cause I deliver for Skelly's." He waved and ran toward the dunes and the road.

"Skelly's is a liquor shop," Beth said.

Ed moved close to her. "I want to thank you."

She nodded, still shivering, and he saw her tears. He glanced back at the house, then took her in his arms and held her quietly. She put her head down, lips pressing his chest, and said something.

"What?"

Her head came up. "Nothing very important. I was talking into your flesh, into your heart. I was telling your flesh, your heart, that I'm not going to see you any more."

"Why? I thought you gave us a year, or at least until September?"

"That was before I thought you'd drowned."

He began to talk her out of it, began to use his mind on her, then stopped. He would never coerce Beth Hammermill again. He would never influence her thoughts, her actions again.

Later, changing for dinner, he told himself it was merely that he didn't want to complicate an already sticky situation. He'd made love to her, and received the invitation to East-hampton, and that was all he'd ever wanted. And whether it was strictly the truth or not didn't matter, because it would certainly *become* the truth in time—a relatively short time. Ed Berner, being what he was, could no more content himself with one woman than return to his old life of frustration and failure.

With that settled, he buttoned his sport jacket, ran a comb through his thick hair and walked into the hall. A woman was just backing out of the room next to his; the last room before the staircase. She was short, curvy, about thirty-five. Her hair was shoulder length and deep black. She wore a skin-tight orange sheath, orange lipstick, dramatic green eye-shadow. Her shoes were orange and stiletto-heeled. She turned and smiled. "We're neighbors, I see."

They went down to dinner together. Before they reached the big dining room and huge table with eighteen settings, she'd informed him that she was a friend of a friend of Roscoe Hammermill, and here alone, and looking forward to a moonlight stroll on the beach. "You're hardly dressed for it," Ed murmured, looking around at people seating themselves.

"The dress comes off," she said, her ample bosom pressing his arm. "Rather easily, for the right situation."

They sat together near the head of the table and Roscoe Hammermill. Beth was at her father's right, directly across from Ed. She looked at him, and at Cora Stanton, the woman in orange, and then helped in the introductions. During the meal, she ate little and talked much to her father and a ruddy, good-looking man on her right. The ruddy man was a television producer. He leaned past Beth and said, "Roscoe, I was telling your daughter she could easily do a few spots for me on the new Ray Wallach show. 'And now, here's Ray,' and stuff like that."

Roscoe Hammermill was tall, lean, with a long, sardonic face enhanced rather than spoiled by pitted skin. He had a full head of grayish-brown hair and a thin, totally-gray mus-tache. "She's working for an ad agency, like her daddy. Mr. Berner can tell you whether she's any good."

Ed glanced quickly at Beth. She had her head turned to the maid, just then serving the main course.

"A girl like Beth is good at everything," Ed said. "I think those who know her know that."

Roscoe Hammermill nodded. "Ever since she was ten."

"She told me she's a typist," the TV producer said. "A girl like Beth is too pretty to be typing."

"Beth will dispute that," Roscoe said, and turned to his daughter.

"Beth has left the ad agency," Beth said, poking her fork into a helping of lobster thermidor. "I'll call them this Monday."

Roscoe looked surprised. "I thought you liked the ad game, honey?"

"I do."

"Then why leave, and without adequate notice? After all, I made the contact for you and it ill behooves . . ."

"That's show biz," Beth said, smiling thinly. She looked at the TV producer. "Were you just talking, Mr. Veblan, or should I report to your office Monday?"

"Wednesday," the ruddy-faced man said, looking pleased. "Who knows, you might find yourself taking dramatics instead of . . . what was it you said you studied?"

"English literature."

"Yes. Waste of time, really. Good actor's workshop and you'll be right in the thick of the greatest business on earth."

Beth smiled. The TV producer grinned at Roscoe. Roscoe said, "If you're thinking I might swing a little weight in filling those commercial time spots, Roy . . ." He paused. "Well, let's eat."

It was foolishness, totally unimportant, and Ed divorced himself from the whole thing. He ate quickly, heavily, depleting the bread and hoping no one noticed his appetite. But Cora Stanton murmured, "I love a man who eats big, and doesn't show it. Means he burns up lots of energy other ways."

He gave her the sly grin she expected, but he was wondering how to suggest a poker game without appearing anxious about it.

Beth excused herself before dessert, pleading weariness. Veblan said, "Mark my words, Roscoe, she's going to enjoy every minute at the studio." Roscoe Hammermill nodded unhappily. He glanced at Ed, began to say something, and then stopped. Ed wished Beth hadn't made her announcement just now. She was complicating what should be a simple operation of separating Hammermill and several of his guests from their extra money.

People began leaving the dining room. Ed had a second helping of pie and asked the maid to bring him a large glass of milk. Cora Stanton was talking to him; Roscoe Hammermill was sipping a brandy and chewing an unlit cigar; in a moment they were alone at the long oak table.

"Now for that walk," Cora said, her leg brushing Ed's.

Ed glanced at Hammermill, who was glancing at him. "Not just now," he murmured. "I . . . ah, want to speak to Mr. Hammermill."

Cora batted her dark eyes. "I'll wait on the porch. All right?"

He nodded.

She gave him a very definite press with her leg, and left. Hammermill said, "Did I hear you say you wanted to talk to me, Mr. Berner?"

Ed smiled. "In a way. What I actually wanted to do was smoke a cigar, and I've left mine upstairs."

Hammermill produced a panatela from his inside pocket. Ed thanked him, lit it, shook his head as Hammermill pushed the brandy bottle toward him.

"For a man who sells whisky, you drink remarkably little, Mr. Berner. Or did Beth err in saying you handled the Wylitt account?"

"I handle it, and new business too."

"Ah, yes, she mentioned you were given a promotion recently. Congratulations. Sure you won't toast the good news?"

"I have all the other vices, Mr. Hammermill. I smoke, I look at women, I gamble." He waited, hoping Hammermill would pick up a cue, but the agency owner had other things on his mind.

"Perhaps you can tell me, Ed; what happened to make Beth want to leave P.B.S.? Just last weekend she was saying she really enjoyed the place."

"It surprised me too, Roscoe."

Hammermill looked at his cigar, struck a match, spent a moment in getting an even light. "Beth has invited only four men here since she graduated from high school. The other three were boyfriends. Do you consider yourself in that category, Ed?"

Ed laughed. "I'd certainly like to." He shook his head and

laughed again. "No, of course not. I just helped her out a few times and she mentioned your summer place and I told her I love the shore where it's not inundated with humanity, and she asked me to come."

Hammermill tossed off a brandy. "Don't misunderstand me, Ed. I won't set myself up as judge of whom my daughter sees, as long as the man declares himself. To be more explicit, she can fall in love with, or sleep with, anyone she damn well pleases to choose, but that someone can't be playing a double game. He's got to be free to be with her, free to fall for her, free to marry her if it works out that way. He's got to be able to come here and say he's Beth's date. Otherwise, I'd be a little unhappy. I'd do something about it too."

"May I remind you of my declared vices, Roscoe? I said I smoke, *look* at women, and gamble. I've had a look at Beth, and enjoyed it, but poker is my real passion. And speaking of poker, does anyone here indulge?"

Hammermill was still looking at him. Ed sent him a strong thought—a thought of Ed Berner's broad-spectrum naïveté, high morality, and low voltage.

"Mean to say you're looking for a poker game with Cora Stanton waiting on the front porch? I think you should be apprised of the facts. Cora buried a rich husband last year. Herb was twenty-two years her senior, and an invalid the last eight years of his life. She's been making up for lost time ever since."

Ed shrugged. "The evening's still young. Care for a game?"

Hammermill rose, the cigar clamped in his teeth. "Stay put. I'll gather a few of the faithful. I should warn you we generally play table stakes. I don't know your financial situation . . ."

"I carry between five hundred and a thousand when the possibility of a game exists. I have eight hundred in my pocket at the moment."

"A checkbook would do as well," Hammermill murmured, and went to the door.

"The hell you say," Ed chuckled. "Your daughter isn't that good a judge of strangers."

Hammermill smiled. "Well, the other gentlemen I hope to bring back to this table are known to me. Their checks are good, Ed. I vouch for that."

Ed nodded. "I know where I am, Roscoe."

Hammermill returned with three men; two of them big names in advertising, the third Roy Veblan, the TV producer. The male servant brought glasses, ice, soda and a tray of bottles. Everyone drank, except Ed. He paid strict attention to the game.

They played five card draw, jacks or better, table stakes with a fifty dollar limit on openers. Ed lost the first three hands; then adjusted to working on four minds simultaneously and began to win. He bet heavily when he was sure, and dropped out when he wasn't. He had all the cash in the game by eleven-thirty—forty-two hundred dollars, with Veblan the heavy loser at eighteen hundred. Then the checkbooks came out and the betting increased as everyone tried to make up his losses.

By two a.m., Ed had added eleven thousand to his winnings. Until then, he'd been too busy playing cards, and minds, to notice any change in the atmosphere. But he paused to ask Hammermill if there was any chance of grabbing a sandwich. Hammermill said, "Help yourself. The kitchen's down the hall and on your left."

Ed nodded and rose, smiling around the table. Three of the faces that met his were grim, closed, guarded. In Roy Veblan's there was outright hostility. Ed paused to light the stub of his cigar, and sent out thoughts of Ed Berner's honesty, vast good luck, intense good will. There was some slight change, but Veblan, for one, remained hostile. Ed left, feeling he couldn't stop them from suspecting him. Damned unfair too, just as with that thug, Gordon. He *wasn't* cheating, insofar as what they knew about methods of fixing a game, so why should they suspect him? A man could get lucky, couldn't he?

He found the kitchen and wolfed down three beef and cheese combinations and drank two cans of beer. He hurried back to the dining room, and the voices stopped as he entered. His seat was occupied by Veblan. The other men had also moved around. The empty seat was now the one previously occupied by Hammermill.

He smiled. "Not the usual thing to do, gentlemen. Still, it's quite all right with me."

No one smiled back at him, but Hammermill seemed a little embarrassed.

Veblan said, "Your luck seems just short of phenomenal, Berner. We've opened a new deck too."

Ed sat down, maintaining his smile. "Just as long as you haven't reclaimed my winnings."

Veblan flushed. "I moved your pile myself. Want to count it?"

Ed spent a moment doing just that. When he finished, he looked at Hammermill. "I take it you suspect me of cheating, Roscoe?"

Hammermill's eyes dropped. "We do."

"You've lost only five hands in four hours," snapped Cletis Failes, who was sole owner of Loeser, Baird and Failes, Advertising. "That goes beyond the laws of probability."

"But not beyond the laws of possibility," Ed replied. "And the possibility that a man can have one hot evening shouldn't escape you gentlemen."

Failes began to answer. Hammermill cut him short. "Let's play. Let's get those laws of probability and possibility working for someone else."

"I hope they *do* work for someone else," Ed said. "I hope they work for you, Roscoe, because I'm occupying your seat, and probability knows only position, not personality."

Hammermill chewed his cigar. Veblan glared. Failes said, "This is getting damned unpleasant." Andrew Cohen, a partner in Copy Masters, Ltd., rose and said, "I feel I've been had but I can't prove it. I don't intend to accuse Mr. Berner without proof, or to continue being had through lack of it. Goodnight."

Hammermill also rose. "My feelings exactly. I apologize if we're wrong, Mr. Berner."

"Goodnight, Mr. Cohen, Mr. Hammermill," Ed said, and though he smiled, he was raging inside; at them, and at himself. They were right, and they were wrong. He'd been discovered, and he'd been falsely accused.

Veblan stayed seated. So did Failes. Hammermill and Cohen left. Veblan poured himself a Scotch, tossed it down and sighed. "Well, maybe things *will* even out. Maybe we *will* apologize before the night is over."

"Yes," Failes murmured. "I've never turned my back on facts."

Ed understood that they were inviting him to throw a few fat hands, return their losses and so regain his good name. And he might have done just that, if he'd felt there'd been anything to gain. But there wasn't. Not a thing. It would only confirm their suspicions of his dishonesty. He said, "I still feel hot, gentlemen. If you can't afford the losses, better quit."

Veblan began to deal. Ed said, "It was *my* deal when I left. If you please."

Veblan slammed the cards on the table. Ed reached for them, shuffled, dealt under the intense stares of his opponents.

Veblan got good hands. They won him a few small pots from Failes, but Ed always dropped out. By four-thirty, Ed had won six thousand more, and Failes jumped up and shook his fist and shouted, "You lousy swindler! I don't know how you're doing it . . ."

"But he's doing it," Veblan finished, also rising. "We both know it, Clete. I say we take back what he stole."

Failes was in his forties, tall and heavy. He was a big man who'd had no opportunity to learn he was in lousy shape since leaving the activities of college. Veblan was shorter, broader, tighter in the gut and chest.

Ed stayed seated.

"All right," Failes said. "All right!"

Veblan said, "You going to give back what you stole, Mr. Berner?"

"My, my, what bad losers. I guess good losers just don't gamble. I'm going to have to give up poker."

Veblan said, "We're not kidding. You're not walking out with our money."

Ed stood up and began putting his winnings in his pocket. Veblan started toward him. Ed finished putting away the checks, raised his fist and brought it down on the massive oak table. Bottles and glasses bounced; the heavy wood split. He did it again, and the table caved in at the center, scrambling liquor and glassware. Once more, and it fell in two separate pieces.

Failes turned and walked out, the back of his neck white. Veblan stood absolutely still. Ed said, "I hope you won't make it necessary for me to look you up, Mr. Veblan? Any trouble with the checks, and I'll feel terribly put upon. The accusations were bad enough. Your threat of violence was worse. But going back on your written word will be too much."

"I've never welshed yet," Veblan said, voice high and weak. "You can't blame us . . ."

"I can, and I do." He walked out.

When he got to his room, he slumped to the bed. He felt ashamed. He felt diminished. It was the end of his dream of Instant Money.

He emptied his pockets and counted his winnings: a total of twenty-two thousand two hundred dollars. With the eight hundred from Gordon, he had an even twenty-three thousand.

He put it all in his jacket, and the jacket in the closet. He began to take off his shirt, and heard sounds from next door, from Cora Stanton's room: a man's voice; footsteps; someone moving into the hall and away in stockinged feet.

He went to the wall and placed his ear against it. He heard lighter footsteps, and then a shower running. He buttoned his shirt and went downstairs. Except for the light in the dining room, the house was dark and silent. He entered the kitchen and the walk-in refrigerator. He'd seen three bottles of champagne there earlier this evening. Only one was left now, but one was enough. He found wine glasses in a cupboard, put champagne and glasses on a tray, and made himself three sandwiches. He ate quickly, returned to the second floor and stopped at Cora Stanton's door. He didn't hear the shower, and tapped softly.

Footsteps approached. Cora said, "You could have waited till morning for your damned tie." The door opened.

Ed smiled. "He couldn't have been much. You're not happy."

She was leaning around the door, a tie held out in her hand. She stared at him.

"May I come in?" He showed her the tray of champagne and glasses.

"Kind of late, wouldn't you say?"

"It's never too late, for the right situation. You did say the dress came off for the right situation, didn't you?"

"The dress *is* off. I think the whole thing is off."

He felt her annoyance, but it wasn't with him. She'd had less than the perfect lover this evening. She wasn't in love with love this evening.

He countered her annoyance with heated thoughts, saw her lips lose their tightness, and pushed forward.

"Wait a minute," she whispered. "I haven't a stitch . . ."

But he came in, kicked the door shut and watched the big, naked rear run for the bathroom. He opened the champagne, began to fill the glasses, and then stopped. He no longer liked wine. And besides, he was in a hurry. He had things to forget. And what better way than on a woman's body?

He went to the bathroom and tried the door. It opened, and Cora turned from the mirror. She was wearing a knee-length terry cloth bathrobe and holding a lipstick. "Really, Mr. Berner, this is too much!"

"Please shut up," he said, and reached her and ripped off her robe.

She cried out and raised her hand and struck him. "I'll scream the roof off this place if you don't get . . ." He cut her short with his lips and pulled her against him and held her immobile, arms pinned to her sides. He put his hands under her buttocks and raised her a few inches off the floor and backed out of the bathroom, across the bedroom to the bed. He turned and fell on her.

She did scream, about the time the sun was rising, but it was soft and deep in her throat. She screamed again at noon, into her pillow, after he'd learned she liked a little pain and improvised an exotic spanking.

He left her at one-thirty, ravenous for food, but didn't go down to lunch. He packed his bag, deciding to avoid embarrassment and eat on the road. But he felt he had to make at least an attempt to see Beth. Her room was at the other end of the hall, facing the dunes. He went there, certain she'd be either at the dining room or the beach. He began composing the note he'd leave her as he knocked at her door, but she answered. She was wearing a tan slack outfit and had a book in her hand. She looked lovely, and unhappy; her eyes pink, watery, underscored in black.

He said he was leaving.

"I heard about the poker game. I told Father you'd never cheat, and he asked how I could be sure, and of course I couldn't be sure. Did you cheat?"

"No."

"Did you . . . influence their thinking during the game?"

"That's nonsense. I never influenced your thinking and I can't influence anyone else's. Where did you ever get such a ridiculous idea?"

"Then there's nothing more to say."

"Except goodbye." He leaned over and kissed her cheek.

"I'm reading Petrarch," she said, turning away and raising the book. "Have you ever read him? Love sonnets to Laura."

"There's no time for that now," he said. He wanted to

leave the ocean and Beth and the smashed table in the dining room. He wanted to take his money and get back to the city and go on to triumphs unadulterated by fear, shame and nonsense.

"There was time for Cora."

"Was the keyhole large enough for comfortable viewing?"

She kept her back to him. "I left my door open and listened for you. I was going to come to you. Then you went downstairs and I waited for you to return and you went into Cora's room. I don't blame you. I know I said it was over. And it is."

"Don't dramatize it, dear. It was little enough to begin with, and it's less now. You'll be meeting dozens of attractive, successful men through Roy Veblan. Have a ball. But don't ever get dramatic about a quick affair."

She turned then, her face flushed. "I don't believe you, Ed Berner! I don't think you're the sophisticated Don Juan. I feel you're someone else under all this."

He laughed to cover his shock. "You mustn't read too much poetry, Beth. It's giving you delusions. Whatever I am or am not under 'all this,' you can't see it. Just as I can't see inside you."

"You don't have to see inside me. I'm all on the surface, for you."

"Oh, Christ," he muttered, and went to her and took her hand. "Let me say goodbye. I just want to leave and know you understand that I never wanted to hurt you, that we're friends. You saved my life yesterday. I want to thank you. Can't I, without all this confusion?"

She nodded. "You're right. I will forget you, and I will have a ball, and . . . goodbye, Ed."

"Goodbye." Yet now he hesitated about leaving, feeling there was something more to be said. "I'll read Petrarch. I'll drop you a line, to let you know what I think of him."

"No, don't."

He went to the door.

"Read de Sade instead."

He'd read de Sade. He'd remembered de Sade during the last hour with Cora. He intended to remember de Sade again, perhaps with Gladys. The total spectrum of erotic experience awaited him, and Beth was only a momentary detour.

He said, "Yes, thank you," and walked out. She had tried

to shame him, and instead had reminded him who he was. She'd intended to hurt him, but instead had freed him. Because Beth didn't fit; Beth wasn't one who burned; and he and his partners had to burn, and burn white hot.

He stopped at a roadside stand and bought a dozen hot-dogs and five containers of orange drink and took them to the car to avoid comment. He drove and ate and smoked a cigar and patted the bulge in his jacket. He had survived the sea, and survived . . . was it love? Whatever it was, he had survived. Now nothing could stop him!

chapter 8

THE FOURTH WEEK of Ed Berner's new life was a second re-birth. Freed from whatever vestiges remained of his old life —its restraints, romantic dreams and morality—he worked toward increased power and self-gratification.

Nick Bandson returned to work, and found Ed firmly entrenched as group head over his old accounts. A brief meeting with Ed robbed him of his indignation, courage and will to remain at P.B.S. He had a querulous and unimpressive meeting with Stennis, and gave notice that same Monday.

The new-business group arrived early and left late every night, slaving under Ed's mental and verbal stimulation, his induced dreams of money and glory. As the week drew to a close, they put the finishing touches on an exciting presentation for the preliminary Dennison Motors meeting, which was set for Friday morning. At that time, Ed and Stennis would meet with Evan Purcell, Jr., ad manager of the giant automotive company, and present print and television campaigns, as well as a general prospectus of what P.B.S. could do for a major car account.

In addition, Ed met twice with Sy Roverstein, drawing extravagant praise and the statement, "How the hell did Wylitt ever get along without you?"

Since he no longer worked at the typewriter, using any copy man in the agency for any job that had to be done, Ed had considerable time for fun and games. He had taken possession of his furnished apartment on Monday morning, and had a long pleasant dinner there that night. He had picked up his sports car Tuesday afternoon (a hundred dollar tip expedited matters considerably), and given it a few trial runs along the East River Drive. In both apartment and car, he'd had the company of a statuesque model who was initially interested in employment and soon willing to settle for Ed Berner.

He'd spent hardly any of his twenty-three thousand dollars. Stennis had caught the new-business fever and was allowing Ed to use his expense account in pre-Kennedy Administration fashion.

At home, Ed kept Edith drugged with calm thoughts; shut her up whenever she began to complain of his late hours and nights in the city. He found time to take a drive Wednesday night, meet Gladys (who was supposedly at the movies) and lead her to a little-used country lane. The Olds station wagon was confining but adequate. He thought of de Sade again, and Gladys ending up whimpering and begging and, as they dressed, worrying that Harry would ask about the bruises sure to emerge. Before he went back to his own car, she said, "I'm not sure I can take this kind of thing, Ed." Her face was puffy in the darkness; her voice thick and shaky. "I never thought I'd *ever* get enough, but now I don't know. Do you have to be so . . . violent?"

He shrugged and said they'd discuss it the next time.

"Well, all right. I won't be able to see you for at least a week. . . ."

That was the way he wanted it. Once or twice and then finished. It was the newness, the novelty of a different woman, that made the game sweet. It was the clinging, the hanging on, that turned it sour.

He stayed in the city Thursday night, using the Friday morning meeting on Dennison Motors as his excuse. He entertained his model until one A.M., then drove her to her home in Greenburgh. She feared speed, especially in the low-slung, full-throated, open-topped Triumph, so he kept to a sedate forty-five miles an hour. But on the way back, with the highway almost deserted, with Manhattan sleeping on his left and the Hudson glittering darkly on his right, he did what he'd been wanting to do ever since getting the car. He put the accelerator to the floorboard. He intended to keep it floored until she reached her maximum—well over a hundred. He didn't. He couldn't. At eighty-five, fear swept over him; fear of smashing up and being scattered over the roadside; fear of swift and violent death.

He slowed, and was disgusted with himself, and tried to accelerate again. He drove at fifty, inching toward sixty several times but always letting up, always giving in to the fear; a new fear even for the old Ed Berner.

He parked in the elevated garage two blocks from his apartment and walked and wondered at himself. He was so much man in so many ways, but there were the imperfections: the need always to be eating (he was hungry again); the inability to drink liquor (which was an embarrassment for an ad man); the fear of violent death (new, and growing stronger); and the dreams. The dreams were the worst. The dreams came twice a week, which was as often as he slept. They always started out as triumphs, and ended with a Presence threatening him, an Unknown of tremendous power which made him run from his triumph in weakness and terror. He was glad tonight was a reading night. He had the last volume in Durant's *Story of Civilization* series. And he had the slim volume of Petrarch's poems to Laura.

He was in the office by eight Friday morning, checking the layouts and storyboards. By nine he had four artists making rush changes, and another doing tissue layouts on several additional thoughts. At eleven he and Stennis sat down to review the presentation. Stennis was impressed, but not hopeful. That was because Ed allowed him to think independently. Then he fed him a large dose of confidence, and Stennis ended by saying what Ed had been pressing him to say all week:

"Man in your position can't be underpaid. We'll make it seventeen thousand, and that's only temporary; until we land a good piece of business."

Ed took it calmly. It was small change. Within six months, he would be making *fifty* thousand, and running this show.

The noon meeting with Evan Purcell, Jr., went beautifully. Ed and Stennis received the ad manager in the client conference room, with one other person present—an aging writer with some small experience at J. Walter Thompson on the Ford account. His function was to greet Purcell, whom he'd met once when Purcell worked for Ford, and then pin up the layouts as Ed talked them.

Purcell was in his early fifties, short and thin, with reddish hair and nervous eyes. He had a shrill, birdlike voice, a sharp mind and a wicked tongue. As soon as he cracked wise on the first layout, suggesting that it required a staff of twenty writers to implement, Ed began feeding him thoughts of a small staff of creative geniuses, led by Edward Berner, the hottest copy mind in advertising; a core of leadership which would help Dennison displace one of the big three. And if Dennison didn't take the "Berner Group," General Motors, Ford or Chrysler would.

Purcell stopped making jokes. The print ads were as good as any being run, and the television storyboards were better. Along with the mental enthusiasm beamed his way, the ad manager began to nod, to smile, to murmur compliments. Finally, he walked to the corkboard wall and went down the row of ads, saying, "Best I've seen yet. Best by far, gentlemen. P.B.S. may be small, but it's got everyone licked, so far." He turned to Stennis. "I can't say anything more at this early stage—we've got many other agencies to see—but I'm certainly going to be positive in my report to the board."

He'd have let it go at that, but it wasn't enough for Ed. Purcell had to swing for P.B.S., and swing in a big way. Otherwise, Dennison's board of directors would bring up size and that would end it. Also, the board itself had to be subjected to the ads, and to Ed Berner, as soon as possible.

"Thanks, Mr. Purcell," Ed said. "We're seeing other people ourselves. You may have heard . . ." He fed Purcell the thought that he *had* heard. Ford, was it?

"Yes. Best of luck." Purcell hesitated, his eyes darting around the room. "The board meets this Tuesday. Could you be in Detroit at, say, three P.M.?"

Stennis flushed with excitement. "Perhaps. What do you think, Ed?"

"It means canceling out something else, Paul. Remember?"

There was nothing else, but Stennis played along. "Yes, of course, but perhaps . . ."

"If you think it's important, Mr. Purcell."

"I think it's *very* important, Ed. And I also think it's important to get on a first name basis."

They ate lunch together. Ed kept his consumption of food to a minimum, but Purcell still commented on Ed's being as strong a trencherman as he was an ad man. At the end of the meal, Purcell said he hoped Ed would suspend his teetotalism long enough to drink a toast to the success of Tuesday's meeting. Ed tried desperately to feed him distasteful thoughts connected with liquor, as he had when they'd considered cocktails before the meal; but this time he was caught by surprise, and Stennis quickly compromised him by saying, "Ed's no teetotaler, Evan. Just a little stomach trouble. The ad man's malady, you know—tight gut. But it's loose today. No sweat today."

They all laughed; Purcell called the waiter; three brandies in snifter glasses were soon on the table. Purcell raised his glass, inhaled, said, "Gentlemen, to a meeting of the minds at the meeting of the board." Stennis said, "Well put," and raised his glass. Ed brought the snifter to his nose, inhaled, fought down a wave of nausea. He drank along with Purcell and Stennis.

"Have to catch a plane," Purcell said, looking for the waiter. Stennis said he would handle the tab. Purcell rose and said he would normally argue the point but he was very short on time and would they mind if he ran right now.

They shook hands all around. Ed nodded and smiled and waved . . . and as soon as Purcell left the restaurant, ran to the men's room. He'd become thoroughly ill as soon as the alcohol hit his stomach. He'd fought it during the moments of Purcell's parting. Now he reached a sink and vomited.

Luckily, Stennis remained at the table. He questioned Ed about the precipitous dash for the men's room, and Ed said it had really been a dash for the phone booth in the anteroom. "Kid's been ill. I've been dying to find out what the doctor said." Stennis looked doubtful, but a quick thought or two and he dropped the subject. There were more important things to think of, anyway. The trip to Detroit, for example. The trip that could lead to an eighteen-million-dollar pot of gold.

Stennis wanted a weekend push to double their layouts and storyboards. Ed said it wasn't necessary.

"Confidence is all right, Ed, but this is Dennison Motors! We're going to need a *ton* of good stuff! We're going to need an avalanche. . . ." He went on, but Ed didn't listen. No amount of ads, no matter how high the caliber, would bring a major automotive account to a minor agency. It was Ed Berner who would do it. Ed Berner alone. If he was at that board meeting, Dennison was in the bag. And nothing on earth would keep him from that meeting!

He returned to the office and told his secretary (the blonde, Anise, who was now his private property) to arrange for jet flights for himself and Mr. Stennis to Detroit on Monday, for hotel reservations Monday and Tuesday nights, and for the return flight Wednesday.

"Whew, those jets!" Anise said, sticking her chest out at him. "Couldn't get me to fly six hundred miles an hour!"

He was fully recovered from his nausea, and that chest in its snug white sweater was becoming more appealing by the second. "Flying's an everyday affair, Anise, and much safer, statistically, than driving. I flew during the war . . ." (he'd hitched rides home on furlough from Texas and the West Coast) ". . . and I flew jets twice while on vacation. Smooth and lovely, and you get there in no time."

"Maybe, but I still can't see it. If anything goes wrong, *boom!* you're scattered over half the country."

He began to laugh; and then stopped. He was suddenly unhappy about the flight to Detroit. But he reminded himself that he'd flown and enjoyed it, and leaned over the desk. "Make those reservations, honey. I want to show you the cutest little apartment."

He went to his office and called Edith to say he'd be late tonight. She was bitter about it, and he couldn't beam any calming thoughts over the phone. He heard her out, and explained that it was part of the extra load of work connected with the Dennison Motors pitch. When she heard he was going to Detroit Monday, she hung up on him. He sat back and told himself she had a right to be bitter; then he wondered what sort of a man he'd been to choose such a woman. It was already difficult to remember himself as a failure, a Milquetoast, a coward; someone who deserved a woman like Edith.

The weekend went well. He took the kids to a fair over in Dutchess County. Edith thought it too rustic to bear, and stayed home. He enjoyed the children, and they him . . . to a certain point. That point was reached about two P.M., when Miri began talking of her "best friend" Pam, and Matty wanted him to pick up a Hereford bull to prove his strength. Both were bored. Ed, too, was bored.

They returned home earlier than he'd planned, the kids ran

off to play with the friends, he went inside to tell Edith about
the fair. She was on the phone, talking to her brother Harold.
She covered the mouthpiece with her hand and whispered,
"I'd like a little privacy, please!" He went outside and read.
She joined him half an hour later. He suggested she start the
Durant series, and she jumped up and said, "If you can't talk
to me for even a minute!" and went back into the house.

She drove to the city Sunday, taking the kids on a visit to
her brothers. The three Mainer boys got together once a
month in a family circle affair, from which Ed had respect-
fully withdrawn some years back. Edith's brothers were hulk-
ing lads with high school football in their background. He'd
heard about their touchdowns, their crucial tackles and their
fist fights until it became unbearable. Also, they never bothered to hide their contempt for him.

He considered going with her this time and tossing them
into the hospital, one by one, but decided it was beneath him.

She returned home in a vicious humor, full of talk of her
brothers' devotion to their wives and of their advice to leave
him if he continued his late hours and occasional nights away
from home. "And Harold said if you ever dared run off again
like you did to New Mexico, he'd personally teach you a lesson!"

Ed leaned back from the dinner table. "Now what do you
think would happen if he tried that?"

She stared at him and wet her lips. "I'd tell him to bring
Ralph and Vinnie. You'd better change your ways, Ed!"

She was happier after they went to bed. He served her for
two reasons: because she desired him, and because a vestige
of guilt still remained. Later, he slept, and dreamed.

Settling himself on the train Monday morning, he tried to
reason away the dreams. They were based on his amnesia; his
lack of knowledge as to what had happened to him in New
Mexico. That much was obvious, even to the patient. In time,
he would get over his dreams. Ordinary men worried over
similar questions, but rarely for long. They asked who had
created them, and why. There was never any answer, unless
death brought one. And there was never any point to their
worrying.

It comforted him, and he turned his thoughts to the Detroit trip as the train started with a jerk. Tomorrow, after the

meeting, he would be the fair-haired boy of advertising. Both the *Times* and *Tribune* would carry the story in their advertising columns (he would see to that!), and Stennis would double his salary as a defense against the offers he'd get from other agencies. And the right offer might change his plans. He wasn't wedded to P.B.S. . . .

The train stopped at Tarrytown for its last load of commuters before the run to Grand Central. He looked out the window . . . and his thoughts of Detroit and everything else came to an abrupt end. He got up and pushed his way through the boarding passengers, oblivious to their muttered complaints. He left the train, entered the parking lot and walked down a long row of cars, trying door after door until one opened. He got into the car, a two-year-old sedan, and bent under the dashboard. He found the ignition wires, tore them apart, jumped them and started the engine. He left the lot and headed for the Tappan Zee Bridge. He had stolen a car in a cool, professional manner, though he'd never before considered such an act.

He drove to New Mexico in slightly under three days, stopping only for gas. He left the highway at nine P.M. of the third day and bumped along through the sand and sagebrush country. It was an overcast evening, a black evening, yet he didn't put on his lights. He knew exactly where he was going.

He drove another half hour through deserted badlands; then braked to a halt, stalled the car and got out. The hole opened some ten feet in front of him and the Druggish emerged. "Mr. Berner! How nice to see you again! Welcome, welcome!"

That's when Ed remembered everything: the Druggish, the reason he'd changed, how he'd gotten here, everything.

"Do you know what you've done?" he said, leaning weakly against the front of the car. "Tuesday I had a meeting with the fourth largest manufacturer of automobiles. . . ."

"We only landed a few hours ago. We hovered while you made the trip, and now we're operating on a ten-chort—a twelve-hour—atmospheric treatment. Come into the ship, Mr. Berner. Your report may take up to eight hours, so there's dangerously little leeway."

"But . . . you interrupted my life at a crucial moment!"

"There's no helping that, Mr. Berner. We have no way of keeping tabs on your personal involvements. We hover above

Earth, start you on your way here and land shortly before you arrive. We haven't time for anything more. Once each month, give or take a day, you must make your report."

"Once each month," Ed repeated dully. And then the full import of this came home to him. "Once each *month?* I'm going to live almost a thousand years, and once each month . . . with travel to and from here, that means six or seven days out of every thirty . . . that means I can never complete any . . . can't go abroad for more than . . . and I can't even prepare for it because I won't remember . . . and I *stole a car!* I'm a criminal!"

"Ah, yes, the means of transportation. There's just no way of controlling that either, Mr. Berner. It has to be by the first available automobile."

Ed was weak with hunger, stunned by shock, and his mind began to pick on little things. "I could fly. Send me to an airport. I'd be here in a day."

"Public means of transportation are too regulated. Records and such. And you won't always have the fare. Besides, traveling alone means less chance of being spied upon. No, automobiles are best. As for any trouble with the authorities, that will be minor."

"Minor? Car theft means jail."

"You have great advantages in mind and body. You will probably manage to avoid detection. And if you should have to spend some time in custody, it will be a very small percentage of your life span." The Druggish paused. "The Education Panel mentioned institutional life. Experiencing it would enrich your reports."

"My God," Ed whispered. The fairy tales came back to him then; the three wishes leading to disaster, to death, at best to a return to poverty, failure, mediocrity.

But his beautiful life couldn't be wrecked! There had to be a way out! He pushed himself away from the car, made himself stand erect, forced himself to think.

"All right; so I might get away with stealing this car. But if you continue making me report once a month, without any warning, probability dictates that I'll steal many cars. I can't get away with it forever. Sooner or later I'm going to be caught, and caught again, and again. I'll end up in jail for *years!*"

"The reports are of overriding importance, Mr. Berner. The reports come first, always."

"Yes, I understand that." He smiled triumphantly. "So how will you get those reports if I'm locked in a cell?"

"I should think the answer is obvious. You will escape."

"But . . . I'll be a hunted man! I'll be shot at, perhaps killed. . . ."

"We will face that contingency when it comes. Now, please, the report."

Ed stared at the huge beetle. "Civilized, you said. Aware of the worth of the individual, you said. *My* worth. Yet you're consigning me to destruction."

The Druggish sent no answering thought for quite a while. When it came, it seemed defensive. "You will think of something, Mr. Berner. You will not remember us, but you will remember that you end up in New Mexico every month. Eventually, you will come to live here. That will help somewhat."

"For the love of heaven, why didn't you choose someone who *already* lives here? Why me?"

The beetle turned to the hole. "The Leadership Panel is aware of the point you raise. They claim that an Eastern urban man was needed, not a Western rustic one, but that is only partially acceptable. Mistakes happen, Mr. Berner. Not often, but they happen. It begins to appear as if you are one."

"I see. And because of your mistake, I'm to suffer imprisonment, and eventually death!"

"Let us not be so pessimistic, Mr. Berner. Let us wait a while. If life becomes insupportable for you, the Leadership Panel may yet authorize a decision of change."

"What sort of change?"

"I am not on the Leadership Panel. And it's time to report. You must come now."

Ed wasn't going to move, but he did. Strong thoughts entered his mind and made him move. "No coercion, you said."

"That was for the initial decision, Mr. Berner. You are now obliged to fulfill the articles of your agreement."

Ed Berner did just that. He slid down the ramp behind the Druggish and entered a ship far smaller than the first. He stooped half over as he walked under ceilings just high enough for the beetle to a small room with a table totally out of keeping with everything else around it. A table made for a laboratory specimen. A table made for an animal that thought itself free but ran on a leash thirty days' long. A table made for Ed Berner.

He lay down. The Druggish turned to leave. "We'll talk after I'm finished, won't we?" Ed asked.

"I doubt if there'll be time."

"Just for a few minutes. We've got to find a solution to this · mess. We've got to make a few changes so I can survive. Nothing drastic, of course. Maybe reporting twice a year instead of once a month. I'll spend much more time with you during those reports to make up for . . ."

"I'm in no position to effect changes, Mr. Berner."

"Then let me talk to the Leadership Panel."

"They are involved in other projects. I am here with a pilot and astrogator." The Druggish moved to a portal.

"Man, how am I to live!" Ed shouted, and his voice echoed back at him and he heard the word "man" and he wasn't speaking to a man.

The Druggish replied, the defensive note stronger now: "You agreed to report. We did not take the time element into consideration. You should have questioned it. Now the agreement is in effect. The reports are of overriding importance. The reports come first."

Ed sat up, bellowing Anglo-Saxon defiance. The Druggish shouldn't have understood, but the incredibly cold air came and washed Ed Berner away.

He was behind the wheel of a totally unfamiliar car. It was night. He rubbed his face and felt the stubble and said, "Please, please, don't let me be changed back." He got out, touching himself all over. He slammed the front fender. It dented. He seemed the same.

He looked around, and recognized the highway. He was in New Mexico, at about the same spot as before.

He remembered the meeting in Detroit, and punched the fender again, in anguish this time. "Why?" he shouted. "Why?"

But there was no sense in punching fenders and shouting at the sky. He had to return to New York. He had to make some sort of explanation to Stennis. And Edith—she'd really raise the roof!

He got back in the car, found the dashboard lights, counted a little under two hundred dollars in his wallet. Fortunately, he'd had two hundred and fifty as expense money for the trip to Detroit, and seemed to have spent only enough for gas. Gas for a car which wasn't his.

He went back to the last thing he remembered before waking up here: pulling into Tarrytown station on the commuter train. He might have gotten off there, after the amnesia struck. He might have gotten the car there.

Had he rented it?

He searched his pockets for a rental contract, and the car for a company tag or label. Nothing.

How would he get a car if he hadn't rented it? How . . .

He couldn't have stolen it!

The ignition key; that would have the rental agency tag.

He had no key, other than those for his Chevy and Triumph. He searched the car thoroughly, front and back, under sun visors and mats. He found a map of New England, a package of cigarettes, two sticks of gum, a plastic raincoat, and a program for a Tarrytown drive-in theatre. Chewing the gum, he returned to the front seat. That was when he noticed the wires dangling under the dashboard.

God, his mind was sick! With everything going so well, he had suddenly blanked out and stolen a car and driven to New Mexico! And why New Mexico?

This was his chance to find out. He could spend a few days in the area, driving around, questioning people. If anyone recognized him . . .

But that was dangerous. There were those two men he'd fought off the highway last time. What if they had died? And even if they hadn't, what had they told the police? He might be wanted for assault, battery, murder! And what about the car? The police had lists of cars stolen all over the country, and the longer he drove this one the better his chances of being picked up.

The gum had lost what little food value it originally possessed. He spit it out, saliva flooding his mouth as he thought of meat and bread and milk. He had to drive, and he had to eat.

He bent to the ignition wires, remembering stories of car thieves. Was this the way he'd taken the car in Tarrytown? If so, he could do it again.

He fiddled with the wires until the engine turned over and caught. He was on his way.

He reached the town he'd stayed in a month ago; it lay dead and dark under an overcast sky. He wondered what had happened to Lois, the waitress; whether she'd lost her job or made it up to her fat boss or what. He didn't even slow down. This was dangerous territory.

He checked his wrist watch. Four A.M. He wasn't looking forward to the new day. It could mean new trouble.

He was beginning to feel hunted. And another fear was beginning to grow; fear of his own mind. When would it betray him again? When would he blank out again; do something crazy like stealing a car again; drive to New Mexico again?

And why, why was it New Mexico?

The sky was growing light. He saw the neon sign up ahead: "Biggie's Eats."

He grinned and slowed and came to the aluminum-and-glass diner. Two trucks were parked outside, and a highway patrol car. He almost wept, he was that hungry, but he drove on.

It was eight o'clock before he came to the shabby stand. He wouldn't have passed this one if a convention of sheriffs had been meeting there, but the Negro counterman was all alone. Ed parked beside the small frame building and walked over. The counterman looked up from a newspaper, and stiffened. Ed knew he must look pretty bad, what with three or four days' growth of beard and rumpled clothing. He smiled and said, "Hey there. Been driving from the Coast. Haven't had time for more than a few catnaps side of the road. What's on the menu?" As he talked, he took a ten from his wallet and placed it on the counter.

The sight of money reassured the young Negro. "Hamburgers, franks, chili. Coffee and orange drink. Got cheese too."

"I'll have a few hamburgers and a few franks. Any milk?"

"Yessir. Pour you a glass?"

"Just bring the bottle." Ed chuckled, and the man smiled uncertainly.

"How many burgers and franks you want?"

Ed felt he could have eaten fifty of each, but he didn't want to impress himself too vividly on the man's memory. At the same time, he just had to have plenty of food. "Make it ten of each."

The man blinked.

"Don't want to stop again," Ed said. "I'll eat some on the road later."

He intended to do just that, but his appetite took over and he ate them as fast as they came off the grill. He had a second quart of milk and a cheese sandwich, despite the man's startled gaze.

As he pocketed his change, he asked for the rest room, planning to borrow a razor. There was no rest room. That was a bad break, because he would have to face more startled looks at his next stop.

He drove away, glancing into the rear-view mirror. The man was leaning out over his counter, staring after him. Was he getting the license plate number?

The sweet life was turning sour. The Great Dream was becoming a nightmare. As soon as he got home, he would have to prepare for the next amnesia attack. He would put together a survival kit: a battery-operated electric razor, tins of biscuits, meat and beans, a few hundred dollars in cash.

He came to a gas station. There was just one attendant on duty, and Ed used his mind on him immediately. He got a razor and shaved and came back out to the car feeling better. But not for long. Leaning against the car was a tall man in suntans, cowboy hat, five-pointed star and hip-slung gun. Ed paid for his gas; the officer looked at him; Ed smiled and said, "Going to be another hot day."

"Not according to the radio. They say rain and cool."

Ed chuckled and waved his hand and got back into the car and drove off. He glanced back. The officer was looking after him. He began to sweat.

He was Superman, and he was running scared. He felt he would run scared from now on; that his life would be a buildup of tension until the next blanking out. He didn't see how he was going to lick this thing. How could he, when he didn't know what it was?

He stopped at a motel toward evening, unable to keep his eyes open. He parked the car behind the L-shaped building and checked into a room under a false name and just did get his clothes off before falling into bed, fast asleep. He slept for ten hours, and might have slept even longer if hunger hadn't gnawed him awake. It was three in the morning. The motel dining room was closed. He bought seven bars of candy from a vending machine. He drove and ate and thought.

Could a doctor help him—a psychiatrist? But how could he explain the *changes* to a doctor? Amnesia, yes, but what about the other things, the good things, the impossible things?

They'd put him in a mental institution, or make his life miserable with publicity.

Besides, the very thought of confiding in anyone set up strong resistance in him. He knew he could never do it.

His mind ran in circles for the next two hours; and then, after a huge breakfast at a good diner, he calmed down and settled on a plan of action. First, he would call Edith. Second, he would drive to Tarrytown and put this car in the parking lot, where he'd probably gotten it. Third, he would take a taxi home and soothe Edith's feelings. Fourth, he would go to the office, handle Stennis, and get his career back on the track. Fifth, he would continue with the good life, hoping the amnesia attacks would end with this one.

He lit a cigar he'd bought at the diner. It had rained while he'd slept and the dawn skies were crystal clear, the air sweet and fresh. It was going to be a beautiful day.

Confidence returned. What was the worst that could happen at home? Edith would walk out. Stennis would raise a little hell.

There were better women and bigger jobs.

At three o'clock, he pulled into a good-sized town and found a steak house. He had a T-bone, rare, and double orders of potatoes and salad. On the way out, he stopped to talk with the cashier, a dark, plump woman with a soft Spanish accent. She was about to take her two-hour break. They spent those two hours in her room across the street.

When he drove out of town, he was back on top of the world. He felt too good to be sick. The amnesia wouldn't happen again. He was in control of himself, and of everyone who came in contact with him. How could it happen again? No, it wouldn't happen again. No.

chapter 9

HE NEVER called Edith. The prospect was too unpleasant. He telegraphed her instead, giving his estimated day of arrival. He reached Tarrytown station at seven Monday morning, having traveled in easy stages the last day, wanting to arrive during the crush of business-day parking. He felt a crowd was his best cover; would give him his best chance to park and leave undetected.

He sweated a bit, pulling into the lot and seeing the officer directing traffic up the road. But then he was walking away and hailing a cab and settling into the back seat. In half an hour he was stepping out on his own driveway, where he saw with distaste that the car in the garage wasn't the Chevy but dear brother-in-law Harold's white convertible.

His key wouldn't open the front door. After struggling a moment, he bent for a closer look and saw that the paint around the lock was chipped and the lock itself new.

He pressed the bell button. That always brought shouts from the kids. This time there were no shouts; just footsteps; heavy footsteps.

The door opened. Harold said, "Well, the native returns." That was as clever as he got.

Ed stepped forward. Harold didn't move, and then Ralph and Vincent moved into view, backing him up. Harold was the oldest and biggest; about six-two and well over two hundred pounds. He was a high school fullback gone to fat, but still retaining enough basic sinew to make him a dangerous opponent, especially with his vicious temper. Ralph was just an inch and fifteen pounds smaller, with the same heavy chest and massive arms. Vinnie was almost a twin to Ralph, but he had more basic intelligence, and less antagonism to Ed, than his brothers. The three together made interesting competition.

"Are you going to let me into my house?" Ed asked.

"It isn't your house," Harold answered. "It's Edith's house."

"That's the same thing, isn't it?"

"Harold," Vinnie murmured, "can't we talk inside?"

"Edith said no," Harold said. "Edith said to throw the bum out."

"Come on now," Ed said. "Let me speak to her. I didn't run off or anything like that. I *had* to leave."

"We're not interested. If you really had a good excuse, Edith would know it, wouldn't she? And she wants out of this marriage. And we're here to protect her rights."

"Protect them, but get out of my doorway."

Harold smiled, his big mouth cracking wide. "Oh I been waiting for this for years. I told Edith she should never have married such a little punk; a punk who never played ball, not even golf. A punk who tickles a typewriter."

"Look at me," Ed said, still trying to make excuses for them; still telling himself they were doing this out of brotherly love and it was understandable and he didn't want to hurt them. "How little a punk am I now, Harold?"

Harold looked. "Yeah, she told us you'd put on a few pounds of muscle. But you don't think, buddy-boy, that brings you up to snuff against a *real* man?"

Ed pushed him. Harold staggered backward, knocking his brothers into the wall. Ed moved past them and into the living room. "Edith!"

The door closed behind him. He didn't turn. "Matty, Miri!"

Something hit him in the back of the head. He stumbled forward, stung but not hurt, and turned to catch Harold's punch full in the mouth. That hurt, and knocked him down. He spat out teeth.

His beautiful teeth!

He got up. Harold said, "The damned fool wants more." He was pleased. He hunched forward, jabbed professionally with his left, prepared to throw his massive right. Vinnie said "Don't, Har. You're gonna hurt him bad."

Ed took that warning for himself. He didn't want to hurt Harold badly, and his anger dictated that he would. He remembered what he'd done to Gordon, and caught the left jab in his right hand and squeezed. Harold screamed and flailed with his free hand. Ed squeezed harder. Harold choked and fainted, falling on his side.

"Okay, *now* you get it," Vinnie said, brotherly partisanship flaring up.

"Together, Vinnie," Ralph said, moving cautiously. "He's got some sort of judo training. We got to rush him together."

They did, and they screamed together too. Ed leaped high in the air, clear over Vinnie's onrushing bulk, and landed and turned and struck them both, one with each hand, in the small of the back. Vinnie got the right and passed out. Ralph fell, conscious but barely able to breathe. Ed bent to him. "I'm sorry, Ralph." (He wasn't. Not at all. He was just sorry he couldn't let loose without doing them permanent injury.) "Where are Edith and the kids?"

Ralph couldn't talk too well, but he was desperate to please

Ed and tried very hard. He managed to gasp out that Edith was at Harold's home; that she'd decided on a divorce.

"Just like that? And I suppose she wants everything—house and car and bank account?"

"Don't be mad," Ralph wheezed, terror coming into his eyes. "Please, Ed, she took the money out of the bank and she's got a lawyer and he's got the house and car tied up."

"I see. Am I supposed to give up my children too?"

"She'll let you visit. But this lawyer says if you don't agree he'll have you investigated—your trips and all. Edith says something fishy's going on." Ralph said more, pleading all the while that it wasn't any of *his* doing, but Ed was no longer listening. At first he felt a terrible wrenching; a tearing of the fabric of his life. Twelve years of that life had been spent with Edith. An instant later he felt a surge of rage. She was stripping him bare without giving him a chance to explain. (Not that he *could* explain.) And then he felt relief. It was over, the hypocrisy of a union that had always lacked fire, lacked communication, lacked reality. It was over, a marriage which no longer made even minimum sense to the new Ed Berner. Of course he'd agree!

Besides, he couldn't allow anyone to investigate him and his trips to New Mexico. He was afraid of what they'd learn. That knowledge, whatever it was, was for him alone. And there was the fight off the highway that first trip, and the stolen car this trip. Edith had him over a barrel, without knowing what the barrel was. She probably thought it was a woman, when it was much more dangerous to him than that.

But he would get unlimited visiting rights with the children. She could have everything else; or what she thought was everything else, since she didn't know about the twenty-three thousand dollars, the apartment and the Triumph. She could walk away with whatever he'd made of his old life, except the children.

He revived Harold and Vinnie, and asked if anyone wanted a doctor. They said no, though Harold could barely control his groans. His hand was certainly broken, and Ed pointed it out to him. Vinnie said they'd take him to their own doctor. They wanted out of here.

Ed said to tell Edith she could have everything, if she agreed to let him see the children as often as he wanted, and to take them with him occasional weekends and vacations. If she didn't agree, he'd fight her for house, car, bank account and every last item right down to her engagement ring. And then there was her living allowance. Let him see his kids whenever he wanted to and she could name any reasonable figure.

Vinnie looked surprised. "She said you'd . . ." He stopped.

"She said I'd take my beating and beg for a reunion. And when you said no to the reunion, I'd fight for some part of what I worked all my life to get. Is that it?"

"Vinnie wasn't going to say that," Ralph muttered, but none of them would look at Ed. They were wondering how generous *they* would be in similar circumstances. They couldn't know he would soon be earning more money than they'd ever dreamed of.

Which reminded him that he had to speak to Stennis. Not on the phone. He had to be in the same room with him and work on him and smooth things over.

The brothers left. At the door, Vinnie turned and held out his hand. "No hard feelings, huh, Ed? I never wanted this sort of a beef, honest. But Edith was so damned mad and Harold . . . you know Harold."

Ed nodded and shook the hand and began to close the door.

"Oh, say, what sort of school did you go to? I mean—jumping over us and handling us so easy and all." He spoke just a little too casually.

"A home study course."

"What books? I'd like to . . ."

"They're in the library, under Miracles." He closed the door, went to the bathroom and looked at his mouth. His lips were slightly puffy, when they should have been swollen to twice their normal size. And while he'd felt his front teeth break and had spit out several pieces, all he could see was that the front three uppers and lowers were a little short and failed to meet on the bite.

He washed, dressed and took the big old trunk from the attic. He packed it with all his things, thinking back and experiencing memories of his life with Edith. Most of them were bad, and none good enough to make him feel more than a little nostalgia.

He phoned for a cab to the station. When the horn beeped out front, he took one last look around, and then another look at himself in the mirror. He wasn't surprised to see that all his teeth were now normal size.

He hefted the trunk onto his shoulder, took it out to the driveway and set it down. The cabby, a squat young man in jeans and cowboy boots, said he'd put it in back. Ed returned to the house to make sure all the doors and windows were locked. He wondered whether Edith would sell or live on here. For the kids' sake, he hoped the latter was the case.

He returned to the cab to find the driver blue in the face and the trunk still on the driveway. Ed raised it with a hand pressed flat against each end, said, "The boot or the rear?" The driver stared, muttered something about a bad back and opened the boot. Ed tossed it in.

At the station, he carried it to the platform and onto the waiting train. The conductor blinked at the size (it should have gone by baggage car), but said nothing as Ed put it up against the wall in front and took the nearest seat. There wasn't much you could say to such a man. There wasn't much you could do, either, except be his friend or get out of his way.

He left his apartment at one-thirty and stopped by the garage to see if the Triumph was all right. The attendant said it had developed a flat on the left front wheel. Ed asked how come. The man shrugged. "Y'know, just settin' around. New car, ain't it? Sometimes those little foreign ones got shit tires."

Ed said, "Let's see it."

The man took him to the third floor in the car elevator. The Triumph had a flat all right. Ed asked why they hadn't fixed it.

"Boss says customer has to okay all work. We park 'em, that's all."

Ed leaned in the front window and looked at the mileage. "That's not all. You drive them too. I didn't have five hundred miles when I left. It's over six now."

"Now listen, mister. You wanna complain, go to the boss. I never took this pile of junk anywhere."

Ed looked at him. The man wasn't more than twenty, lean and hard and tattooed on both arms. He considered himself tough. He was looking to cow this middle-aged, white-collar worker.

Ed walked past him and gripped the front bumper and lifted the Triumph off the floor. "Fix it," he said.

The man froze.

"Fix it," Ed repeated. "And don't ever take it out again, you or your relief. Pass the word. The next time it won't be the car I'll lift."

The man muttered sure and he was sorry if someone had taken it out and he'd see to it no one ever did again. Ed rode down with another attendant. The last he saw of the first one, the man was straining at the front bumper of the Triumph and the Triumph was still solidly on the floor.

He strode into the waiting room of P.B.S. with a smile. "Nice to see you again, Miss Carlsbad."

Her mouth fell open. "I . . . uh . . . nice to see *you* again, Mr. Berner. We were all worried about you, not having received any word . . ."

"Sorry my wife couldn't call to explain my absence. Family crisis. Mr. Stennis in?"

"Yes," she said, a glint of the old vindictiveness returning to her eye. "He asked to see you."

"Fine."

"He said, 'If Mr. Berner ever shows up, send him to me immediately.' "

He widened his smile. "Mr. Berner will *always* show up, Miss Carlsbad. Like the proverbial bad penny. But bringing good luck."

The vindictiveness held on. "Let's hope Mr. Stennis agrees, Mr. Berner. Go right in."

He went right in. Stennis was on the phone, and stared at him. "Listen, Nick, can I call you back? I still think we can make a deal, but first I got a little unpleasant business to finish." He hung up.

"Was that Nick Bandson?" Ed asked, settling into Stennis' black leather couch.

"If anyone's going to ask questions, I am! You think you can just walk in here and take up where you left off?"

"I've had a rough time, Paul. My wife is leaving me . . ."

"I'm not interested in your goddam personal life, though I think she's showing excellent judgment!"

"You presented to Dennison Motors, I presume?"

"You presume correctly, and too damned much! They laughed me out of Detroit! I never in all my life . . ."

Ed began feeding him soothing thoughts, thoughts that he was risking losing the best ad man in Manhattan. "You have every right to be angry, Paul. I can't tell you how sorry I am.

I'd have given anything to make that meeting, but I was fighting to save my marriage, and then to hold onto my kids . . ." He went on, beaming the strong thoughts all the while, and soon Stennis was muttering, "Too bad. Yes, understandable."

When Ed finished, Stennis rose and spread his arms, fighting, though he didn't know it, more than a reasonable explanation. "Couldn't you at least have *phoned?* I'd have tried to put off the presentation. But thinking it over, I was sure you'd gone off on a drunk. That first five days' French leave, and your avoiding liquor and having a violent reaction after one brandy, and then another long absence . . . I was positive you were an alcoholic. Now be honest, Ed. You have a problem, don't you?"

Ed decided he had to give the man something convincing. He dropped his head. "You guessed it, Paul. One drink and I'm off. And this business with my wife . . . I just went to pieces." His head came up. The thoughts of his value to P.B.S. were stronger than ever. "But it'll never happen again. And even if it does, one toot a month or so doesn't mean I can't function for the agency. Listen, I've got some new ideas for that toy account . . ."

He left the agency at four-thirty. He'd smoothed things over with Stennis, and assigned his group the toy presentation, and received a call from Gladys. She was in the city and not expected home until ten or eleven. Could they get together? He stopped at a delicatessen, bought an enormous amount of food and went home. He phoned Bert Raines, a lawyer, to ask for the name of a good divorce attorney. Bert said he could handle the job. He gave Bert the details, and Bert advised him to fight for more. He said, "No, Bert, that's just the way I want it. You'll have enough trouble keeping some hidden assets hidden." Bert said, "You sly dog you," and chuckled, and then remembered he was supposed to feel badly.

Gladys arrived at five-thirty, and didn't leave until twelve. He drove her to Grand Central in the Triumph, and she was glum and subdued; not only because she was late, but at the news of his divorce. "You don't think Edith suspects anything about us, do you, Ed?"

"She suspects, but she can't prove."

"My God! What if someone was watching your apartment?"

He shrugged. "You know what they say about the cookie crumbling."

Gladys barely nodded when he asked her to call next week. She was already hurrying away from the car. He drove back to the garage, wondering if he'd ever see her again, not caring one way or the other. He began thinking of the hostess at the Chinese restaurant near the office. Lovely oval face; terrific little figure; incredible voluptuousness on a small scale. He hadn't had Chinese food since the change. He thought he'd try it tomorrow.

As he was walking back from the garage, two dark-skinned youths came out of a doorway. One blocked his path. "You got a light?" The other looked up and down the deserted street. Ed knew what they were going to do.

"You boys have a gun?"

The one looking around drifted behind him, murmuring, "What kinda talk is that? All we want . . ."

"If you don't, leave right now. If you do, show it."

The one who stood before him pulled out a knife. "Your money," he whispered, shaking and frightened and hopped up and dangerous. The other threw his arm around Ed's neck.

Ed left them in the doorway, the knife-man unconscious, the other whimpering over a broken arm. He had a cut on his cheek, but it didn't worry him. He threw the knife in a sewer grating and walked past his apartment house and down to the United Nations. It was a beautiful night. He wouldn't sleep. He would read, but there was plenty of time. He'd always wanted to walk the city by night, when its shout had diminished and its mobs had gone. But who could walk Manhattan by night? Who could risk the hop-heads, muggers, queers and psychotics that came looking for prey in the black hour? No one. No one, that is, but Ed Berner.

He walked until three, and then returned to the apartment and settled into his easy chair and began to read. He snacked on cold cuts, bread and beer, and only once did he experience anything but pleasure. That was when he came across a reference to amnesia in his novel.

He raised his eyes from the book. Amnesia was common enough. Others must have suffered periodic attacks of mindlessness similar to his. How had they handled it?

Doctors, of course. But . . . the thought of revealing himself to a third party, no matter how scientific and detached he might be, set up certain inner tensions, inner barriers, almost as if a pre-set inhibition existed.

What if he were to seek aid *without* revealing himself? What if he were to hire a companion, a guard, a male nurse, and say only that he went off on occasional binges and wanted to be protected against rash actions?

Yes! A male nurse was the perfect solution. . . .

But his enthusiasm died before it had fully developed. Too many negatives became apparent in the next instant. The amnesia attacks could take place any time, any place, so his nurse would have to be with him twenty-four hours a day. He couldn't have anyone living at the apartment and retain freedom of action with women. He couldn't have anyone tagging along at the office without creating concern in Stennis and gossip throughout the agency. He couldn't take a companion along on a business trip without expecting the client to ask questions. And, most important of all, he couldn't allow anyone to learn what the new Ed Berner was. Just couldn't, as he couldn't tolerate the thought of fame, publicity, any degree of limelight.

And there were other considerations, based not on vague inhibitions but on the vital specific of self-preservation. God only knew what he did during those blackout trips to New Mexico! Allowing an outsider to be in a position to observe him could be a quick ticket to prison or a mental hospital.

He thought a while longer, and shrugged, and returned to his book. He would have to fight it out alone.

Tuesday, he solidified his position with Stennis and returned a call by Sy Roverstein. The ad manager wanted to discuss a trip to Kentucky and the Wylitt distilleries. "Thought you should see the actual physical operation, Ed, and meet management, and address our sales convention. We can fly down together and have a few fun days. That's three weeks from today, which gives you plenty of time to prepare."

Ed said it was fine with him; then realized the flight would take place roughly one month from the date of his second amnesia attack, which had taken place about a month after the first.

But what did that mean? Amnesia, or whatever the hell it was, didn't run on a time schedule!

Roverstein asked if Ed was free for lunch.

Ed thought of the inevitable toasts in Wylitt booze, and of the delicious Chinese hostess just across the street, and said, "Working on those ads of yours, Sy. Don't want to let go now, not even for lunch. I'm having a sandwich in. How about a rain check?"

Roverstein said he understood, and that he'd make sure Ed relaxed when they got to Kentucky. "I know a few chicks in Louisville and Lexington. . . ."

Ed went to Stennis and told him about the Wylitt meeting. Stennis said the invitation was a terrific compliment, indicating they were really happy with the agency. "I go every year, of course, but they've never asked any member of the creative department before." He patted Ed on the back. "I can forgive you anything if you keep them happy. They're our bread and butter, you know." He thought of something. "Listen, there'll be drinking there. You don't think you'll . . ."

"I'll use my stomach as an excuse. Ulcer. No one'll expect an ulcer patient to drink."

"I'm not sure that's so smart, Ed. Would Wylitt like a sick creative head? We'd better play it by ear. You can always nurse a drink, or fake it—put it to your lips and get rid of it later."

Ed lunched at the Chinese restaurant. He was shown to his table by the lovely little hostess. She was wearing a long yellow gown slit daringly up the right side. He complimented her on it, and she murmured her thanks, and he got the feeling she was worried about relatives on Formosa. He said, "Do you have family in China or Formosa?"

She looked at him in surprise. "Formosa," she replied, her voice thin and delicate. He felt she wished they were anywhere but in the land of Chiang Kai-shek.

"Well," he murmured, "I know it's not a popular opinion, but I'd as soon live on the mainland as there. The absence of freedom is about equal."

She blinked her eyes nervously, and he fed her strong thoughts of his liberal tendencies, sophisticated approach to Asian politics and intense admiration for the Chinese people —especially the seductive little Chinese person looking at him now. She said, "Most people do not understand how difficult . . ." She glanced about and wet her lips. "There are people waiting for tables."

He took her hand, said, "Couldn't we talk sometime after work?" and let her hand go.

She hesitated. He looked at the slit in her dress; at the glimpse of warm brown thigh. He fed her his desire; willed that she desire him. She nodded. "Perhaps. I finish at seven."

He said that the next six hours would be long ones. She smiled and moved away, her body rolling smoothly inside the tight gown.

He learned a good deal about China that night.

The week went quickly, and marvelously. He met three new women, read three new books, and explored the city from Lincoln Center to the Battery.

On Friday, he and Stennis made their presentation to the Baby-Marvel Toy Company. The following Friday, they got the million and a quarter account. Stennis raved about the television storyboards, but Ed knew why they'd scored so quickly. Only two men had been involved—the owner and his ad manager, who was also his son. He'd been able to handle the two minds very easily. He'd practically put the words of acceptance in their mouths.

"If only you'd been in Detroit," Stennis began; then clapped Ed on the shoulder. "To hell with Dennison. We'll land a car account, and a big one. But first we'll build P.B.S. to fifty, sixty million. I'm trying to set up a meeting with Harry Bryant of Abmanter Chemical. They make a dozen consumer drugs. Land that one and I'll put you in the high-income tax bracket."

Ed could have pushed for another few thousand right then and there, but he wasn't in any hurry. Money would come.

He heard from Edith's lawyer. The man phoned to say she wanted to set definite limitations on the days and hours of his visits with the children. Ed suggested they meet the next day for lunch.

They were cordial with the appetizer, friendly with the entrée, positively buddy with dessert. The lawyer, Simon Handsdeck, promised to make Edith see reason. "A man like you, Mr. Berner, can do so much in shaping the character of his children. I would be remiss in my duty to them—and I do represent them, as well as Mrs. Berner—if I failed to create a situation in which you could affect their attitudes and character. Trust in me, sir."

Ed hoped the mental suggestion wouldn't wear off before Edith was convinced.

The Thursday before he was to leave for Kentucky, Ed received word that Edith had agreed to his terms, if he would give one hundred twenty dollars a week toward the children's support and an additional sixty a week toward her own. Simon Handsdeck was somewhat apologetic about this figure, and held out the promise of immediate visitation rights (until now denied Ed) if he signed the proper papers. After that, the divorce would be instituted out of state.

A hundred eighty a week represented about half of Ed's current salary, but wasn't as much as he'd planned on giving —either directly or by means of savings accounts—to the kids alone. There was his twenty-three thousand to tap, if it became necessary, and the certainty that his salary would grow. He agreed, after complaining a little to allay suspicion.

On Friday, he left the office at three-thirty, assuring an increasingly more worried Stennis that he'd meet him and Sy Roverstein at Newark Airport in plenty of time for their ten A.M. departure Monday. He had previously discussed taking his vacation before the end of August in order to spend it with the children. Stennis had grumbled about "losing my key man for two solid weeks," and suggested long weekends instead, but Ed wouldn't consider it. A week, at least, with Miri and Matty at a seaside cottage. He would teach his little boy to swim, and improve Miri's style. Afternoons, they would picnic on the beach; evenings they would dine in good restaurants. Westhampton had both the beach and the restaurants, as did Easthampton. Perhaps he'd get a sitter one night and meet Beth. . . .

That last thought caught him unawares. Beth didn't need him and he didn't need her.

He arrived at the house in somewhat less than the best of spirits. Edith surprised him with a correct, if not warm, greeting. She looked past him at the Triumph and said she was glad he'd finally gotten "a little car" that suited him. She said she hoped he was well and harbored no ill will toward her and that their future relations would be friendly. She said she'd prepared dinner and that Miri would help him serve it. As for herself, she was spending the evening at a friend's house and would return at ten. Or should she make it eleven, or twelve? No bother, really.

He said ten would be fine, and they walked out together, he to move the Triumph from the driveway, she to back the Chevy to the road. He had never seen her look better, and her thoughts proved she had never felt better. She was as pleased to be rid of him as he was to be rid of her. She had what she wanted of him; enough money to live on comfortably, without having to hunt for another husband. Not that her mind was closed to another husband, but candidates for that post would have to search her out. And someone might yet do that, Ed felt, if she continued in her present state of grace.

He watched her drive away, and returned to the house and the children. They'd remained in their rooms, on Edith's instructions, and now came bursting out to kiss him and scream in his ear and, in Miri's case, to wet him briefly and wound him deeply with tears over the end of the family.

Despite the real love felt on both sides, they were glad of Edith's return: the children bored with his intensity to please and their own need to please what was no longer an everyday personage; he tired of the effort needed to keep them happy every minute of the time they spent together.

That night he sat in his armchair and read, and his mind slipped away from the book and touched on many things, among them the changes that had taken place in the eight weeks since the first trip to New Mexico; changes in his dream of life. He was glad for some of them, and sad for others. He no longer felt it necessary to look up people from his childhood and impress, hurt or make love to them. That was good. That was growth.

He no longer thought of making a quick fortune and traveling the world and doing nothing but sipping the pleasures of life. Power and triumph in the office had begun to please him. Money made in advertising had begun to please him. That too was good. That was reality, and a widening of goals.

But his irrational fear of speed, of air travel, of anything which might conceivably splatter him over the countryside, that was bad. And his growing tension over what would happen every fourth week, his expectation of further amnesia attacks, that was bad. And his harking back to an eighteen-year-old girl who wasn't half the woman Gladys was and certainly no better than Yin and Anise and any of the others, *that* was bad.

He returned to the book. He read, and relaxed. What were minor irritations compared to all he had? He was set for life; the most rewarding life in human history!

chapter 10

HE WAS AT Newark Airport at nine Monday morning, a full hour before flight time. Stennis arrived twenty minutes later, his worried face lighting up when he saw Ed. "Glad you made it all right, boy!"

Ed didn't say he himself was glad, and rather surprised. "You didn't think I'd miss this trip too, did you, Paul?"

Stennis chuckled and said of course not, and then Roverstein arrived. They went to the second-floor restaurant and sat at a table overlooking the runways. A jet came in for a landing. "I'm always a little jittery before a flight," Roverstein said, lighting a cigarette. "Silly, really, but that's the way I am."

Stennis said a certain degree of anxiety was natural. "Feel that way myself, even though I've flown a hundred times. How about you, Ed?"

Ed turned from the window and the plane streaking over the macadam. His insides were twisting; his pores open and sweating. "A little nervous, yes," he muttered. When the waiter came, he merely shook his head.

Their plane wasn't more than half full, which gave Ed the chance to sit alone in the double seat behind Stennis and Roverstein. He appreciated this, because his fear was growing and he didn't know how he was going to react once they got into the air.

The take-off was abrupt, four powerful jet engines thrusting them into a steep ascent. Ed doubled up, face twisting, mouth rigidly open. He just did manage to choke back a scream. And no matter how often he reminded himself that he'd flown a dozen times before, he couldn't lose the terror. It was as if something outside himself were fighting to keep him from moving so fast, so high, into a situation where trouble could lead to his body being utterly destroyed. The image of that type of destruction kept flashing before his eyes. He couldn't understand it. He had left cowardice behind when he'd awakened that first time in New Mexico. Why should he fear what he hadn't feared in his *old* life?

The captain's voice came over the loudspeaker. They were flying at thirty-two thousand feet, at six hundred miles an hour, and would arrive in Louisville at ten-thirty—an hour and a half trip, allowing for the one-hour time differential. "You may remove your seat belts and smoke."

The hostess came by; a big brunette with a glowing complexion and marvelous figure. She smiled at him. Smiling back was out of the question. *Thirty-two thousand feet! If they fell . . .*

He moved from the window to the outside seat. Stennis rose to look back at him. He closed his eyes. "Sleeping," Stennis said to Roverstein. "Nerves like steel, that man."

Roverstein cracked that Ed would need his nerves to face the hoopla of a Wylitt sales meeting. Stennis chuckled. Ed kept his eyes tightly closed. He was shrieking inside. He was begging for the flight to end.

The landing was almost unbearable. On their approach, they slipped away to the left, the patchwork-green earth lurching up at them. He tried to keep his eyes shut, but fear made him glance out several times. Each time was hell.

Stepping off the plane, he vowed he would never fly again. In three or four days he would have to find a way to *drive* back to New York, without admitting the real reason to Stennis or Roverstein.

But the worry, the memory of fear, drained quickly away. He had a major triumph to celebrate. He hadn't blanked out and gone to New Mexico. It was four weeks since the last amnesia attack, but he was safe. Compared to that, fear of flying was a minor matter!

They stayed at a downtown motel. He swam in the pool and snacked in the dining room and read in his room. Then he joined Stennis and Roverstein out front, where they were picked up by Wylitt in his air-conditioned limousine and driven to a good restaurant. Everyone started off with cocktails. Ed ordered a Wylitt Old-fashioned and shook his head when the waiter wrote out the second round and shook his head again for the third round and all the beers and wines thereafter. No one seemed to notice. He laughed at jokes and told jokes. He raised his glass in toasts, and had the waiter remove it untouched when dessert came. He was extremely cheerful, and since he poured out strong and encouraging thoughts, so was everyone else.

Back at the motel, Stennis was suddenly drunk and Roverstein half asleep. As for himself, he was glad to say goodnight to both and get to his room for an evening of reading. The talk and jollity had bored him toward the end. He knew he would be spending many such evenings as he grew in importance as a new-business specialist, but he wouldn't think of it now. He would read now. He would enter that special world of variated pleasure now.

He came down at midnight for sandwiches, and at three a.m. for twenty laps in the flood-lighted pool. By morning, he was ready to face the world of whisky again.

After breakfast, their bags were taken out to Wylitt's limousine. The president of Wylitt Beverages had stayed at his Louisville residence, maintained for his frequent visits and occasional amours away from Manhattan and Mrs. Wylitt. He sat beside his colored chauffeur, turning to chat with Ed, Stennis and Roverstein. "We're driving to Frankfort, where Ed can tour the bourbon distillery. Then on to Lexington for a combination dinner and executive meeting with my local people—district and distillery managers. After that . . ." He grinned at Roverstein. "Well, Sy takes over. He's the grand procurer for those who indulge."

Roverstein flushed, chuckled, murmured, "Just know a few young ladies . . ."

Everyone guffawed.

It was noon, and hot, when they reached the distillery on the quiet country road outside of Frankfort. Ed was turned over to a guide, and the others disappeared into a stone building whose window air conditioners looked totally out of place. Ed followed the guide through various odoriferous sections of the bourbon plant, and tipped him two dollars to cut his spiel short. He rejoined Wylitt, Stennis, Roverstein and the plant manager in a conference room where lunch was being served by a stout but attractive Negro waitress. Ed was beginning to want a woman badly, this being the longest he'd gone without one in eight weeks. He divided his attention between the food, Wylitt's profundities, and the waitress' abundant rear end. He sent her several thoughts, and she responded with quick glances as she removed the dishes. When she left the room, Ed excused himself and followed.

The building was old, spacious, staffed by the plant manager, his assistant, a half-dozen other men and women. Almost everyone was out at a springhouse across the road where picnic tables afforded a pleasant place for lunch. Ed came up behind the waitress, who was carrying the platter of dishes toward a door at the end of the hallway. There was a smell of sun on old wood, of dust in corners, of country greenery. A summer smell; an unhurried, curiously relaxing smell. He said, "Let me get that for you."

She smiled, her round cheeks dimpling. "Thank you."

He squeezed by her, the back of one hand brushing her soft rear. He opened the door and pressed against the wall. She went inside, and their bodies touched.

The room was lined with shelves and the shelves filled with ledgers. There was one window, its shade up. A large wooden table had been cleared, a tablecloth thrown over it, various food containers placed there. Ed closed the door. The waitress put down her tray. "My, it's *specially* hot today."

Ed knew that wasn't just talk; not with the heated pictures he'd placed in her mind. "Yes. You live in town?"

She nodded.

He looked at her wedding band. "Husband work out here?"

"Wish he did. He's a carpenter. No work for the last two months."

"I'm sorry to hear that."

"Oh, well, we get along."

There really wasn't anything more to say. He couldn't do it with words. She either wanted him now, for the simple sake of pleasure, or she never would.

The door had a snap bolt and he used it. She turned to the table and fiddled with a pot. He walked past her to the window. "It's all right," he said, his thoughts flowing to her; his burning, desirous thoughts. She put down the pot. He lowered the shade, and the room was suddenly dim. He came back to the table and put his hands on her round arms and pulled her to him. "Now, mister," she whispered. "They gonna be looking for you."

"Not for five or ten minutes. Can you spare five or ten minutes?"

She smiled, and he kissed her on the smile. Her arms stayed at her sides awhile, and then she put them around him.

She was a fine woman. She took him with pleasure, lying on the table and making that table as comfortable as the thickest mattress. She said, "My, my," when he went on. "You get quite a bit out of five or ten minutes." She got quite a bit out of it herself, and it was actually half an hour. As he was leaving, he asked if he could give her twenty dollars to help out until things got better at home.

"Sure thing. If it was me had the money and you hard up, I'd do the same. I'd pay fifty, after this sweetness." So he made it fifty. She covered her mouth and whispered, "My God. I been in the wrong business all these years." They laughed together.

He returned to the conference room, saying he'd wandered over to the springhouse and looked around a bit. Roverstein said, "You missed some fine old bourbon, but you'll get another crack at it tonight. We've got to be going. Everyone's meeting at the Danton House in Lexington."

Ed was relaxed and happy during the hour drive. There was more talk about whisky and sales and meetings, and he nodded and smiled and thought of that fine, fine woman and how good it had been and hoped Roverstein's "young ladies" weren't too worked out and knew that whatever they were he'd enjoy them and make them enjoy him. Life was the way he wanted it again. Life was the Great Dream again. The few problems he had could be solved, now that the fear of amnesia was slipping away.

He interrupted Stennis to say that reminded him of a joke, and told it, and had them all, including the chauffeur, roaring.

The Danton House was gracious and roomy; a rambling, two-story hotel on the outskirts of town. Wylitt led them through the main dining room, which was already bustling with a large, dinner-hour crowd, to a hallway past the kitchen. A door at the end of the hall brought them into a private dining room where six Wylitt managers waited at a table set for ten. Ed saw the dozen or so bottles of Wylitt liquors standing on a sideboard, but they didn't worry him. In such a large group, it would be easy to fake drinking, the way he had last night. And the more everyone else drank, the easier it would be for him to lose himself in the general uproar.

Wylitt took his place at the head of the table, facing the door. He waved Stennis to the seat on his immediate right, Roverstein to the one on his left, and Ed to the remaining empty seat beside Stennis. Ed nodded at the man on his right, who introduced himself as Greer Vangus, Open States Manager. "Best thing about these meetings," Vangus murmured, "we get to sample some of the old man's private stock." From his redolent breath, Ed knew he'd been sampling *somebody's* stock, private or otherwise. Which was fine; just fine. They all would soon be in such a condition as to give him complete freedom of action.

Wylitt tapped the table for silence. "The first order of business is Sy Roverstein's report on next year's advertising."

Roverstein rose, said that reminded him of a story, told a joke that lacked discretion and went overboard on excretion. Ed laughed with the rest, but raised his eyebrows when Stennis glanced sideways to see how he'd taken it. Stennis shrugged slightly, as if to say that was the ad game. Roverstein launched into a preliminary buildup of the new campaign, describing as major aims the improvement of sales figures in markets now leaning toward Scotch and Canadian. "We're going to hit the medicine taste and the no taste! We're going to get our flavor story across as never before! And tomorrow, we're going to fire up our salesmen and send them out ready to rip the guts out of the opposition! Tomorrow, we're going to kick off the greatest sales period in Wylitt history! Thank you."

He sat down to thunderous applause. Wylitt rose, nodding and smiling. Silence descended. Wylitt's lined, ruddy face grew serious. He touched his thinning gray hair, cleared his throat, took a deep breath. "Gentlemen, imports be damned!"

The room rang with whoops and cheers.

Wylitt then settled down to a routine report on the corporation's financial condition. Tomorrow, he would follow through on the sell-America theme with a rousing speech written for him by the P.B.S. public relations department. Now he contented himself with describing the success of the blended whisky, the new emphasis on Wylitt's three bourbons, the growth of the gin and vodka, the higher corporate profits since the reorganization of 1963, and "the banner year fast approaching, due to all of you, and to the intensified efforts of our advertising agency, Prior-Bailey-Stennis." His expression lightened. "And not to play down the contributions of old man Stennis . . ." pause for laughter, loudest and longest from Stennis ". . . who is not only president of P.B.S. and our esteemed account executive, but also one of our best customers . . ." pause for further laughter, with Stennis slapping the table and shaking his head at the richness of the jest ". . . I want to introduce to you a man new to these meetings. A man who has grown to major importance in the Wylitt profit picture in a very short time. A man who has done more to inject excitement and real hard sell . . ."

"Yahoo!"

"Amen!"

The managers recorded their approval for a full minute, ending the demonstration only at Wylitt's upraised hand.

"Sell with *heart* as well as brain. Sell with real *American* feeling. Sell with a special touch of *genius*. That man is our new creative supervisor, Ed Berner. Stand up, Ed, and let the boys see what a real cocker-knocker looks like!"

Ed rose, grinning and nodding amidst the applause, and began to sit down again. But Wylitt said, "Stay up there, Ed. I've finished my little spiel. Now we're going to do you a major honor. Something we've never done for a man at his first, or even his second, special meeting." He looked at Stennis. "I believe you had to wait four years for your initiation, Paul. That right?"

"Five," Stennis said, smiling. But the smile didn't seem quite natural. Not to Ed, who felt shock, fear and tension emanate from the man's brain. "Maybe we should wait until Ed's a bigger boy. . . ."

Wylitt chuckled and pressed a bell cord at the side of his chair. Stennis looked up at Ed, still smiling, and said, "This was one thing I never figured on." His eyes begged for Ed's fortitude and strength.

A Negro waiter entered, carrying a cut-glass decanter on a silver tray.

Wylitt raised his arm. "Ah, here it is! The oldest, smoothest bourbon in the world. Distilled and barreled by my granddaddy, not too long after James Crow made his first, rare distillation. Granddaddy also originated this little ceremony . . ."

"And it laid him in his grave!" one of the plant managers bellowed. The table dissolved in laughter. Stennis laughed with the rest, but he still looked frightened. "You'll have to fish or cut bait now, Ed," he said. "You'll have to show what you're made of."

"And what Wylitt's best bourbon is made of," Wylitt added. Ed saw he had taken the decanter from the waiter and was pouring straight bourbon into a water glass. "The aroma alone," Wylitt murmured, "is enough to make a confirmed drinker of a Carry Nation."

"Gentlemen," Ed said, desperate for a way out, "I say we *all* drink a toast to the man who . . ."

Wylitt looked up, surprised and displeased. "Not now, Ed. You're about to be taken into the Wylitt upper echelon. You're about to drink about six ounces of the finest bourbon whisky ever made. No man could fail to appreciate it." He held out the glass, three-quarters full. "Take it, drink it down, and as you do remember you'll never get another glass like it in all your life. It's 100-proof manna. It's ageless, priceless and irreplaceable. I've had only four drinks of it myself, and no other man has had more than one."

Ed took the glass. Wylitt turned to the waiter. "Fill these gentlemen's glasses with their preference from the sideboard. I'll have the blend."

Ed stood there as the waiter went from man to man. He racked his brain for a thought to beam at Wylitt; a thought that would make him cancel out this ceremony. But could anything stop it at this late stage? If only there'd been some warning; just a hint that this *might* take place. Then he'd have made Wylitt feel Ed Berner was still undeserving of so great an honor. But there had to be another way. . . .

Wylitt was facing him, a smaller glass held aloft. And Ed found a way. Immediately, he beamed a strong thought at Wylitt; of Wylitt's feeling sick, weak, dizzy; of his being in imminent danger of a stroke or heart attack.

Wylitt dropped into his chair. He still, however, held his glass. And he said, "I envy you. Now raise your glass."

Ed obeyed, and continued pounding thoughts of sickness into Wylitt's brain.

Wylitt blanched. "Quickly," he muttered. "Give the toast honored in antiquity. The toast . . ."

Roverstein was leaning toward the old man, asking what was wrong. "Sy," Wylitt whispered. "Tell him the toast. *Now.*"

Roverstein said, "Confusion to the dries."

Ed said, "I think Mr. Wylitt needs a doctor."

Stennis leaped at the opportunity. "We can do this some other time. Get Mr. Wylitt . . ."

But Wylitt thought more of the ceremony than Ed believed possible. He shook his head and raised his voice. "The toast! If I have to go, I'd rather go here, watching this, than any other way! Hurry!"

Roverstein turned to Ed, nodding violently.

Ed had run out of time. He said, "Confusion to the dries," and put the glass to his lips. The fumes rose to his nostrils, and he hesitated. Roverstein said, "Go on, man! Go on!" and others at the table raised their voices, urging him to hurry.

Ed threw back his head and drank. Fire filled his throat. He drank again, and the fire reached his stomach and touched off an explosion and vomit rose in a sour, stinging wave. He didn't even have time to turn away. As Wylitt began to straighten, recovering the instant Ed's thoughts let up, Ed retched and was sick on the table. He forgot Wylitt and Stennis and everything but his intense disgust with the poison in his glass. He flung it down into the pool of vomit, gasping, "Filthy stuff! Goddam filthy stuff!"

Wylitt whispered, "My God!" and looked sicker than before.

Roverstein pushed back his chair, face twisted, brushing at splatterings on his shirt and sleeve. Stennis moaned softly.

Ed managed to take a deep breath, and only then realized what he'd done.

Stennis jumped up. "Forgive him, gentlemen. I thought something like this might happen. That's why I tried to stop it. He's been nipping at a flask of Wylitt blend all day. Just too much of a good thing."

Ed nodded, head down. "Yes, sorry. Best bourbon I ever . . ." He gagged, and felt he was going to vomit again, and lurched to the door. As he opened it, he heard Stennis speaking frantically: "Just a momentary indisposition, boys. He'll be back in a minute . . ." And Wylitt interrupting with: "If he does come back, get me an umbrella!" No one laughed, and Ed could imagine the look on the old man's face.

He ran down the hall and through the swinging doors leading to the kitchen. He pushed past startled cooks and waiters to an open door leading to the outside. There, in the darkness beside a row of garbage cans, he was sick to his heart's content.

When he finished, he found his way to a path and walked around to the front of the hotel. He had to return to that dining room. He had to face Wylitt and the others. He had to apologize; had to assure them he hadn't meant what he'd said about their revered bourbon; had to put himself back in Wylitt's good graces. But not right now. Not for half an hour or so.

He reached the parking area. The limousine was there, and so was Clark, the young Negro chauffeur. Clark got out and opened the rear door. "Take you somewhere, Mr. Berner?"

Ed said no, he just wanted to sit and smoke a cigar in the cool of the evening. He got in back, took two cigars from his breast pocket and held one through the window for Clark. The chauffeur said thanks and he would smoke it later. Ed lit up. Clark cleared his throat. "Guess I'll walk around a bit, stretch my legs." Ed said he didn't have to, on his account. Clark said he wanted to, and began walking away. Ed didn't answer. He sat absolutely still, the cigar half-raised to his mouth. Then he threw it out the window, opened the door and slammed it shut behind him.

Clark was about fifteen feet away, and glanced back. Ed was getting into the front seat, but he didn't know he was doing it. He'd stopped knowing anything a moment ago, when the Druggishes had reached him with their probe. He started the big car.

Clark called, "Mr. Berner."

Ed backed from the curbing.

Clark waved his hand. "Mr. Berner, I'll drive you . . ."

Ed roared forward, tires screaming as he twisted the wheel toward the exit and the highway.

Clark shouted, "Mr. Berner, Mr. Wylitt don't 'low anyone to drive his . . ."

But the limousine was at the highway, its stoplight stabbing red. An instant later it leaped into traffic. Clark stood with hand raised, face shocked. "Mr. Wylitt sure gonna be mad," he muttered. "Should I tell him now, or should I wait till that nut come back? I better wait, just in case he told him he could use the car. Yeah, I'll wait. . . ."

He had a long wait. Ed Berner was on his way to New Mexico.

It took a little under two days this time, since he started from Kentucky instead of New York. He arrived early Thursday evening and sat in the big car in the middle of the empty land and blinked at the spectacular sunset. He didn't get out until it grew dark, which was when the Druggish finally appeared. Its greeting reflected an awareness of Ed's frame of mind. Gone was the glad-to-see-you approach. "If you're ready, Mr. Berner, we'll get on with the report."

Ed knew then, of course, everything that had happened. He said, "I'm not ready. Every time I come here, I create terrible problems for myself. And there are other things. I've got to be able to drink alcohol without getting sick. And why am I so afraid of speed, of flying, when I never was before? Those things must be changed." But he said it without real hope.

"Alcohol is not a natural part of the human diet, Mr. Berner. In your case, because of changes made to give you full potential of strength and longevity, alcohol takes on the properties of a poison. As for the speed and flying, the more we learn about your incredible accidental death rate, the more we must inhibit you against self-destruction. During the process of the last report, we strengthened the inhibition. We may strengthen it further this time."

"Aha! You *can* make changes!"

"That much of a change, yes, because it is minor, a matter of degree. But to reverse a basic decision, no. I can increase protection of a valuable recorder, but not decrease it. We're actually helping you, can't you see?"

"I don't think you believe that yourself."

"I most certainly do! I would not express an untruth. . . ." The Druggish seemed to judge its own vehemence, and stopped.

"All right," Ed said. "I can live with everything, except the monthly reports. I can even adjust to them, if you'll allow me to remember that I must return here. . . ."

"I have explained to you, Mr. Berner, I am without authority to effect such changes."

"Why won't you at least *try?*" Ed said, voice beginning to tremble. "It's not just a matter of my comfort, you know. It's a matter of survival—actual, literal, physical survival."

"I *have* tried."

Ed was surprised into silence.

"I was in contact with the Leadership Panel after your last report. They are satisfied with the situation as it is, Mr. Berner."

"Satisfied! But didn't you explain . . ."

"I explained. Let us get on with the report."

"But how can they be satisfied if I'm being destroyed?"

The Druggish sent a command and turned to the hole. Ed followed it down the ramp, into the small ship and through the low-ceilinged room to the table made just for him. He lay down, and the Druggish turned to leave, and he said, "Just explain to me, please, how can the Leadership Panel be satisfied?"

The answer didn't come right away, and when it did it seemed subdued, reluctant. "They are in favor of a high degree of stress. They find it enriches your reports immeasurably." A pause. "One thing more, Mr. Berner. I am not of First Stature. By that I mean I am not in the confidence of the Leadership Panel; not in possession of all the facts. I can answer your questions only from a limited fund of knowledge."

Ed had nothing more to say. His Dream Life was finished. His life itself, probably. And the worst part was, he wouldn't know it once he left this ship. He was a blind dog being prodded toward a cliff. A laboratory mouse being driven to insanity and death. A fool, a pigeon, a victim!

The Druggish read his thoughts. From the portal, its answer snapped back at him: "But all within the letter of our agreement! All perfectly correct! You might be a fool, Mr. Berner, but you are not a victim! Not of the Druggishes, certainly!"

"Go away," Ed said wearily. "Go away, civilized being. You're no different from us. You fit the jungle. You're a beetle. A carnivorous beetle."

"It is not permitted . . ."

"The letter of our agreement. Men strip each other of

everything, including life, with those words. The letter of our agreement. A child agrees to let you see its heart, and so you cut it out. The letter of . . ." The incredible cold came then, washing him away.

He was stopped by a state patrol car and taken into custody twenty minutes after awakening on the highway early Friday morning. He was held in a two-cell jailhouse in the same town in which he'd met the waitress and defeated the local strongboy at arm wrestling. The charge was driving a stolen vehicle. And what a vehicle to steal! Wylitt's custom limousine was one of six in the whole country!

He sat at the edge of his cot, head in hands, and waited for someone to tell him he'd killed Warner or Pat or both thugs who'd attacked him two months ago. He no longer wanted to understand why he came here. He was afraid the answer was quite simple. He was insane. That was why he thought he'd grown muscle and hair and teeth and virility. That was why he thought others noticed such changes. That was why he thought he could read thoughts, and influence them. That was why he was sitting here, waiting for an end to his freedom, perhaps his life.

When the questions finally came as to how then had he been able to win at cards, at business, at physical combat and with women, the answer was that anyone who believed so strongly in himself was bound to triumph, for a while. He had always had great strength and never used it. He had always had luck and never tried it. He had always had untapped potential. His madness had released that potential and his madness had given him two months of glory and his madness would now destroy him.

A young man in baggy suntan trousers and T-shirt brought breakfast on a tray. He unlocked the door and walked in and put it on the cot beside Ed. Ed raised his head. He could strike this body down. He could walk out of here, unless someone shot him. Why not take the chance?

The jailer left, locking the door after him. Ed ate the soggy scrambled eggs and two slices of white bread and gulped the tepid coffee. He was starving. He had to have more to eat. And when would they let him wash and shave?

He got up and went to the bars. "Hey! Hey, jailer!"

No one came.

He pressed his head to the bars and tried to see the cell to his left. He saw nothing but the corridor. "Anyone here with me?"

No answer.

He shouted, "If someone doesn't come, I'll rip this goddamned . . ." He looked down at his hands. He'd pulled two bars far apart—and at that moment the bar in his right hand snapped. He backed away.

He reached the cot and lay down. He was both mad and inhuman. He could tear out that door and walk into the next room and destroy whoever was there and drive away in the first car he saw and . . .

And be hunted and shot at and eventually killed.

Mad or inhuman or what, he was doomed. He knew it, and there was no use fighting.

But he was so damned hungry and uncomfortable! If he had to kill someone to get enough to eat and the chance to wash and shave. . . .

Footsteps sounded. The young jailer was back. He opened the door and began to speak, and then noticed the bars. He stared. "I searched you myself. How'n hell did you do that?"

"I didn't," Ed muttered. "Was that way when I came in."

"But I never noticed . . . and anyway, it's not cut or burned through or . . . it's bent, so how . . ." He looked at Ed. He began to slam the door, and then stopped himself. He opened it all the way. "You're sprung. Why didn't you say it was your boss' car? He changed his mind about pressing charges. Lexington police wired us you're to drive the car to Louisville. Otherwise, you'll be back in the can in no time."

Ed drove the limousine back to Louisville, and Wylitt's suburban home. Clark was the only one there. The chauffeur said, "You sure didn't look bagged, Mr. Berner. If I'd known . . ."

Ed asked if he could phone for a cab to the train depot. Clark said he was driving that way. Ed thanked him and sat up front, wondering if Stennis would allow him to stay with P.B.S. Small chance. And even if he did, the next amnesia attack would finish it.

He could always get a new job. The announcement of his part in landing the toy account had reached most people in the business. He could go to half a dozen agencies. But again, what good would it do? In a month or so he would lose his mind and drive to New Mexico. In a month or so he would queer any deal, any job. And there was no way of avoiding it; no way of preventing it. All he could do was prepare for it. And that was best done by forgetting about jobs and staying close to his own apartment, his own car. That way, at least, he wouldn't steal anything; wouldn't end up in jail. He had enough money to live on a year, perhaps longer, even with the payments to Edith. During that time he would enjoy food and women and books and his children. And he would think of ways to get money for another year; maybe a new try at poker with new victims.

Which reminded him of Roscoe Hammermill, and then of Beth.

He thought of Beth awhile, at the station and on the train pulling out of Louisville. He missed her. Just a little, of course, and only because he was shaken; but still he missed her. He wondered if she ever wondered about him.

He went to the dining car and ate an enormous meal, and remembered he hadn't had a woman in five days. He struck up a conversation with a tall, lean, sunburned blonde of thirty or more. She was from Texas, and laughed a good deal about the curious ways of her fellow Texans. They walked toward the club car together, bumping against each other as the train rocked. In one inter-car passageway, they were alone and she stumbled into him and he held her. She said, "Ed, I'll tell you straight, I don't much care for men."

He fed her his thoughts, his needs, and kissed her and gave her rough caresses.

She was big and hard in his arms, unresisting but unresponsive. He said, "Let's go to your compartment and talk it over."

She hesitated; then turned and led the way. In the compartment, she seemed bigger, harder, totally unfeminine. He smiled. "I'm going to like this."

"But am I?"

"I really don't give a damn."

She'd been sitting, but got up and shook her head and began to speak. He grabbed her again. She said, "It's a mistake. I don't know what the hell got into me, but it's just not possible."

He didn't answer for quite a while. She struggled and said, "You bastard!"

He said, "One thing is certain, it's possible."

"Get out of here," she gasped. "Get out, you . . . lousy stallion!"

He didn't. Not for two hours. She was crying when he left. She was crumpled on the berth, big and lean and hard in her nudity, and trembling like a frightened child. She felt like a woman. She hated the feeling. She would never forget the feeling. The pattern of her life was torn.

He knew all this from her thoughts, and felt a little sorry for her. But her struggle, her convulsive battle which had turned, somewhere, into convulsive lovemaking, had been exciting, satisfying, different.

It had stopped him from thinking.

He didn't go to the office Monday or Tuesday. He wanted relaxation. He spent the time reading, walking, eating, moving his car from one parking spot to another. He'd taken the Triumph from the garage. It was too far away. He had to keep it right outside his apartment house. If it meant an occasional parking ticket, so be it. He also picked up five women, and had one minor altercation with an enraged boyfriend. The boyfriend saw reason after Ed explained he hadn't known Maria was waiting for someone. That and a gentle push which sent the big youth slamming into a parked car ended the dispute. He was beginning to tire of such matters. In two months he had lost a lifelong need, an intense dream of proving himself with other men. The proof was overwhelmingly conclusive. There was no longer any doubt as to the outcome of a fight.

Wednesday, he went up to P.B.S. Miss Carlsbad rose from her desk, a thin little smile on her thin little lips. "I'm glad you stopped by to say goodbye, Mr. Berner. Strange how things work out. Only the other week you suggested I might be the one leaving. And now . . . well, better luck on your next job. If there *is* a next job."

"Aren't you being a little premature?"

Her smile never wavered. "I was told to remove your name from the time sheets last Thursday. My friend Olivia in Payroll said your final check, as of last Tuesday, plus two weeks' severance, has already been made up."

"Ah, but I haven't spoken to Mr. Stennis yet. And you know what the golden tones . . ."

"Mr. Bandson was rehired as group head on Wylitt Beverages."

"Mr. Bandson and I can both work for P.B.S."

"Mr. Stennis made no secret of your activities in Kentucky. He, ah, called them reprehensible, but in stronger language. Everyone, but *everyone* in the company knows you were fired, Mr. Berner. Permanently, Mr. Stennis said. And he gave his word to Mr. Wylitt you would never again work for us, in any capacity. Now shall I tell him you're here? Not that it will do any good. He won't see you."

Her eyes were glittering, her hands clenching and unclenching in sheer vindictive delight. She was having her revenge.

He said, "I'll tell him myself."

"You're not to enter our offices! Your personal possessions will be sent . . ."

He went by her. She picked up her phone. As he entered Stennis' office, the phone rang. Stennis picked it up, and saw him, and said, "I know, Miss Carlsbad. No, you needn't call the police. He's quite sane, except when he's been drinking. But thanks for your concern. Very well, if he isn't out in fifteen minutes, you *can* call the police." He hung up, leaned back in his chair, said, "You can pick up your check at Payroll. Let's not have a scene. I promised Wylitt, on pain of losing the account, that you wouldn't be employed by this agency. Even without the promise, I believe I'd have let you go. Stealing the man's car was just too much."

Ed began sending him thoughts; strong thoughts of new business ten times the billing of Wylitt's. Stennis got up and strode to the door. "I don't care how much new business you can swing! I can't trust you and I don't want you here!"

"I haven't said a word," Ed said, but he stopped trying. He hadn't expected to stay on anyway.

"Well . . . I was thinking what you were about to say. And it makes no difference. Just get out of here, Ed. You can go to most agencies in the business. I won't smear your name. If anyone calls and asks about you, I'll say we had a personality clash. But no matter where you go, you'll end up on the street. You know that, don't you?"

Ed stood up. "Yes," he said, and walked out. He got his check from Payroll and stopped to say goodbye to Anise. She agreed to cook dinner at his apartment Saturday night. He went on to the reception room. Miss Carlsbad was just telling a middle-aged photographer's rep to have a seat as Ed passed her desk. "Adieu," she said sweetly, mockingly. "I'll be sure to tell everyone I know in advertising that you're looking for a job. You can count on it, Mr. Berner."

Ed decided not to leave just yet. He stood beside the desk as Miss Carlsbad dialed and spoke.

"Mr. Vanders is here. Yes, thank you." She hung up. "Mr. Tryser will see you as soon as he gets out of conference, Mr. Vanders. He has . . ."

Ed sent her a thought, intensely, straining to burn it into her mind.

She cleared her throat.

"He has a cosmetic client . . ." She faltered, and began to redden. "He . . . another ten minutes . . . I . . ." Her hand came to her mouth. "No," she whispered. "No, what is . . ."

Vanders looked at Ed, eyebrows rising. Ed shrugged. "Are you all right, Miss Carlsbad?"

Miss Carlsbad nodded. "I'm perfectly . . ." And then, "If there's nothing else, Mr. Berner . . ." She put both hands to her face. "Why don't you leave?" she whispered. "Why?"

"You're rather quick to kick a man when he's down, aren't you?" His thoughts beat into her mind; his graphic, searing, erotic thoughts.

"I'm not . . ." Her head shook violently, as if to throw off the images there; the never-before-experienced images. "I just can't . . ." She jumped up. "Men!" she screamed. "Filthy, rotten, ugly . . ." She shoved past Ed and rushed to the door. She stopped, whirled on Vanders, struck him full in the face. She turned to Ed. "And . . . you! You, of all people! *Stop it!*" She ran out.

Vanders was standing, touching his cheek. "I never said a word to that woman in all the years . . ."

"Neither did I. I believe she's lost her mind."

"In self-defense, I'm going to report this to Bill Tryser! I mean, I can't have her running around telling people I did something. . . . Did you see her face?"

Ed nodded, moving to the door. "As if we'd both been attacking the hell out of her."

chapter 11

EDWARD BERNER was not a very lovable person during the early weeks of September, though he engaged in the act of love a record number of times. Only with his books, reading of lives both far less and far more than his own, was he at peace, at pleasure. He ate enormously, making a vice of it. He had woman after woman, occasionally two a day; once three, when a cosmetic saleswoman came to his door. He had girls of seventeen and women of fifty. The saleswoman was fifty-eight, and quite satisfactory. But his totality of pleasure had dropped. Books, and a few moments of each visit with the children, were truly good, truly satisfying. Even the city, explored and re-explored, had begun to bore him.

He was sleeping one night in five, and looking forward to those nights as he had once looked forward to having a woman. This, despite the dreams of interrupted triumph and headlong flight. To sleep *every* night now seemed a gift, a blessing. But that was because his days were incredibly long and he had more than enough time to read. (He decided that even if he worked all day and slept each night, he would have enough time to read. He would *make* enough time to read, now that he knew what it was.)

He was aware of the humor of his situation. He walked the streets, a juggernaut of strength and sex and brain-power, and wasn't happy. (If he really was what he thought he was. If he wasn't insane and dreaming.)

He thought of his old life with a certain degree of nostalgia, but with no wish to go back to it. Insane or not, amnesia or not, he wouldn't want to be the pitiful, defeated man he'd been.

Besides, the amnesia might disappear, and then he would again trust his sanity. There was always the hope. Only a week—or was it four or five days?—remained before the month between attacks was up. If it passed without incident, if the sickness ended . . .

He decided to visit the children the next night, Friday, just in case he went to New Mexico and there was trouble and he didn't come back. He phoned the house. Edith wasn't there. She was in Reno, establishing residence. Her Aunt Gertrude was taking care of the kids. Gerty was a plump old doll, all sweetness and light, and particularly pleased with Ed because of the size of his subsistence checks. She said he could come up Friday or any other night of the week. She'd be glad to prepare a big dinner, or take in a movie. Anything he wanted was fine with her.

He said he would take the kids out to dinner, and to expect him by six. But he'd forgotten how much slower he drove these days.

On Friday, he moved along the Taconic Parkway, hugging the right, disgusted with himself, wondering why he'd ever bothered buying the speedy Triumph when he couldn't move it over thirty-five miles an hour. Gentlemen of seventy driving battered old sedans passed him with contemptuous looks. When an old lady with spastic head did the same, he tried stamping down on the gas pedal. The Triumph roared and surged forward; and the vivid picture of a fatal accident—with Edward Berner the fatality—flashed before his eyes in full color, the creamy whites of viscera and brilliant reds of blood making him break into a sweat. His foot lifted. The Triumph bucked, belched, sighed, and settled into its shameful thirty- to thirty-five-miles-an-hour pattern. Ed kept his eyes from the cars that passed him.

Crawling along that way, he had plenty of time to think; which gave him no joy, except as pertained to one area of his life. He'd received four offers of jobs this past week. Y.&R. would pay twenty thousand. The others at least that, maybe three to five more. He could go places with a big agency. He could move fast.

Yeah, right to New Mexico, and then right out of the advertising business as his reputation for being a drunk, or a kook, spread around. He couldn't take a job until he was certain he'd finished with the amnesia attacks.

He reached the house at a few minutes to seven. He took the kids to a new Chinese restaurant and ordered a huge variety of dishes—ribs and duck and beef and shrimp and lobster and egg roll and five different kinds of rice and three kinds of chow mein and two soups and two desserts. The kids tasted and he finished. He ate far more than he needed, almost more than he could hold. He was disgusted with himself when they left the restaurant, and the kids began to quarrel. He scolded them; they grew sullen; he took them to a drive-in movie. Matty fell asleep and Miri didn't like the picture and he brought them home at nine-thirty. The evening hadn't been a success. Goodbyes were quick, and then he was out of the house and walking to his car.

He would return to the city and have a woman and read straight through until Sunday. He wouldn't look into himself any more, examine himself any more, worry any more. He had his survival kit in the Triumph, and the Triumph close at hand, so even if he did go to New Mexico it wouldn't be dangerous and he could enjoy the country on the way back and . . .

And stop thinking about it, damn you!

He stopped thinking about it before he reached his car. A familiar voice spoke from the black shadows off the driveway. A familiar shape came toward him with a familiar object in its hand.

"If it isn't Ed. You told me I could call you Ed, didn't you?"

"Not you," Ed said. "Only Gordon." He tried to reach Dick Nelson's mind with soothing thoughts, but it didn't work. He kept trying. Nelson jabbed him with the gun.

"Walk down the driveway. Or maybe you want to die right here? I wouldn't mind right here. I wouldn't mind anywhere. I got a ringing in my ears and headaches and one eye don't see so good. What'd you hit me with that time? Brass knucks? A sap? A rock?"

"The weight of my intellect," Ed said, and turned and walked ahead of Nelson and his gun. It wasn't a very funny joke, nor was Nelson likely to appreciate it, but he'd had to say something to convince himself he wasn't afraid. Terribly afraid. He felt he was going to die.

"I been waiting for this," Nelson murmured. "How I been waiting for this!"

Ed shrugged, but inside he was screaming. *He couldn't die! He had so much to live for! So much more than anyone else!*

They reached the end of the driveway, and he saw the dark Lincoln Continental. His body tensed. He would turn swiftly and smash Dick Nelson with one blow. Then he would race around behind the Amory house. Let Gordon follow if he dared!

He took a breath, writing off the risk of a possible bullet wound and preparing to act. But he didn't act. He walked to the car and got in back with Nelson. Gordon, wearing a black glove on his right hand, drove to the highway and turned toward Putnam County. "Finding you took time," Gordon said. "And then we had to wait for the right setup, but now it's gonna be good."

Ed began beaming thoughts at him, but was interrupted.

"Yeah, good," Nelson whispered, and slammed Ed's face with a blackjack, breaking his nose. And slammed it again, smashing his forehead and his right cheekbone. And again, breaking his jaw and teeth, splitting both lips wide open. And once again, sending him to the floor, choking on his own blood, moaning, consciousness slipping away. *Why hadn't he fought? Why hadn't he run?*

He heard Gordon say, ". . . blood all over the car, dimwit! We gotta think ahead! And pocket that gun. *I'm* putting the bullet in him."

Ed tried to raise his head, but too much was smashed, and before it knit together sufficiently for a renewal of strength, he would have that bullet in him.

He felt regret; blanket regret for all that could have been and would never be. Regret for the women and the food and the books and the kids. And for one woman, a girl really, who had managed to touch him deeply. Regret . . .

The car stopped. He was pulled out and dragged by his feet over rough ground. Gordon said, ". . . looks dead to me. By Christ, if he isn't alive to see me blow his head off, I'll do it to *you!*"

"He ain't dead. He's breathing. Wait, I got some smelling stuff in my car. That'll bring him to. I go blooey sometimes . . ."

"We both know *that* story. Get the stuff."

His feet were dropped. He opened his eyes. He was lying on his back, looking up at the sky. The stars were out. A tree branch cut into the heavens. And a peaked edge of roof. He moved his head. He was outside Gordon's summer place in Putnam County. He was going to die here. *But why? How had he allowed these thugs to bring him to this? What had kept him from fighting?*

Gordon's thick face swung down at him. He shut his eyes,

but not in time. "So you're up, Eddie boy. I'm glad. We won't wait for Dick. We'll say goodbye right now, you and me." He held up a flat automatic in his left hand. "Do you remember all the fun you had back in July—taking my dough and the girls, busting my hand and knocking Dick's few brains out? Now I get *my fun*. See the gun?"

Ed said yes and couldn't they talk and he was sorry about everything and he'd give back the money, much more money, twenty thousand dollars.

"It's not money I want from you, Eddie boy. It's what you're giving me now." His face glistened with perspiration. "Look at the gun. It's the end of everything. It's finish, dark, goodnight mommy and daddy and sugar candy." He wet his lips, and put the black barrel against Ed's bloody forehead. Ed whimpered. "That's what I want, Eddie boy, so I can stop hating myself and everyone else and get to sleep nights again. That's what I need to live."

Ed said, "I can't see you. What are you doing now?"

"You can't see me? The gun blocks seeing? That's bad. I want you to see." He took the gun from Ed's head and pressed it to his chest. "Look down. Can you see now?"

Ed whispered, "Please. Anything. Please." But he no longer felt true horror, true fear. Which made no sense. Not with a gun at his heart.

"Then we'll put two, three slugs in the chest, Eddie boy. It's the same thing, and you might live long enough to feel them tear your heart out. You might see my gun kick and hear yourself scream before you die. That's a break, ain't it?"

Ed sobbed a little, and waited.

"Goodbye," Gordon said, and bending low to watch Ed's face, he squeezed the trigger. The pain was incredible. Ed screamed high and shrill above the gun's roar, and felt a lesser pain, and died.

Regaining consciousness was a shock, because he remembered his death. He was lying on cold concrete in total darkness. When he sat up, his clothing pulled away from his body, stiff and caked. It was his own dried blood. But he was alive. *Alive!*

He put his hands beneath his shirt and undershirt and felt himself. A small, puckered scar; two of them. Reaching around back, he could just touch a larger scar, where one

slug had emerged, and feel the stiffness of a second one, out
of reach. He touched his forehead, nose, cheeks, lips, teeth.
Everything healed. Everything normal. And the scars would
be gone by morning.

He stood up and felt his way along a rough wood wall. He
reached a plank door and opened it and began to see a little.
Pale night light came in through a half-window across a long
room. He was in a basement, and had just come out of a
storage bin. He heard voices: Gordon's and Nelson's.

He made his way to a staircase and up it. He moved softly,
quietly, once again strong and sure. He reached a door. He
heard Gordon, at least a room away, say, ". . . dig up the
floor and put him there."

Nelson answered, "Why not the lake? A few lead
weights . . ."

"You jerk! The ropes or something rot and he floats right
up and then we got cops!"

"I know three Mafia guys put away in Lake George! Three
guys, and not one ever come up or nothing!"

"Lake George's like the ocean compared to this stinking
puddle! I tell you we're gonna dig up the floor . . ."

He was in Gordon's cellar. They were planning to dispose
of his body. But this body wasn't ready for disposal. This
body was getting out of here and going . . .

Where?

He didn't know. If he killed these two, he'd be in danger
of the police and prison and maybe even the electric chair. If
he slipped out and went back to the city, they'd find him
again and do a better job—blow his head off. (Which would,
he knew without doubt, be final death; death without hope of
reprieve.)

He had to run. He had to get out of here and grab a car
and travel far.

New Mexico! That was it! He'd never gone there of his
own free will. He'd never searched for answers to the many
questions of his new life. It was time he did.

He put his hand on the knob and turned until the tongue
was clear. He opened the door slowly and looked into Gordon's kitchen. It was dark, but through an archway to his
right came light and voices. To his left was the door leading
to the outside. He moved into the kitchen. Gordon's voice
said, "I'm not arguing any more. C'mon and we'll . . ."

Ed was a step from the outside door when the light went

on. He turned. Gordon stood facing him, hand frozen on the light switch. Nelson came up behind him. "You oughta listen just once to me maybe. I got experience in . . ." He saw Ed. He wet his lips and giggled shrilly. "It's a gag," he said.

"A gag," Gordon repeated, and backed up, bumping into Nelson. Both stumbled backward, an inept vaudeville team, into the living room.

Ed could have left then, but decided not to. He would take a chance on their pulling guns again. He would gamble for high stakes—ridding himself of them forever.

He came forward, walking stiffly. He raised his arms a little; set his face in rigid, inhuman lines. He played the monster. His blood-caked clothing was all the makeup and costume he needed.

Gordon shoved Nelson aside and broke for a door across the room. Ed moved forward. Nelson raised his hand; a traffic cop for monsters. Ed came forward; inexorably forward. "A gag, ain't it?" Nelson said faintly, and backed into a couch and sat down. Ed came closer. Nelson drew his legs up, little-boy fashion. He hugged himself and said, "I wasn't the one who killed you, remember? He was the one. I hit you a few times, so you do that to me. But *he* killed you, not me. Not . . ."

Ed reached out to touch him. Nelson threw himself face down on the couch and sobbed into the cushions. Ed waited a while. When Nelson didn't stop, he went to find Gordon.

A locked bathroom door on the second floor ended the search. He knocked softly, three times.

"Dick?" Gordon called, voice hoarse.

Ed knocked again, receiving waves of terror from the other side of the door.

"Listen, you had your laughs. Now go away."

Ed knocked. The terror rose to crescendo pitch.

"Dick and you!" Gordon screamed. "Don't try to kid *me!* It's Dick and you, screwin' around! A gag! I know its a gag 'cause I put two bullets in your heart and you bled all over the place and no one can get up after that. No one!"

Ed knocked and leaped aside, knowing Gordon's intentions a split-second after Gordon did. A roar of sound erupted. The door splintered ten times; then there were clicks and harsh breathing. Ed kicked the door under the knob. It flew inward.

Gordon was sitting on the closed toilet, face ashen, shoulders slumped. He held his empty automatic in both hands and rubbed it with his thumbs. He didn't look up as Ed entered the bathroom. He didn't look up as Ed stopped before him. When he felt the hand on his shoulder, he raised the gun to his temple and pulled the trigger. Then he dropped it to the floor and whispered, "Okay? We even? Both dead? Okay? I'm off the hook now? Okay?"

He continued his anxious questioning as Ed walked out.

Nelson was still on the couch, still sobbing, though more quietly now.

Ed went outside. He would take the Lincoln and drive back to the house and get his Triumph. Then he would return to the city, change clothing and pack for an extended trip to New Mexico.

The keys were in the Lincoln, and he started up and drove down to the dirt road. There he forgot the Triumph, his apartment, fresh clothing, everything. He even forgot his trip to New Mexico . . . though that was where he was going.

It was a luminous night on the New Mexico wasteland. Moon and stars shone brightly, making it easy for Ed and the Druggish to see each other. The Druggish came up out of the hole and said, "Hail and farewell, Mr. Berner, to quote humans of a rather interesting place and time."

Ed smiled wearily. "You misuse the phrase, Druggish. That would mean we are about to part."

"And so we are, Mr. Berner. Permanently."

Ed had always tried to avoid looking directly at the giant beetle. The sight never failed to disturb him. But now he did —directly and intensely. "I don't understand."

"This is your final report. The agreement between us is hereby terminated."

"Terminated?" Ed whispered. "You . . . I'm not going to be called to New Mexico any more?"

"Never again. And the inhibitions against speed and flight, nicotine and liquor will, of course, also terminate. Satisfied, Mr. Berner?"

"Yes!" But then he thought of something; something terrible. "I'm to be as . . . as I am, right?"

"Certainly not. That would be giving you the fruits of the agreement without the labor. That would be cheating the Druggishes."

Ed began to argue, but the Druggish cut him short. "We could under no circumstances leave behind a human so capa-

ble of satisfying its hungers. You constitute a menace to
other humans, Mr. Berner."

"Does the Leadership Panel . . ."

"Here, and tuned in. The big ship is here too. The disassembly and reassembly equipment is ready."

"But *why* have I lost my usefulness? Wasn't I supposed to
report over a period of *years?* You said you could make me
live almost a thousand years!"

"And so we could, if necessary. And you would, indeed,
live between four and six hundred years as you are, if left
unaltered, and live even longer under further treatment. But
we never planned to leave you unaltered past the conclusion
of our agreement. It is not our fault that humanity is too simple a subject to sustain interest for six months, not to say six
hundred years."

"You can't possibly know all there is to know about humanity after only three months!"

"We know all we want to know. Your kind is motivated by
multiple hungers—derivations and extensions of the basic
hungers for food, shelter and sex. You hide them, and so
hide most realities of yourselves from yourselves. Your lives
are spent in pursuits of objects and the opposite sex and in
creating fables to mask these pursuits. It is repetitious beyond
belief."

"For a beetle," Ed said, suddenly angry.

"We will overlook the insult. You have suffered much in
the past five days. Your death was especially trying. But you
can feel satisfaction in knowing it was the necessary conclusion to your reports, the logical termination of the file on Edward Berner, human."

"You didn't *plan* it, did you?"

"We allowed it to happen. We were in probe contact, and
subverted your will to resist Gordon and Nelson. But we
were also determined that you would recover."

"Of course," Ed said bitterly. "How else could I report?"

"Exactly. Now we can conclude our business, Mr. Berner.
You have run off a human life for us in high-speed photography, as it were."

"Think nothing of it. Just throw me back in the tanks. Just
fulfill the letter of our agreement. . . ." But his anger fled as
he suddenly accepted what was going to happen. He began to
tremble.

"Do not fear the reverse process, Mr. Berner. It is safe."

"Safe," Ed whispered. "I hope not. I hope I never come out of those tanks."

The Druggish was silent, reading his mind. And his mind was full of agony. To return to what he had been, to be *less* than other men after having been so much more, now frightened him as much as death had.

Multiple minds spoke to him. The Leadership Panel said, "Modifications will be made, Mr. Berner." Then they withdrew, leaving Ed with the single Druggish, and faint hope.

"What did they mean?" he asked.

"Come, Mr. Berner. It is time for your report."

"But shouldn't we discuss those modifications?"

He was stilled. He followed the Druggish into the ship and through several rooms to the large room crowded with slim metal tanks. The table was there, and he lay down on it.

The Druggish said, "You must trust our wisdom, Mr. Berner."

Ed's voice was freed. He said, "It's not your wisdom I mistrust, Druggish. It's your compassion."

"Goodbye, Mr. Berner."

Ed didn't have time to answer.

chapter 12

HE AWOKE behind the wheel of the Lincoln Continental. It was night. He was in New Mexico again—same highway; same spot. He remembered frightening Nelson and Gordon and taking their car. But after that . . .

He felt different. Nothing specific, but an overall difference; a compendium of far-reaching and important differences.

Had he reverted to his old self?

He began to get out of the car; then changed his mind as the overhead light went on. He kept the door open with his foot and examined his face in the rear view mirror. His hair was the same. His teeth too. And under the usual stubble of beard, he looked strong, confident, more man than most men.

Than most men.

Why hadn't he thought: *Than all men?*

The feeling of difference. The knowledge of change.

He got out and raised his fist and brought it down on the front fender. He grunted. It hurt. And while the car rocked a bit, the fender didn't dent.

He hit it again, as hard as he could. A good blow. A blow powerful enough to break a man's jaw, perhaps. But not the blow he would have struck a few days ago. And the fender didn't dent.

He was weaker. Definitely weaker. What else had changed?

He touched himself all over; then smiled in relief. Outwardly, at least, he hadn't changed. And that was important. Very important. Though something else came to him immediately afterward. The feeling that he was now susceptible to wear, time and damage.

How could he know this? How could he be so sure of it?

He looked around, as if an answer would appear on the road, or out of the flat, black countryside. But there was no answer. He just knew.

"What the hell does it mean?" he said aloud. "Changing once and changing again? Where will it end?"

Again he knew, though there was no answer. This was the last change. From now on, changes would come with time, with accident, as they did to other men. From now on he was normal.

Or was he? How about women? Would he be the same in that respect?

And what about his mind? Could he still control others? Did he still have that wonderful edge?

As if to provide an answer, a sound made itself heard. An engine. It grew louder, and then he saw the battered pickup truck moving out of the east. He laughed in shock, and hesitated, and then stepped around the car to the edge of the road.

The pickup truck pulled to a halt. One of the two men leaned out the window and peered at him and jerked his head back inside and said, "It's him, Pat! It's him!"

The driver said, "The hell you say!" and looked for himself.

Ed beamed the strongest thought possible at them. *Cut the engine. Get out. Nothing to fear.*

The driver jerked into motion. The engine roared. The gears ground. The truck sped away.

He'd failed to control them. And he hadn't been able to pick up the slightest sensation of their obvious fear and terror. All he'd learned was that Pat and Warner were alive, and very much closed books to him.

He got back in the Lincoln and looked down at his clothing. He was still wearing the suit he'd "died" in. A mess! It would scare anyone who saw it clearly.

He started the car and pulled onto the road. He had to find a change of clothes before daylight. And he had to get out of this area, where he'd already been arrested for car theft. He doubted whether Gordon or Nelson had reported the Lincoln stolen, but he might be stopped for any of a dozen reasons and he couldn't produce ownership papers.

He drove well below the fifty-mile-per-hour speed limit, and passed through the tiny town a short while later. He saw the boxlike house on the eastern outskirts, and slowed and saw the clothesline off to the side. He couldn't be certain, but he thought trousers and shirts, as well as towels and underthings, were hanging there. He went past the house, stopped, and walked back. It was an awful chance to take, but if there was no dog . . .

There was no dog. He opened the low picket gate and walked straight to the line and unpinned a pair of light work pants and a matching work shirt and took out his wallet and found a ten dollar bill and pinned it to the line. He started back toward the gate.

The front door opened. A woman's voice said, "All right. Hold it there, mister."

He turned. The woman threw a light switch with her free hand. He saw she was reasonably young, reasonably attractive, and held an enormous pistol in her right hand. She wore a long, striped bathrobe and pulled it tight around her. "Gil," she said, turning her head slightly to the interior of the house. "Gil, do you hear me?"

Ed moved toward her.

"Now you stay there! This thing works. I practiced plenty on tin cans, and if I can hit them three times out of four I can hit you the same! Just 'cause a woman's alone don't mean any dirty tramp can . . ."

She stopped as a boy of ten or twelve came up behind her. He wore gray pajamas and a frightened expression. "Call Bill Tomlins. Hurry. This man . . ."

"Please," Ed said, beaming thoughts as hard as he could.

"Let your boy check the clothesline. Let him see what I left there."

"I don't care what . . ."

"I paid," Ed said, and felt the thoughts weren't getting through. He would have to do it with speech. "I left ten dollars for a pair of old work clothes. My own clothes were ruined a while back. I'm not a thief. Let him check."

The boy came around her. She pushed him back. "I didn't tell you to do that, Gil! He's got some sort of trick up his sleeve. If your father were here . . ."

"Just check the line," Ed begged.

She hesitated. Her bathrobe was old and worn. Her house was small and shabby. The ten dollars would make a difference in the way she judged a man.

"All right," she said.

The boy ran around her and over to the line. The woman kept the gun on Ed. The boy came back, holding the bill. "Ten dollars all right, Ma!"

She looked at it, then back at Ed. "Well then, why couldn't you go to a store?"

Ed tried answering her with soothing thoughts. She said, "C'mon now, speak up! You can get better than a boy's old pants and shirt for ten dollars!"

"I didn't know it was a boy's outfit. I thought the man of the house . . ."

"Gil is the man of the house," she said, and her pistol dropped a bit, and Ed knew the moment of danger was over.

"Will they fit me?" he asked.

"Hardly. Big man like you."

"I'm five feet, maybe more," Gil said defensively.

She rubbed his hair with her free hand. "Sure. And you do a good job helping me." She looked at Ed. "You want to buy some clothes? I can use cash. I can always use cash, since my husband passed away."

"I'd be very grateful," Ed murmured.

"Then come on in. But remember, I'll have this gun all the time. I'm no babe in the woods."

He came into a square little living room with worn, cheap furniture. He put the boy's clothes on the couch. "You can go to bed, Gil," she said, and pushed the gun into her robe pocket. It bulged half out, and she kept it there with her hand. "Go on now. I'll call you if I need you."

The boy handed Ed the ten dollars. Ed said, "Keep it, Gil."

"Gee! Can I, Ma?"

The woman began to remonstrate, but Ed said, "For frightening you this way."

She nodded, and the boy whooped and ran up a flight of stairs near the front door.

"You're still frightening me," she said. "That blood on your suit, mister?"

He said it was mud and oil and other things and that he'd been ashamed to go into a shop in broad daylight.

"Well, maybe," she murmured. She told him to come along, and walked out of the living room and into a bedroom. The light was on. The bedclothes were rumpled. She stepped around the double bed and pointed at a closet, her right hand still on the gun. "Look in there. Steve wasn't as big a man as you, but almost."

He began to feel good. Twice now she'd spoken of him as a *big* man. He hadn't been big in a woman's eyes three months ago.

He went to the closet and opened it. He took out two suits, a blue and a brown. Both were made of cheap, stiff material. Both were clean and serviceable. He put the brown one back. "May I take this one?"

"You better try it on, 'less you want to change in your car."

"You saw my car?"

"I see lots of cars." Her expression had grown less tense, and more tired. She brushed at her light brown hair. "I sit at the window lots and look out. I hate being alone, and Gil don't help much at night."

"I understand." He tried a warm thought on her. Her face didn't change. "A woman alone . . ."

"One of these days I'll get a dog." She jerked her head at the living room. "You can change in there."

"I'd better pay you first."

"I'm not worried. The ten you gave Gil covers it."

He took another ten from his wallet and put it on the bed. He had more than enough to get back to New York. "You wouldn't happen to have a shirt?"

She turned to a dresser and opened a drawer. She brought out a white shirt, freshly laundered, and tossed it on the bed. He picked it up and reached again for his wallet. "All right now," she said angrily. "This ain't no fancy house where you have to pay for every little thing!"

He took the shirt and went into the living room. Off in a corner, he stripped to his underwear; then realized they were even worse than his suit and shirt. The top had holes front and rear; top and bottoms were black with dried blood. He pulled them off and rubbed himself free of flaking blood. He reached for the blue trousers, unable to see himself bothering her again.

Her voice startled him, made him cover himself with his hands and turn. "You better take this, mister." She came toward him, holding out a suit of underwear. The bulge was gone from her pocket. Her eyes were down. She was pale. He used one hand to reach for the underwear, and their fingers touched. She turned away. He put his other hand on her arm.

"You don't owe me a thing," she said, her voice shaking. "You can get dressed and go on." But she didn't move.

His hand tightened on her arm. He felt her trembling. He felt her need, but not by reading her mind. He dropped the underwear and hoped he was man enough to make her happy.

Later, she got up from the bed and slipped into her robe. "I got to get Gil off to school. Can you wait a little bit?"

He had shaved and showered and was ready to go. "Well . . ."

"We'll have some breakfast."

His eyes widened. How had he gone this long without food? And now that he thought of it, he was starving! He doubted she had enough to feed him.

She left and he looked at the window, at daylight behind the dark shade. He had enjoyed her thoroughly. Twice. He hoped she had enjoyed him as much. Because it was over for now.

She served hotcakes and coffee. She made him two big stacks, and he couldn't finish the second stack. "One thing," she said. "My Steve out-ate you. By plenty."

He finished his second cup of coffee. It tasted good. He wondered why he'd avoided drinking it all these months. "And . . . in other ways?" he asked.

She shrugged, smiling. "Oh, he did all right with less than you." She dropped her eyes and her smile grew. "Much less than you."

He got up and came around the table and kissed her neck.

She looked up at him, hopefully. He straightened and said he had to be going. She nodded. "I hope you're not in big trouble, Ed."

"No, Bea. Honestly. No trouble at all, any more." And how he knew it he couldn't say, but it was so.

She took out cigarettes and offered him the pack. He began to say no; then accepted one and lit up. He smoked it as he said goodbye, and while in the car. He smoked it right down to the filter, and it was fine. But he decided cigars were even better.

He drove at his usual cautious speed for a while. The highway was empty; the big car hummed smoothly; he began pressing down on the gas without being aware of it. When he glanced at the speedometer, he was shocked to see he was doing sixty. Without fear! He pressed down even harder and the needle climbed to seventy, eighty, ninety miles an hour. And still no fear!

He dropped back down to sixty-five and grinned and put on the radio. The changes weren't all for the bad.

That afternoon he ate at a drive-in restaurant. A leggy blonde with knowing eyes served him in his car. He tried beaming thoughts at her, and smiled a lot, and attempted a subtle proposition. She confirmed what he'd learned with Bea last night. He was no longer Casanova. Bea had needed him. The leggy blonde didn't. He got no more than a "Yeah, sure, come around again some day when I got no fiancé."

It hurt. No denying that. The irresistible Ed Berner was gone. The Dream Life was over.

But the hurt didn't last long. He ate at a motel dining room that night and the waitress laughed at his pleasantries and looked mildly interested and he felt he could make out if he stayed a few days and pressed the issue. Instead, he stopped at the bar and ordered a bourbon and water and waited until the bartender went back to his discussion of baseball at the other end. Then he took a cautious sip. No nausea. He sipped again, and smiled, and finished the drink. He ordered a double and got into that discussion of baseball. "The Yankees finished? Let a native New Yorker set you right on *that,* buddy!"

The discussion grew rather heated toward the end. A gentleman of reasonable height and enormous girth took umbrage at Ed's position. He asked Ed to step outside. Ed began to laugh it off and say goodnight, but the heavy gentleman proved he was no gentleman at all by punching Ed in the head. Ed went down, ears ringing, everything getting rather remote. He got up as the bartender called for cool heads. He hit the fat man in his fat belly, pulling the punch so as not to kill him.

Not only didn't he kill him, he barely made him wince. And he certainly didn't stop him from delivering a second solid blow to the head. Ed got up off the floor again, determined to end the fight before he lost some of his precious teeth; teeth which wouldn't grow back. He hit the fat man in exactly the same spot as before, but as hard as he could this time.

It made quite a mess. The fat man was helped out by a friend, green in the face but already recovered sufficiently to pledge a return later that evening.

Ed drove on to another motel, in order to avoid any chance of further trouble. In his room, he examined himself minutely in front of the mirror. He confirmed all he'd learned in the past two days, and mourned his losses. But he was still a very strong man, by normal standards, and he looked it. The same went for his genitals, his mind and his total personality.

He went to bed, exhausted, but woke only an hour later, chilled by gusts of night air coming through his wide-open window. He closed the window and used the extra blanket and was asleep before he could note that this too was a reduction.

The next day was clear and sunny, and he was hot in the car. And he slept the next night, and the last night before reaching upper Westchester, where he left the Lincoln on a side road before hitching a ride to the house and his Triumph.

He spent two days in the apartment, resting, reading and meditating. He ate normally and slept normally and adjusted to his new self and began to think of how to order his new life.

Friday morning, he phoned the smallest of the agencies which had offered him a job, and set up an interview date. He'd chosen that agency carefully, for its growth potential. He felt he too had growth potential, of the gradual sort.

Then he put aside thoughts of business and turned to important things—women. He thought again of all the wonderful women he'd had. Women by the ton. Women endlessly different and exciting. He regretted their loss, but with less anger and anguish than he'd anticipated. After all, he'd had more, in his three months, than most men have in a lifetime! And with that, he turned from the contemplation of women in general to one in particular.

He could call Reno and ask Edith to give their marriage a second chance. But he decided against it. She didn't want him. He was still too much man for her; not nearly reduced enough to provide her with the Milquetoast she needed. She was happier this way, and so was he.

He struggled with himself Friday afternoon and evening. Would Beth Hammermill be at her Easthampton home for the weekend? Or would she be at the Central Park South address listed in the Manhattan telephone directory under Roscoe Hammermill? Or would she remain at her college dormitory in New Hampshire? And wherever she was, would she be interested in hearing from him?

It took all of Saturday before he got up the nerve to call Easthampton. No one was there. He called the Manhattan number and waited an interminable five minutes while the maid went to see if Beth had left for her "appointment." Then the cool voice said, "Hi. Anything new?"

He said yes, and told her as much as he could as quickly as he could—about Edith and his new approach to life. She listened without comment, and he finally said, "Am I boring you?"

"Not boring me. Straining my credulity."

He asked her to come right over and see for herself. He gave his address as part of the invitation.

"Sorry. I've got a date. Harvey Stiltoe Hagens—a popular television writer. Very interesting man. The type you advised me to enjoy."

"I'm now advising you to forget him."

"I can't. At least not until after I've watched him be brilliant on a new network interview show. It ends at eleven."

His confidence slipped away. He would never be interviewed on television. "I see. Well . . ."

"And after that we're attending a producer's party. Big stars and lots to drink. You know."

"Yes. I'll call some other time."

"And after that he'll take me home."

He said nothing.

"Father is very fond of him."

He said goodbye and hung up.

He wasn't going to, but he watched the television show. The writer was there all right—young and glib and, in the moderator's words, "good looking enough to star in any of the shows he writes." Ed turned off the set and went to bed. He didn't sleep. Nor did he feel like reading, or eating, or drinking. There was only one thing he felt like doing, and with only one woman.

Being normal was hell!

His doorbell rang. He got up and put on the light and looked at his watch. One-thirty. He went to the door, and Beth's voice said, "Let's not ask who's there and such nonsense."

He opened the door and she came in and he kissed her before it had closed. "Go brush your teeth," she said.

He brushed his teeth. By the time he came out of the bathroom, she was in his bed, her clothes heaped on a chair. He was suddenly afraid. "Listen, Beth, I'm not the man I was. I mean . . . you'll notice changes. I've had . . . a serious illness and it affected . . ."

She raised her eyes to the heavens. He shut up and got in beside her. He was frightened and excited and unsure, and he couldn't seem to do more than kiss her cheek and try to find verbal substitutes for the fiery thoughts he had once put in her mind. "Beth, we should talk a bit about . . ."

Her hand came to him. She said, "I thought for a moment you were someone else. But you *can't* be someone else. There's no one else like this." She kissed him hard, pressed her warm body against him, said, "It's exam time, Mr. Berner. Pass it and you have a wife. Or wasn't that what you had in mind?"

It was exactly what he had in mind. *She* was exactly what he had in mind. And together they were even better than they'd been before. Because now she was half the team, not an unimportant fraction. She felt this, and worked hard for him and for herself. She cried out toward the end, not in pain and exhaustion, but in pure pleasure. She held him, fought to keep him with her as long as she could, gave him up with regret and understanding.

It wasn't the erotic marathon, the limitless delights, the superhuman chain of climaxes as before. He would never have that again, and he would always think back to that and marvel at it and, in time, long for it as all men longed for it.

But it was the best he had ever had, in quality if not quantity, because he was in love.

At three A.M. she shook his shoulder, kissed him, said, "Hey, wake up. I've got an important announcement to make."

He opened one eye.

"Congratulations," she said. "You are now a human being."

He smiled and closed the eye and slept.

Made in United States
Orlando, FL
19 December 2021

12180469R00117